THE
TAME CACTUS

El Nopal Manso

by
ESPERANZA ZENDEJAS

Ric —
Shared your
for all your
help!
Espereny

Published by Ojo por Ojo
5326 White Marsh Lane
Indianapolis, Indiana 46226

ISBN 0-9670467-0-X

First printing: April 1999
10 9 8 7 6 5 4 3 2 1

Printed in the United States of America.

DEDICACIÓN

This book is dedicated to my brothers and sisters, Maria Elena, Gustavo, Cuca, Rodolfo, Alfonso, Luis, Hector, and Blanca (*viejos los cerros*), and to our parents, Silvino and Maria, with deep admiration, respect, and love for the spirit of life you have inspired in all of us.

PREFACIO

A
s the old pickup neared the western outskirts of
Houston, a train bound for California left the station.
The passengers were still settling in for the overnight
ride when the engineer began the progression for halting the
train in a manner he hoped would not disrupt or alarm anyone. He pulled on the horn and engaged the brakes in hopes
of avoiding a one-sided disaster. But in a matter of seconds,
the pig iron's pointed cowcatcher smashed itself against the
passenger door of the truck. The impact brought the
screeching noise of death.

The stalled locomotive dragged the wreckage more than a
hundred feet until it fell off to one side of a wooden bridge.
When the train finally rolled to a standstill, the rubble
looked like a broken accordion unable to sound.

Small mesquite trees huddled under the gigantic limbs of
two enormous trees growing on the south side of the tracks.
The truck landed upside down in the shadows that the trees
cast on a small creek bed nearby. Its cabin was crumpled
against the truck bed in a vise of catastrophic destiny.

• • •

ADIÓS, AMAPOLA
Goodbye, Amapola

News of the accident arrived in the village of Amapola as it celebrated Mexican Independence Day in 1957. The festivities had begun before dawn with the traditional Catholic mass. *Cohetes de trueno* rocketed skyward, the thunder of their fireworks signalling the start of the fiesta. By midday the cobblestone streets were filled with the laughter and chatter of young and old celebrating their allegiance to the community and patriotism for their country.

Everyone was dressed in colorful new garments on this very special day. Tissue-paper decorations swayed from one end of the street to the other. Many small Mexican flags decorated the homes of Amapola. Some of the more prosperous families flew large green, white, and red satin flags in celebration of Mexico's independence from Spain.

A musical band played the songs of the revolution to stir the innermost emotions of the people. At the same time, rockets made of long bamboo sticks filled with gunpowder thrilled the celebrating families with each mile-high explosion.

As was customary in every fiesta, men, women, and chil-

3

dren were excited by the music, food, and celebration. Young children ran through the crowds and tagged each other. On one corner of the decorated square, huge cracked clay pots had been transformed into beautiful star-shaped piñatas for the young children to break. The piñatas were filled with peanuts, candies, sugarcane sticks, and fruits. The young hombres courted the señoritas by tossing colorful confetti in their long, dark braids.

Many people came from near and far for the celebration in the peaceful village nestled in a lush mountainside. Signs of the fiesta were in the air. The white-painted adobe homes of the small village glistened as thin puffs of gunpowder smoke lingered in the blue skies.

The road to Amapola was a dusty one. It had enough rocks to prevent automobiles from using it and enough shrubbery for the roaming animals to survive a dry season. The road was lined with small mesquite and skinny oak trees. Green beaver-tail cacti were also abundant along the edges. An occasional truck delivered products and transported passengers to the neighboring villages for market days. The road by truck was not a pleasant one either. The lizards seemed to be the only ones enjoying the Mexican sun, darting back and forth across the road at the sight of a moving speck of dust.

Six days a week, news from the rest of the world arrived by horse. The mail was brought in canvas sacks carried behind the saddle of the mailman's horse. The people of Amapola knew that the tri-color canvas sack contained letters from America and the plain khaki sack contained letters from surrounding villages and other Mexican towns and cities. Urgent messages were communicated by messenger to the remote mountain village.

On this day of celebration, only a few noticed the unfamiliar shadow of a small man riding a palomino toward the plaza. He was bringing a message to Amapola for the village priest. The gaunt rider wanted to deliver the message without hesitation so that he could return to his own village's celebration.

At the adobe church of San Juan, the village priest was busy preparing the altar for the next mass. He was surprised by a young child running toward the altar. "A messenger is looking for you, Padre." Padre Angel carefully placed the chalice next to the freshly starched linen napkin and stepped outside with the child.

The boy guided the padre toward the group of men hovering around the messenger. The harried priest pushed through the festive crowd. His ankle-length robe kept him from moving faster. The rosary tied at his waist swung from his left thigh to his right as he hurried through the crowd. He knew that only uninvited and undesired news would be delivered on this holiday. His emotions were beginning to show as he approached the visitor. When the messenger recognized the advancing priest, he removed his hat, bowed his head, and extended the neatly folded note held in his other hand.

As Padre Angel read the official telegram, his hands began to tremble and his face turned pale, showing the deep lines of his aging skin. His green eyes began to water and his heart pounded as fast as the beat of the revolutionary music playing in the background.

Amapola, Michoacán, México. 16 de septiembre de 1957. Municipio de San Juan Parangaricutiro. Noticia para la familia de Octavio Luna Amparo, Domicilio Conocido, Amapola, Michoacán, Mexico.

El servco de Emigración Estadouidense informa a las familias de Octavio Luna de Amapola, Michoacán, que el Señor Luna y su familia fallecieron en la cuidad de Houston, Tejas. Favor de informar a los parientes de ésta familia. El servicio de Emigración enviá a los fallecidos por avión a Guadalajara, Jalisco. Por favor de arreglar lo necesario para concluir este traslado. Llegaran el 17 de septiembre de 1957 a las seis de la manaña. Aviación General-Aeropuerto de Guadalajara, Jalisco, Mexico.

The telegram was directed to the father of Octavio Luna, notifying him that his son and all of his family had perished. The message instructed the relatives to pick the bodies up the following morning at the Guadalajara, Jalisco airport. The Immigration Service would ship the bodies back home via the Flying Tigers airplane cargo company, which transported undocumented aliens caught in the United States back to their country of origin.

The priest refolded the note and extended his right hand under his skirted robe to bring forth a couple of pesos. "*Gracias y que Dios te bendiga muchacho.* Thank you and may God bless you, young man." He sent the messenger on his way.

Padre Angel's grief escaped unnoticed in the chaos of the fiesta. He felt his calves weaken under the weight of his burden and his speeding heart felt about to burst. He rushed back to the church, concealing his emotions as he dashed past the joyful people. Padre Angel could only imagine the face of death. When he reached the altar his heart cried out to God as he knelt before Him in silent pain. He felt that God had abandoned the people of Amapola. He recited the Hail Mary in an act of consolation to his desperation. Padre Angel knew that his oversized adobe church, centered in the middle of Amapola, would house the solemn funeral mass, and that he would be expected to provide spiritual nurturing for the families during the difficult time ahead.

He reflected on the last moments he had spent with the Luna Amparo family. He clutched his rosary tightly as he lifted his eyes to the carved wood statue of Saint John. How could he break the news of such sorrowful misfortune to the elderly grandparents? He directed his pain-stricken question to the cross hanging over the holy sacraments. This incident would last forever in the heart of Amapola. The families affected were popular and well-respected. Padre Angel dreaded telling their friends the terrible news.

He did want to act quickly in order to find the resources necessary to bring back the bodies of the deceased family from Guadalajara. His shoulders were heavy with the burden of the difficult situation, and his stomach did not welcome his emotions.

The priest acted quickly to gather four male volunteers from the village. He informed them of the tragedy and instructed that they should stay with the parents of the victims until he arrived to share the telegram. The grandparents were elderly and news of this magnitude would shatter their hearts and pierce their souls.

Padre Angel knew that once the church bell rang outside the regular scheduled callings, the parishioners, the band, and the festive mood would fall apart. Everyone would immediately know that something was wrong. The bell was the call for church activities and emergencies only. As Padre Angel clanged the bell, the sound ricocheted to all corners of the mountain village.

Just as he predicted, the band stopped playing when the bell rang out defiantly. Old and young ran to the adobe church. The chatter turned to murmurs of questions and speculation. Even the monarch butterflies returning to this part of Michoacán seemed confused.

As if the entire universe knew the sad news, the sunny September skies began to fill with gray clouds. A somber mood descended on the clay-colored tile roofs of Amapola.

The grandparents were politely escorted to their homes by several relatives and friends. Nuns from the school the Luna Amparo children had attended also went along to provide needed support.

Padre Angel took small bottles of holy water and huge sanctified candles to the families. When the grandparents were informed of the deaths, their worlds ended at the first understanding of having their children and grandchildren gone forever. They wept as the priest consoled them with prayers for the departed souls. Their cries filled the air of Amapola with sorrow.

The human pain heard emanating from the families' homes was enough to move the crowd of villagers into the church in an urgent but traditional manner. The women always entered the church first. The children would follow the women. The men and the young boys went in last. As usual the women took the right-side wooden pews and the men and boys sat opposite. The pigeons, too, enjoyed the solace of the church as they roosted on the very top openings of the adobe walls.

Leaving the families in the arms of their friends, Padre Angel rushed back to the church to inform the community of the tragic outcome of the Luna family. When the entire village had jammed into the church, Padre Angel lit the huge cream-colored candles that stood tall at attention to Amapola's patron saint, San Juan. The priest sensed the anxious eyes watching his every move at the altar. This brief moment preparing the church provided him much-needed strength to deliver the announcement.

The priest's black robe was highlighted by a thin embroidered band of white material with gold trim. Padre Angel slowly climbed the winding staircase to the old-fashioned carved wood pulpit as if he were going to give the Sunday sermon. He had spoken often from this very old structure while wearing the same robe. The pulpit had an umbrella-like canopy decorated with tiny carved Easter lilies. The canopy and the glint of the gold embroidery gave the padre a heavenly presence. *"En el nombre del Padre, del Hijo, y del Espírito Santo.* In the name of the Father, Son, and Holy Spirit."* He always began services in the same way.

"I am deeply tormented and profoundly hurt by the news regarding one of our families. We were notified by telegram from the authorities of America that our dear friends and relatives, Octavio Luna and his family, suffered a fatal accident." Padre Angel spoke in a tender voice. His usual assertive manner was absent during this somber occasion. He wanted to give them strength through the sad and difficult ordeal. The shock was felt throughout the church as moans and yells flowed from the sanctuary. The priest doubted his effectiveness in convincing his parishioners to be brave. His own confidence was undermined as he tried to hide his emotions from them.

As the parish listened to their spiritual leader, it was evident to many that he was shaken by the news. The entire congregation showed a tremendous amount of discomfort. Men and women knelt down and began to pray. The women bowed their shawl-covered heads and shook in disbelief. The cries of the women created significant uncertainty in the men. The tears in church were uncontrollable while the decorations outside wilted in the wind of confusion. After hearing the news, even the pigeons flew away from their adobe nests. It seemed to the children that the birds could not bear to witness the sorrow.

During his brief announcement, Padre Angel also asked for volunteers to travel with him to the airport to bring the family home for burial. Guadalajara was three hours away as the crow flies and six hours by vehicle. The priest and the volunteers would pick up the bodies and return home, while the village prepared for the worst disaster ever. A strong earthquake had shaken the village in the past, causing damage to homes and frightening many people and animals. But never before had the pain been so deep and emotionally charged. The entire village of Amapola was joined together in pain.

• • •

PADRE ANGEL could not believe his teary eyes as the airport officials escorted him to the coffins. He was not prepared to see the four caskets, orderly and waiting for delivery. He got on his knees and asked for the mercy of San Juan. Seeing just four coffins, Padre Angel was relieved by some hope that two of the Lunas had survived the accident and were waiting elsewhere at the airport.

His mind flashed with the memories of the marriage ceremony he had officiated for Octavio and Dolores. He had also provided all the Catholic sacraments to the family. Padre Angel got off his knees and held on to the two men who had accompanied him. They had driven all day to Guadalajara and their fatigued bodies and spirit were not prepared to see the total destruction of a single family. Padre Angel's stomach muscles ached as if he had not eaten in days. His soul was empty and his heart was heavy. In a matter of minutes, his freshly starched white handkerchief was damp with sentiment.

In the land of the cactus, macho men are not supposed to cry or whimper. Padre Angel yelled to the heavens in pain. "You have abandoned me, San Juan! I was counting on you for strength. You have let your people of Amapola down." Padre Angel was not alone. The airport maintenance men, dressed in somber gray and blue uniforms, cried silently as they watched the priest lay his body on the floor in front of the coffins.

Padre Angel had been assigned to Amapola shortly after his ordination. His twenty-five years in the village had made him a part of all the parish families. He laid his body before the coffins in the same position in which he had received his holy sacrament. It was almost as if he wanted to die along with the Luna family.

Each of the coffins had several official tags dangling from the small side handles. The colored tags suspended by red string stood out against the pale pine boxes. The airport employees had seen an occasional coffin arrive in Guadalajara from the United States, but never before had so many coffins lined the hanger at one time, and all belonging to one family. The scene of grief overwhelmed the entire airport.

Padre Angel was responsible for the identification of the Luna family in their caskets. Before beginning the frightening task, he scanned the four caskets from a short distance. He was prepared to anoint each silent body with a thumbful of ash pressed on the forehead. The coffins were spaced within four feet of each other, carefully arranged by size. He held his rosary tightly in his right hand. On his left hand, he displayed the holy cross as he turned his anguished gaze from one coffin to another. With the help of airport personnel, he could just collect the needed stamina to look inside as each coffin's lid was opened.

The first was Octavio's, whose face still had a deep look of fear despite his cold body. He was draped in white sheet-like material, his hands and arms secured against his sides as if he were standing at some unknown attention. Padre Angel bowed his head in front of the coffin and signaled to the authorities his need to move on.

Fifteen-year-old Antonio was at peace with a sense of destiny and confidence. His lanky figure showed signs of a future stolen from a talented young adult. He had reached a different land of promised opportunity. He had, however, fulfilled his dream of reaching the American soil. No one would have guessed that his heart would also stop in America.

Padre Angel remembered the kindness Antonio had often displayed toward other altar boys. This young man had been dedicated, reliable, and well-liked. For many years he had helped the priest with the early masses. Padre Angel felt an attachment to Antonio for his service to the church and his friendship to others.

The priest moved forward to the next coffin. Sonia was only thirteen years old. She looked like an angel as she rested softly in her coffin, her head draped and bound in the same white material. Her body seemed to shrug sideways with pain. Sonia had made her first communion and was already participating in the religious rituals for young girls. Her excitement on the day she received Holy Communion was forgotten in her coffin. Her rosy cheeks and pink lips now were pale and paralyzed.

The last coffin waiting for Padre Angel's blessing was the most horrid. Dolores was resting in peace with her long raven-colored braids faded on her silent shoulders. In her arms was the motionless body of Silvino, the ten-month-old baby, cradled as if to protect him from danger. To see mother and child in death together left everyone present with a lifelong, painful memory.

"*¡Dios mío, que tristeza!*" My God, what sadness! exclaimed the shocked priest. He lowered his head and leaned it against the edge of the coffin.

Padre Angel took his rosary and placed it in the tiny hand neatly resting at the base of his mother's neck. The small beads signifying the Hail Marys looked like dried beans in the baby's palm.

As he moved from one coffin to another, the weight of the pain made the priest's shoulders sag. His disbelief was visible to all present. Not a dry eye existed in the airport complex center where the bodies waited to be removed.

But in a matter of minutes, Padre Angel realized someone was missing. "Where is Milagro? Milagro should be somewhere if she is not here!" Padre Angel looked around in desperation as he questioned the working men. "Where is the other child?" His tears turned to anger as he realized that she was nowhere to be found. He confronted the airport authorities, who knew nothing of another coffin or child. The message he received had indicated that the entire family suffered in the accident. The officials quickly contacted their superiors about the priest's desperate pleas.

The authorities were sensitive to the nature of the problem and showed much support through their patience with Padre Angel. "There is no other coffin or relative to the family here now or arriving later. We have reviewed the official documents and there are no discrepancies in the count," they told him.

Finally he knelt before the largest casket and softly asked, "Octavio, where is Milagro? What has happened to her? Where did you leave your little girl? I cannot leave without Milagro. Please, someone help us. Milagro must be found."

No one could help Padre Angel. He had four coffins and he was missing a child. The airplane that had brought the bodies had already left for its next stop in Mexico City. At last, one of the men offered the hopeful idea that the child might be alive and would be arriving later. He suggested that perhaps she was hurt and in a hospital somewhere in Texas. But Padre Angel was confused by the telegram and the number of bodies he was taking back with him to Amapola.

The sun would soon rise over the eastern hills of the valley of Guadalajara and the urgency to drive the coffins to Amapola as soon as possible was on the minds of the men. Without refrigeration for the deceased, every minute would jeopardize their condition for the burial. The bodies had been stored in refrigerated equipment. Without electricity, the corpses would begin to swell in the September heat of central Mexico.

• • •

PADRE ANGEL AND THE MEN left the Guadalajara Airport for the emotional trip home. The truck carried the four coffins.

Without the convenience of electricity, the village would tend to the dead immediately. The women would dress the bodies for viewing by placing strongly scented herbal leaves and cotton in the noses and mouths of the dead. Makeup or other adornment of the bodies was unknown to the villagers.

As in most Mexican towns, funerals were family affairs in Amapola. Next to weddings, these were the most important gatherings. Friends would bring food, alcoholic beverages, candles and flowers for the grieving family members. After a night of tearful cries and personal resolutions about life, the men would carry the coffins on their shoulders to the cemetery for burial. For the following nine days and nights, the departed would be mourned and grieved by their friends and relatives.

A musical band played farewell songs for the grieving people as they waited for the Luna family at the main entrance to the village. Having the band play was honorable as the family was returned to their beloved Mexico. Everyone wanted to be buried like the ancestors, in their own country with traditional family rituals. On holy days they would be honored with flowers and food by their children, and their children's children, forever. In Mexican culture, death is almost as important as life.

With their hats in their hands, several men jumped on the back of the truck to help bring down the caskets upon their arrival. The sight of the many caskets turned the crowd into an ocean of hysteria. They could not hold back the tears and cries of their broken hearts at the first glimpse of the wooden boxes. Dark-clothed women were fainting and crying. Young men and the stronger women made every effort to touch the coffins as a symbol of making peace with the dead. Many of the men had prepared themselves by drinking from bottles of tequila, rum and pulque, a cactus-derived liqueur, for the six-kilometer walk back home. The children knew not to run around on this solemn and feared occasion. Amapola had never before seen the sadness of so many people as the bodies were carried to their home for one final time.

Men and women walked alongside the caskets on the rough, dusty road, raising their voices in loud prayer. The people believed that the saints in heaven would hear their prayers, meant somehow to help the dead find a heavenly place for their spirits.

Rockets made from bamboo shoots tied to long mesquite sticks were sent up to the clouds for a loud explosion of gun powder several hundred feet above ground. This sent a message to the heavens and surrounding villages that a young child's soul had passed and an angel had gone to heaven.

Hours later, the bodies lay side by side in their coffins, first the father, then the mother holding the baby, and then the young brother and sister. The small adobe room was barely big enough to hold the five bodies. The room was lighted by candles. The shadows emanating from the candlelight created an uneasy view of the caskets. The smell of recently washed clay floor filled the room with a musky, damp odor.

No one could have imagined that the Luna family would return to their home for their own wake in such a short time. The sight of mother and baby in the same coffin caused so much distress that many women fainted. The women felt their wombs swallowing their hearts at the sight of this multiple tragedy. The men seemed to have little courage to stand in front of any of the coffins. They would just step forward and then backward quickly before their emotions got ahold of them. More than one man held his hat in one hand and a bottle in the other. The liquor conquered and controlled the emotions of many macho men at this funeral.

A haunting pain hid in the shadows cast by sixteen huge candles stationed at each corner of the four coffins. The candles, which Dolores Luna had made, were the last of the supply left for the village to use in future funerals. She had left the sixteen candles with her own mother, asking her to give them to bereaved families. Dolores' mother was devastated at the destiny of her oldest daughter. Moreover, she could not be consoled over her deep grief that her granddaughter could not be found.

Many women huddled around the coffins while the men chose to remain squatted under the moonlight, smoking

hand-rolled cigarettes and drinking tequila. The herbal
smell of yerbabuena and ruda teas mellowed the tequila and
melted-wax fumes in the air. The men talked about the sorrowful outcome the attraction of the United States had
brought to the Luna family. Many recounted the stories of
their trips to America as laborers and the close encounters
with death they had experienced. These conversations made
their pain more tolerable, but they all knew there would be
more deaths as long as America maintained the glitter of a
dream.

At the church, Padre Angel prayed the rosary before a full
house of kneeling people. The gates from heaven would be
more accepting of the souls accompanied by prayers. Fitting
to the occasion, he explained the suffering of Jesus, carrying
the cross as he wore the crown of thorns. But the death of
an entire family was too much for most people to compre-
hend the unfamiliar pain of Jesus at the same time.

The reality was that five loved and respected family members and friends were gone forever. Added to the disaster of
the trip, the child Milagro was lost somewhere between
Michoacán, Mexico and Houston, Texas. The families in
Amapola were beyond consolation. Everyone believed that
God had sent a very difficult lesson for all to keep for the
rest of their lives.

The wake lasted into the early morning hours. Many
drained bottles of tequila left behind seemed to cry in their
own empty sorrow. As the sun rose, the cobblestone streets
filled with friends and family who gathered to stroll alongside the caskets. Amapola's corn-grinding mill was closed

for the day of the funeral and many of the homes showed respect for the dead by displaying large black ribbons tied to their wooden doors, a silent symbol of death and mourning.

The aroma of the calla lilies, gladiolas, azucenas, simplazuchil, and daisies surrounding the coffins was intoxicating to the people in church. The candles Dolores had made were also brought to the church for the ongoing vigil of the family's final sleep. Padre Angel was dressed in his ceremonial clothing as he officiated the emotion-filled mass. Once again he climbed the stairs to give his consoling sermon.

At the end of the service for the *difuntos* (the deceased), the coffins were lifted to the shoulders of their bearers. The trip up the hill to *El Nopal Manso*, The Tame Cactus Cemetery, was not an easy one.

During the early part of the fall season the cemetery often looked neglected. The dried flowers and ornaments from last year's holiday were now unwanted trash. But the seasonal rains always kept the cemetery alive with wildflowers and grassy green shrubs. The evergreen cactus that flowered and gave fruit at this time of year added to the peaceful environment.

The earth mounds of the dead served as great potting soil for the country wildflowers. The amapolas and sunflowers graciously acknowledged the deceased by blooming next to grave markings often represented by old weathered and battered wooden crosses.

Children were afraid of the dead and the cemetery. Young

men on their way to milk the cows tried always to avoid passing through the area of The Tame Cactus.

At the height of the bountiful season, the coffins of the Lunas were carried up the path to the sacred resting grounds. The corn stalks peeked over the rock fences and bushes to see the tragic devastation of the village.

Hidden away on the mountainside, the village cemetery awaited its new permanent residents. It was a quiet resting-place surrounded by many tame cactus plants, mesquite and eucalyptus trees. Volcanic rocks surrounded the cemetery. These porous rocks, like guards at attention, watched the dead. Roaming animals stayed out of the appealing grass only because of the huge rocks keeping them out of the gravesites. Termite-eaten wooden crosses barely standing against the weeds represented many generations back. Few of the families were able to afford the newer cement crosses with inscribed names and years.

Hundreds of people followed in procession. The music played the saddest songs for the mourners. The children carrying calla lilies, amapolas, and gladiolas followed the smaller coffins. Many of the families carried large baskets full of roses, carnations, and azucena. In the rear of the procession, men lighted the tips of more bamboo gunpowder rockets to announce the sadness of the village. The bittersweet songs of the violin players added to the unforgettable torture of pain.

The silent, gliding monarch butterflies chased the colorful flowers. The monarchs usually returned to a festive Mexico.

This year, Amapola welcomed its butterflies with much sadness and emotion.

The bereaved grandparents had selected the northeast side of the cemetery to bury their children. The uncles made space for five members of the family but the men dug only four square areas. The bodies would rest under a tall eucalyptus tree and several tame cacti. During the hot days of summer, the shade would fall graciously over the four gravesites. The families of the victims were comforted by the site and knew that Octavio would also have been pleased with the location.

As each casket was lowered into its freshly shoveled hole, Padre Angel prayed. Each one of the multitude of people scooped a handful of the dark volcanic earth and tossed it over the coffin.

At last the women and children laid their white calla lilies on the powdery lumps of fresh, soft dirt. Never before had a burial lasted so long while the priest gave each of the dead a decent religious farewell. Octavio's father had stationed four wooden crosses on the south side of the gravesite. The crosses had carvings of the names and years of birth and death of each member of the family. Under his arm, Grandfather Luna had carried a cross inscribed with Milagro's name and birth year, 1952, to place on the fifth, unused burial space. He had purposely left the present year out in hopes of finding her alive.

• • •

THE FAMILIES OF AMAPOLA did not have much. Like the Luna family, many worked their *milpas* (fields) by planting corn, beans and squash. The men planted most of their crops by April and waited for the rainy season to end in September to see the corn crops reach above the shoulders of the tallest man. The closer the corn got to the heavens, the better the crop. Autumn provided a time to thank God and the saints for the plentiful rain that produced the harvest.

A fresh-water river ran parallel to the village, from which everyone took water. At the western end of town, men had set up flat-sided rocks against the edge of the river so women could do the wash. The mountains offered two major spring wells that provided drinking water for the people. Women carried huge pottery containers filled with water on their shoulders to their homes. Families with better economic standing used *burros* (donkeys) to carry several of the huge pottery jugs at one time.

Children ran to the river with the intestines of a recently butchered pig. They carefully cleaned the intestines inside-out using a stick and the fresh running water. The intestines would later be used for food and for sausage casings.

Most families had a cow or two for daily fresh milk. The women took care of the children and the home chores. The men cultivated the land and managed the animals. When out on the mountains, men were also expected to find wood for the kitchen hearth.

In 1943, while the world had its eyes on World War II, Mexico was surprised by the unexpected birth of a volcano in the Mexican State of Michoacán. The eruption of Paricutín, the volcano located within an hour from the village of Amapola, broadened the opportunities in the region. Paricutín had caused national and international interest in rural Mexico because of its humble beginnings in a cornfield. The people in the agricultural valley were shocked at the natural evolution of a volcano, which happened so quickly in front of their eyes — from a *milpa* of corn to a mountain of sand.

For many days, the fresh eruptions caused problems for residents of the region. Villages for miles and miles dealt with the troubles caused by the volcanic dust. Mexican men frequently slapped their hats on their bodies or other surfaces to remove the collection of dust. Many thatched roofs were on the verge of collapsing under the accumulation of the fine black powder. Homes of Spanish tile turned gray from the raining ash.

Paricutín had no regard for the crops of the region. The eruptions caused much grief to the poor families who depended on the fertile soils for their annual planting and harvesting. Oxen and horses that normally pulled the plows were busy hauling ash away from the homes and streets of the surrounding villages.

With the eruption of the volcano, Octavio Luna and his father were recruited by the municipal leaders to help governmental workers clean the mess and evacuate the affected villages. They also assisted the Mexican and international geologists during the highly publicized event. The Mexican army, too, was involved in helping make sense of the natural disaster, because Mother Nature's actions had brought many curious sightseers to the area.

Like the overflow of a water fountain, Paricutín poured its lava on a direct path to the town of San Juan Parangaricutiro, the center of the valley and surrounding villages. People from all over the region visited San Juan Parangaricutiro's El Señor de Los Milagros, the Lord of the Miracles. The people considered themselves blessed to have in their presence such a spiritual symbol. Local commerce was also important in this town where many of the indigenous people brought their vegetables and fruits for sale.

The lava eventually buried the town under massive molten rock. But the destruction of Paricutín turned out to be a window of opportunity for many poor peasants of the area, including those from Amapola.

During the months of evacuations from and cleaning of the aftermath of Paricutín, Octavio Luna was assigned to work with one of the Mexican government geologists, Teófilo Gil Fernandez. Octavio was very pleased to be working with the government for this meant that his family would prosper during the upcoming season.

Teófilo was a highly educated Mexican man in his late twenties. He kept the government informed of the "next moves" for evacuation of the villages and towns around Paricutín. Octavio was assigned to be Teófilo's messenger and personal assistant. During this time, the two men developed an indestructible bond of long-lasting friendship. Their closeness would eventually take them to the United States to work as braceros in the federal labor program.

Teófilo developed much respect for Octavio's high level of energy and optimism. Teófilo's wife, Natalia, and their four children visited the Lunas' home on numerous occasions. The older children always had a great time playing many games together and running in the open country. Teófilo's family was of better economic standing. He had gone to school and had a professional career, which was unusual during those days in rural Michoacán.

Teófilo's family brought many valuable goods to the Lunas' poor but happy home. Besides used clothes, they always brought delicious, unfamiliar foods for the family to enjoy. Octavio in return always offered a finished piece of carved furniture he had available for sale. He was proud to have carved a kneeling bench for Teófilo's mother's birthday one year. She was a very religious woman and the kneeler added to her devotion. Dolores always gave up her best cheese and cream for the Gil family, along with her finest wax-dipped candles. The friendship between the families continued to grow over the years.

Only the strong young men of Amapola had ventured to the United States of America in search of a better life. In 1944, many of the men, including Octavio, went to the border cities of Mexico to sign up for work. The United States was recruiting strong bodies for the Bracero Program.

World War II had created a lack of able hands and labor workers were needed in the United States to help with the agricultural crops. The Bracero Program provided Mexican men for much-needed farm help. The program opened the doors to many economically underprivileged men, who returned to Mexico years later with enough money in their pockets to envision a different hope for the future.

Unfortunately, the Bracero Program did not include complete families. The program was limited to the men and therefore the women and children stayed home to cultivate the crops and milk the cows. The older fathers of the braceros helped with the milpas, the animals, and the children during the younger men's long absence. But in many cases fathers and sons joined the Bracero Program together, leaving towns and villages filled with women, children, and the elderly.

Octavio had been a bracero for several years between 1944 and 1951. He had spent most of the time in Cucamonga, California working in the vineyards, helping with the picking and processing of grapes for the wine industry of that region.

For many men who never left Amapola, it was a dream that never came true. They believed that after death they would travel in spirit to the great country of America. Families had buried many of the dead with their feet pointing to the north as a symbol of their unachieved hopes and incomplete aspirations of reaching the United States. The crosses facing south usually marked the graves of children and women who would normally not dream of going to the United States.

AMIGOS HOY Y MAÑANA
Friends Today and Tomorrow

Since the eruption of Paricutín the lands had not given the people the fruitful harvest they needed and deserved. In rural Mexico, the corn crop was always the only hope for a poor family's survival.

When Octavio and Dolores Luna were blessed with another daughter in late September 1952, they named her Milagro — Miracle — in honor of the greatest corn harvest in nine years and in honor of the Lord of Miracles, the patron saint of Paricutín.

Octavio and Teófilo had helped the Bishop move the statue of the Lord of Miracles out of San Juan Parangaricutiro before the lava buried the popular Catholic church in 1943. Therefore, Octavio asked Teófilo and Natalia Gil to be his daughter's baptism *padrinos*, her godparents. In Mexican culture, the *padrinos* present the child before the church and before God for christening. Accordingly, a fiesta was held to celebrate the new *compadre* relationship between the Gils and the Lunas. Milagro's birth secured the bond between Octavio and his best friend and their families.

Just a couple of years later, Teófilo Gil fulfilled his dream of moving his family to Chicago. Many Mexican families had already immigrated to Chicago to labor in the steel mills. Even as a professional Mexican geologist, he could go to work in the United States as a laborer and earn better wages. The Luna family was deeply saddened by Teófilo's departure to the United States. However, by 1955 Octavio and Dolores were receiving monthly letters from their good friends, who sent photos and occasional money orders for the Luna family's well-being.

The Luna children were always excited about the possibility of receiving letters from Chicago. The excitement motivated them to chase the postman as soon as they heard the horseshoes on the cobblestone street. There were few horses in Amapola, and the postman always rode in on his palomino.

During Teófilo's long absence, Octavio and Dolores often spoke of him and his family. They often looked at a photo of Teófilo, his deep eyes bright behind curly lashes, taken at Milagro's baptism. Octavio frequently traveled to Tangancicuaro to visit with Teófilo's parents. He helped them as a way of demonstrating his respect and appreciation for the friendship he treasured.

"Chicago is the place to come for work," Teófilo wrote to Octavio. "All of my family are doing well. My children are learning English in school and I am working in a large building cleaning the offices of important architects. With my limited English, they even named me foreman of cleaning services. Why don't you pack your family and come with

me, Octavio?" The many letters Octavio received from
Teófilo were filled with exciting news about the opportunities for Mexican families. He was confident that his compadre would get him a job. He knew he could live with
Teófilo's family until he was able to get his own home.

It was on Teófilo's insistence that Octavio began to plan his
family's trip to Chicago. The image of the city lights of
Chicago and dreams for his children to accomplish crystal-
lized his mission. Teófilo had convinced him to dream big
and to dream about opportunities. In 1957, after many
years of hardship and difficult times, the Luna family left
Amapola behind for the aspirations of success.

They left their village during the first days of September. In
preparing for departure, they had also made the traditional
farewell pilgrimage to the church, asking for the patron
saint's blessing for the long journey. Moreover, they knelt
before Padre Angel and asked for his blessing by kissing the
religious ring on his left hand. Leaving at the peak of the
corn crop was not easy. Octavio's father and brothers would
have to complete the year's harvest. During Octavio's
absence, they would also take care of the animals left
behind.

Octavio Luna had been Amapola's only carpenter. His father
and grandfather before him had served as the carpenters for
the village, too. They built wooden chairs, tables, coffins,
and church pews. Octavio's great-grandfather built the
church pews out of huge oak trees in the mid-1800s.
Octavio also built a few wooden structures for outhouses for
families who could afford the modern commodity.

On his *milpa* Octavio had planted the traditional crops for his family's food supply. In addition he milked several cows and goats. The family would use two quarts of milk each day and the rest was sold at market.

On his beautiful mountainside land, small white boxes filled with honeycombs adorned the boundaries. He sold the honey to the other villagers. He also took care of many fruit trees his grandfather had planted decades before.

Dolores was a traditional Mexican mother and wife. She took care of her four children and her parents. Beautiful flowers she planted and nurtured always surrounded her adobe home. The children were happy with the flowers because they attracted butterflies, and the butterflies provided chasing games. The monarchs arrived in Michoacán every year. No one knew why or from where they came.

Dolores made guayaba fruit jams for her family and friends. During avocado season, she had the children climb the trees to pick the dark green fruit. Everyone in the village anticipated the great avocados from her tree. Another of her treats was a special quesadilla. At the sight of the first squash blossoms, Octavio would bring some home so that his wife could melt them between corn tortillas.

During the night, she worked with the bee's wax her husband had collected from the combs. She dipped threads into the melted liquid wax until huge yellow candles developed. Under the sunlight, she bleached the yellow wax until it turned white. The white bleached wax was for the special candles. Working with the warm wax was a hobby after her long, tiring days. She offered much of her work to the patron saint in return for the many favors she had prayed for on behalf of her family.

She was the first to rise every day and the last one to rest. Six days a week she shucked dry corn and soaked it in lime to prepare it for the early-morning grinding process. In the shadows of dawn she took this mixture to the village mill and returned home with *masa* (corn flour) to make the fresh tortillas her family enjoyed.

Dolores' parents were also part of the village. Her father fabricated all the fireworks for the region. Her brothers and sisters helped grind the gunpowder by turning huge wooden barrels. Inside the barrels were large rocks that crushed the coal-like material. Her father had become a master in making gunpowder. He gathered the supplies from special plants and trees and processed them along with other ingredients to produce the highly flammable mixture. The fine powder was then stuffed into bamboo shoots for fireworks. Everyone loved the *cohetes de trueno* at the fiestas.

Dolores' mother helped the women of Amapola during their pregnancies, prescribing herbal medicine to help them after their deliveries. She mixed plants with water to create home remedies that worked on adults and children. As an adult, Dolores learned the many secrets of medicinal plants, and became a midwife to help young, expectant mothers.

Her responsibilities entailed the preparation of special herbal teas for the sick. For this she would spend endless hours during the different seasons collecting a variety of plants, leaves, seeds, and tree bark. One corner of the kitchen was always assigned to the hanging and drying of plants for medicinal use.

With the help of her small daughter, Milagro, Dolores would carefully tie the stems of the plants before hanging them from the wooden beams resting on the adobe walls. She would hang the bundles upside down for faster drying. Her garden was filled with medicinal and culinary herbs that grew all year.

Octavio and Dolores were very proud of their growing family. At 15, Antonio was learning his father's woodworking skills in addition to tending the cows and milking them in the early mornings and afternoons. He was also becoming very talented at building the traditional fireworks. Sonia, age 13, was mother's helper and Milagro's favorite playmate and best friend. Milagro was going to turn five years old soon, and was full of energy and life. She and Sonia spent endless hours playing house or school, taking turns in the role of Mother Superior. In autumn they chased orange-and-black-spotted butterflies to their hearts' content.

The baby of the family, Silvino, spent most of his time hanging on to his mother's *rebozo* (shawl) and waiting for his frequent breast feedings. He also took naps on a bamboo crate hanging from the ceiling beams. The entire family took turns giving the occasional push to rock Silvino to sleep.

The Lunas wanted very much to have their children attend school. In their poor village the school was very expensive and most children did not participate because their parents

could not afford the tuition. The Luna children attended
sporadically as harvest success permitted.

Dolores was therefore reluctantly convinced that moving to
the United States, where education was free, would be the
right thing to do for her family, a guarantee out of poverty.
Besides, she could not again face the loneliness she experienced when Octavio worked in the United States for long
periods of time.

Nevertheless, the thought of leaving Amapola was burdened
with the breaking of close family ties and the loss of the
Mexican traditions. Families in Amapola were very close-
knit, with respect and appreciation for all the generations.

In preparation for their departure to the United States,
Octavio instructed his wife to pack only the best clothes in
three small cardboard boxes. Milagro chose the boxes; her
favorite pink marshmallow cookies sprinkled with coconut
were pictured on the sides. Dolores carefully followed her
husband's instructions on the use of a secret compartment
that would hide the family's birth certificates, photos, and
baptism records. She carefully cut between a layer of the
corrugated cardboard in one of the boxes. The slit was large
enough to hold the folded documents. Then she meticulously sealed the secret compartment with hot wax. Milagro
held onto the yellow candle while her mother pressed her
thumb on the edges until the wax cooled.

On the advice of Teófilo, Octavio's plan was to have the
entire family become U.S. citizens. He told Dolores that the
documents were going to be needed in the new country. In

addition, he had painstakingly folded a handwritten note of the names of the family and Teófilo's Chicago address. He showed Dolores where he wore the note inside his sock next to his left ankle.

Milagro did not want to leave her chickens behind. Nor did she want to part ways from her colorful papier maché dolls, and she was not happy giving up her miniature ceramic plates and cups. Most important, she wanted to see the return of the butterflies.

Octavio carried her in his arms at the first sight of the spotted *mariposas* arriving each autumn. He would tell her that the butterflies were for the children of the world. On his shoulders she tried to catch the butterflies, realizing that her unsuccessful attempts were all right.

She was devastated to think they would be leaving their dog behind. Tigre had become like a family member, joining them in the kitchen for every meal. Her brother and father would toss him bits of food and tortilla as a token of appreciation for his good work in hunting and in tending the cows.

The night before they left, many friends visited the Luna home to say farewell. The fireflies were out, providing games for the children after the sun went into hiding. The absence of electricity accentuated the light of the flickering flies. The children's palms often carried the powdery substance left over from accidentally smashed bugs.

During the last few hours before they left, Dolores' eyes were red from the tears she held back. Saying farewell to family was the worst of emotions Milagro had ever seen. She saw that her mother had a difficult time saying goodbye to her own mother and father, crying painfully in silence. It made Milagro feel cold.

Her grandmother, a short and bent, weathered, Indian-looking woman, gazed at Milagro as if for the last time. With tears in her eyes, she told the child she would take good care of her dolls and her chickens. Milagro asked her to promise she would save all the eggs until the family came back. Her grandmother's long braids fell around the girl as she embraced Milagro in her warm arms. The family all knelt before her as she made the sign of the cross on their foreheads. The last inescapable goodbye was her toothless smile and the smell of corn tortilla on her skin.

The family climbed on the market truck. Besides loading the few boxes, they also took a couple of *morrales* (shoulder bags) filled with food and fruits. Octavio, the only one sitting with the driver, acted very important on this occasion as he camouflaged his emotions. It was difficult for him to leave his parents. It was difficult for him to hold back the tears of this farewell.

The children sat on the floor of the truck's wooden plank bed. Wooden chairs were located next to the truck's cabin. Milagro saw her father making all kinds of hand gestures to the driver as they began their journey to the United States of America. It seemed to her that her father was telling the driver about their new destiny.

The truck took the Lunas to the central bus station in

Morelia, the capital of Michoacán, on a four-hour winding road. At Morelia, they boarded a *Flecha Amarilla* (Yellow Arrow) bus to Matamoros, Tamaulipas, which borders with Texas and the Gulf of Mexico. It took three full days to travel the 800 miles. The bus was crowded, noisy, and unpleasant overall. Even so, it was exciting since it was the children's first trip by motor. In Amapola, their only way of transportation was the donkey or the horse, if they were lucky.

Upon arriving in Matamoros, they stayed in a tiny, noisy hotel room, sharing the space with many fleas and wandering roaches. The noises of the city were different from Amapola's. The absence of the distant coyote howling to the moon was replaced by men and women arguing over prices and goods on the streets. The noisy car horns and screeching tires added to the alien surroundings of their room with a limited view. The Gulf Of Mexico humidity covered them like blankets, creating a fever-like sweat.

For several nights Octavio and Antonio went looking for the man who was to guide the family through unfamiliar territory on the route to Houston. He would also show them the way when crossing the Río Bravo. Octavio called these guides "coyotes." The coyote would keep the family out of sight of the U.S. immigration officials.

The river known to all Mexicans as the Río Bravo or the "rough river" divides the entire state of Texas from Mexico. The river serves as a natural barrier from the dividing state line between southern New Mexico and Texas to the Gulf of Mexico. Octavio told his family that the Americans called the river Río Grande, meaning "big river." He also told them that many movies were made from fantasies about the river. By the end of its journey, as it made its subtle entrance into the warm Gulf waters, the river was smooth and tamed.

He was very nervous about crossing the river illegally with all of the children. He was apprehensive as he looked for the coyote. He loved his family and did not want anything to go wrong with this unusual crossing. Milagro had never seen her father so anxious. He tried to conceal his nervousness by treating the family as if they were on vacation. But he did not fool Milagro and her mother.

Octavio was intuitive about the uncharted territory. He had faced the predicament of being caught as an illegal alien and shipped back to Mexico by the American Immigration Service and did not want his family to experience such humiliation.

It was so hot and humid one night that Octavio took the children to the taco stands on the street. Numerous street vendors hauling carts filled with fruit and hot foods were anxious to serve the people on the streets. After a week of waiting in the hotel room, Octavio found the coyote just a few hundred yards away. He had been assisting another family in crossing the border. He instructed Octavio to bring the family at six o'clock the next evening and he would help them cross the infamous river border after midnight. Octavio told the children that the coyotes made lots of money taking people across the river and into the United States.

The coyote — a tall, thin Mexican man with a Dick Tracy hat — was anxious to take them approximately 20 kilometers east of Matamoros. He came across as if he knew the whole territory. From that point they would walk for about two hours north to the mouth of the river delta. This part of the river had, for many years, made illegal crossing easier. The short shadow distance between two countries made this location the ideal crossing, and Octavio had made the trip before. This route would not be as dangerous as some parts of the river and the moonlight would protect the family against the North American officials.

The coyote told Octavio that once they crossed the river, an automobile would take the family to a location in Brownsville, Texas. There they would wait two or three days and then another vehicle would drive them to Houston. From Houston, they would take the bus to Chicago. The coyote had it all set up.

The coyote from Brownsville to Houston did not require any official documents from illegal immigrants just as long as the payment was in cash. The money was always required in dollars and poor people paid a higher price to purchase the dollars with pesos. Street peddlers and vendors were willing agents for this type of money exchange. Border towns were busy with such activity.

To cross legally, the Mexican passport was the crucial document to have. The Luna family would never enjoy the benefits of a Mexican passport because it took lots of money to acquire such a document. For most peasant families, acquiring a passport was only a dream. The only way into the United States would be through the illegal crossing. Many other poor but hard-working people could never get the opportunity to work in America unless they made their trip illegally, too. The coyotes knew all the ins and outs of the crossing points. They knew the areas and they made the necessary arrangements to get individuals and families anywhere in the continental United States.

Chicago was clearly going to be different for the Lunas. Octavio tried to encourage his family with exciting news about their new home. He told them that they would not have to take their wooden stools and chairs to the movies. In Amapola, the movies were shown on white sheets sewn together. Everyone would bring chairs to sit on while the movie was running. The movies did not have any sound, so loud Mexican music was played during the show. He also told them that they would be able to eat ice cream every day. Life in the United States was truly going to be better because the children were going to enroll in school and study English.

As planned, they spent two days in a Brownsville home before they began the trip to Houston on September 12, 1957. An old Dodge pickup would transport them to the train depot there, a seven-hour ride on back roads. Octavio and Antonio sat together in the cabin with the driver while the rest of the family huddled in the open truck bed.

● ● ●

THE RUMBLE OF THE TRAIN and the loud noise of the brakes muffled the dying cries and pleas of the Luna family, but the westward-bound passengers had felt the vicious jolt. As soon as the train came to a stop several hundred feet beyond the rude impact, the engineer and operators jumped off and rushed back to the accident site. All of the cabin passengers had died instantly. The passengers riding on the bed of the truck had been thrown off the vehicle with the impact of the metal engines.

One of the engineers ran back to the train to radio Houston for emergency help. He knew that the rain would make it difficult to get immediate help for the people involved in the accident.

Dr. Jack Wolf and his wife, Katherine, were abruptly shaken by the screeching noise and sudden stop of the passenger train. They knew the train had hit something. The Wolfs were traveling to California. The tall, handsome man with thinning brown hair was a medical doctor and farmer. He and his beautiful young wife were returning from South America, where he had completed two years of service in a rural hospital in the mountains. For the past two years, he had provided medical help to children in the villages of Ecuador. Most of the medical attention dealt with infections caused by unsanitary living conditions.

Jack and Katherine were headed back home to help Dr. Wolf's aging parents run the family farm. He would also begin to help the local doctor with his practice. The couple had arrived early in the morning from Quito, Ecuador and had boarded the night express train for home.

In the late hours and heavy rains only a few curious passengers dared jump off the Pullman cars to get a glimpse of the wreckage. Dr. Wolf's background urged him to leave his wife in their small compartment while he made himself available to help in the emergency.

He quickly pulled his pants on while he forced his feet into his leather shoes. "I'll be right back, honey." Jack sweetly kissed his wife on the cheek, grabbed his medical bag and rushed out through the Pullman's corridor. He jumped off the side of the train onto the Texas land and ran alongside the tracks to the scene of the accident. He felt a tremendous sense of nervousness coupled with responsibility.

He had confronted tragedy on many occasions and could sense a cloud of death approaching him as he neared the area of commotion. The large trees added a haunting feeling of tragedy, hanging over the wreckage like dragons ready to swallow the land. He was guided to the location by flash-lights and loud voices from other men already at the site. "I am a doctor, please let me get to the injured," he repeated as he strode toward the bodies. He pushed his way through the line of curious men in hopes of helping. He moved from one victim to another, desperately hoping to find life. His heart sank as he realized that all of the bodies were lifeless. His medical training had long prepared him for this ugly outcome, yet his internal fortitude was threatened.

The worst part was to see the lives of young children gone in an instant of carelessness. None of the children at the site had been spared, removed from this existence to an unknown resting place. Dr. Wolf's help would not be needed here; he was trained to save lives. On this occasion, he did-n't even get a chance to try. He informed the engineers that all bodies needed to be transported to the morgue and that an ambulance was not necessary. He suggested they contact the authorities and have the coroner prepare the proper reports. As he picked up his leather medical bag he felt useless and unwanted.

Passengers who had jumped off the train to see what happened rushed back to their Pullmans at the sight of six dead bodies. The fresh blood stains on the seats of the crushed Dodge were more than most could handle.

As Dr. Wolf headed back toward his Pullman, he heard the others discussing the status of the victims. "These people must be wetbacks. They have no documents or identification other than money," noted one. "These people never made it to their destination," another pointed out.

Dr. Wolf moved on through the dripping shadows of the Texas mesquite trees, thinking of the steps that could have prevented this accident in which the lives of humans were taken without regard. *What could I have done to save the family?* He thought to himself of the many times children in Ecuador were brought for medical care but to no avail. His mind never let go of the guilt he felt when he could do nothing to help a child survive. As he neared his train car, he paused under the night rain to relieve himself from the collected nervousness.

The shrubbery around him created the perfect place to stand for a minute, out of view of the train and about 200 yards away from the accident site. The need to relieve himself was a priority before he hurried back to the Pullman to wash his bloodstained arms and change his shirt.

The train quarters were crowded and the trip to California was going to be a long one. Due to the accident, the express train was also going to be delayed until all equipment was inspected. Dr. Wolf could just hear the shouts of the men at this distance. The raindrops on the leaves of the bushes were louder.

While his urine poured out under the glistening rain, he was shocked to hear whimpering noises that seemed to come from under an ocotillo tree. He quickly zipped his fly and stepped toward the sounds. His ears confirmed the cries were very close. Baffled, he began to look around, following the moans of a child in pain. As he neared the sounds, he moved more quickly. Then his stoic body froze in confusion.

There, curled up against the manzanilla bushes, lay a small child. Her face was scratched and her clothes were torn and blood-soaked.

To Dr. Wolf, she looked to be four or five years old. Many times before, Dr. Wolf had to calculate the ages of children of Ecuador, as many parents did not have an official birth certificate. In many cases, they would use baptismal records to show dates of birth.

The girl's long braids were familiar to Dr. Wolf because he had worked with Ecuadorian children who had the same hair weavings. She was alive but needed immediate medical attention. His first instinct was to pick the little body up and take her to the crowd of men waiting for the Texas police. He could begin to provide her the needed attention there. But he had immediately guessed that she was part of the family whose lives were stolen by the train wreck and that if so, she was a lone survivor. Dr. Wolf also knew the punishment for illegal entry into this country and had seen the consequences for hired men caught and shipped back to Mexico from his father's farm. He knew that if he turned the child in to the authorities, she would probably be placed in an orphanage until a family was willing to take her.

Jack Wolf picked the frail child up in his strong arms and rushed her to his train cabin. With the alcove light, he would be able to see any possible bone fractures. He would also be able to care for her bleeding injuries.

Katherine was waiting anxiously for Jack. As he entered their quarters, she moved over to make room for his small patient. She was shocked at the sight of blood and bruises on the young girl. She also knew that Jack was the expert and questions at this time were not appropriate. She would help!

Jack quickly pulled a syringe from his bag and drew a liquid from a tiny flask sealed with a rubber cap. Immediately, he began to administer a relaxing substance into the child's bloodstream. "Katherine, get me water out of that container." He demanded immediate support in order to move about his business of caring for the girl. Katherine rushed to comply with his orders. Dr. Wolf was always prepared to deal with emergency situations in the middle of nowhere. His wire-rim glasses rested at the end of his nose while he gently checked the seriousness of her injuries.

The child's small frame was badly hurt. Several of the

wounds on her legs and arms were deep, and her body was reacting by turning blue and purple as blood collected at the bruises. He figured that she would also be swollen by the early hours of the morning. An antibiotic injection would help fight off any potential infection. Jack Wolf not only carried his leather medical bag everywhere but most of his suitcases were filled with lifesaving instruments and supplies he could never find in the mountains. Immediately, Katherine gathered the necessary medical items from several packed suitcases for her husband's use. Dr. Wolf and Katherine set up a provisional clinic in their compartment for the child.

With warm water, Katherine began to sponge away the fresh blood from the girl's skin. As she cleaned the gravel, sand, and dirt from the injuries, Jack quickly covered the area with bandages. His own blood was boiling in determination to watch and care for the little Mexican girl.

Dr. Wolf mentally reviewed the details of the accident. He felt sorry for the sole survivor. He knew that he should inform the officials of his finding. More important, he knew that the child needed his care and delaying it could prove dangerous. He knew they were far from the next major city and help could be too late. He decided to make it his priority to care for the unnamed little bundle.

With careful hands, Dr. Wolf cleaned and dressed the open injuries. He placed the child's head between two sturdy cardboard boxes. He quickly designed another splint for the child's thigh using the cardboard base of his medical bag. The litle girl began to relax from the injection.

Jack and Katherine contemplated the dilemma they were in. "The child's health is at stake and she needs rest for the next few days. The next twenty-four hours are going to be critical," Dr. Wolf told his wife. The couple decided to watch the child for the next day. They agreed to go to the authorities once they arrived at home. The husband and wife embraced each other and cried at the sight of the helpless young orphan girl. She looked like a wounded angel to them. The child rested as the train remained motionless pending clearance from the accident.

When the train finally began to move forward it did so in a very slow and calculated manner, as if wanting to leave death behind without being noticed. For Jack Wolf, it was as if the train knew that a member of the family was on board. Jack and Katherine looked at each other with much love yet with confused thoughts. They knew that they had precious cargo belonging to some unknown family no longer able to care for her. The train had spared the life of the little girl; now, it carried her to a new life.

The train arrived in El Paso on the following day. With a three-hour stop before the train traveled on to California, Jack Wolf got off to purchase additional medical supplies to care for the little girl and to make another contact with his parents to inform them of the delay.

His number-one priority was the well-being of the child. He tried not to concern himself with all the explanations he needed to give his parents and friends about the child. Jack and Katherine had made every effort to conceive a baby but believed they would be childless for the rest of their lives.

Now Jack realized that a bonding was taking place between the child and his wife.

As always, Katherine was very happy to see him back from his adventures. This time he arrived from a quick trip into El Paso with his bag of supplies for the remainder of the trip and fresh fruits for his wife. In the last few years she treasured his return from visits to the Ecuadorian mountain villages. The feeling of completeness always filled her as her husband returned home from foreign territory.

The pensive doctor worried about the ethical nature of caring for a child found at the site of a train accident. Yet he also knew that without his help, the child might have been a lost victim, left without being noticed. She would certainly have died after a day or two of Texas rain and sunshine.

The Wolfs allowed the girl to rest on their sleeping birth while they used the floor of their Pullman quarters for sleeping. When she finally opened her eyes in their presence, "*Amá*" (Mom) was the first word she uttered. She was confused by the two unfamiliar individuals looking at her with such great concern. "*¿Dónde está mi Amá, mi Apá?*" She asked for her parents in a weak and shaky voice.

Katherine could barely hold back her tears. She understood the child's pleas for her parents. Katherine calmly rubbed her hand on the child's forehead with a very soft touch. The couple knew any response at this time would generate more confusion for the child. In their limited Spanish vocabulary they continued to calm her. "*Ya, ya, ya, duerme, duerme.*" (Now, now, now, sleep, sleep.) The child closed her eyes and fell into another deep sleep. Katherine wanted so much to ask her name but held herself from rushing the encounter for the sake of the child's well-being.

The passenger train rolled on its way to the lower desert of California where the Wolfs would end their journey. The trip was filled with the majestic view of the Sonoran Desert familiar to Jack. For Jack and Katherine the trip was also filled with a tremendous amount of ambiguity about their decision to keep the child. As the saguaros, yuccas, and organ pipe cacti of the desert stood at attention to the passing train, the couple pondered their actions and future choices.

The Wolfs met while they were both students at Stanford University in Palo Alto, California, and married in the campus church in 1951. Katherine was from the crossroads of America. Her parents owned a small corn farm in southern Indiana. With her bachelor's degree from Indiana University, she enrolled at Stanford, seeking to move far west to broaden her experiences. Jack was a student in the medical school and she was working on a master's degree in social sciences. They graduated in 1952 with their respective degrees.

Jack was raised in Imperial Valley, California. He grew up on his father's farm. The Wolf family raised steers and planted cotton and sugar beets along with other minor crops in the desert on the California border of Mexico and Arizona.

Early on, Jack was responsible for the care of the animals and for the cotton and sugar beet crops. Jack's father wanted his son to be in charge of the operations of the business. Instead, Jack pursued a degree in medicine. During his stay in Ecuador, Jack realized how much he enjoyed the outdoors and watching things grow. His father's words were becoming more meaningful to him as he grew older.

As the train crossed the New Mexico border into Arizona, the child awoke again. The constant jumping of the wheels on the tracks made her injuries pulsate. "*Amá, yo quiero a mi amá,*" she cautiously whispered. Her eyes were suffering from the unknown as she stared at Katherine's big blue eyes. Her nonverbal expressions reflected the pain of injuries that would not heal in a day or two. Jack had meticulously sewn shut a couple of the deepest cuts.

Somehow the young girl sensed that Katherine would not hurt her and that Jack was helping with her injuries. She had never before seen the pretty, smooth white gauze he applied to her skin. In the past when she had fallen and scraped her skin, her mother had applied plants and small amounts of mud to heal the injuries. She covered the mixture with a larger leaf, depending on the size of the injury. Often her mother would tie the mixture of plants with yucca leaf strips. She recalled the times she was sick and her mother would make brown paper pouches filled with petroleum and coffee grounds. She would wrap these things around the child's feet until the fever and pain disappeared.

"*¿Cómo te llamas?*" What is your name? Katherine asked.

"*Mi nombre es Milagro,*" she responded in a meek and weakened voice. The Wolfs were relieved to hear her name. They smiled at her with compassion. Milagro was a beautiful little girl. Her large hazel eyes looked sad.

"*Soy doctor y te voy a curar.* I am a doctor and I am going to cure you." She smiled ever so slightly at Jack's reassuring foreign words.

The train came to a stop in Niland, California. The small train station in the Imperial Valley's northernmost town was filled with people waiting to travel to Los Angeles. Jack's parents were waiting patiently for the arrival of their son and his wife.

Katherine was first off the train. Jack carried the child wrapped in an Ecuadorian wool shawl. The young girl rested against Dr. Wolf's spacious chest as he greeted his parents.

"Welcome home, son! Welcome home, Katherine!" Jack's parents shouted from a short distance. They were visibly excited about the return of their son and daughter-in law. As they got closer, they were surprised at the small bundle in Jack's arms. "Jack, who is this little one? Is she ours?" Jack's father could not contain his curiosity. The sight of their son holding a child brought tears to Jack's parents' eyes. They had missed Jack and Katherine so much, and were so grateful that they had decided to return to the Imperial Valley.

"Dad, we'll talk later. This is Millie. A very special miracle," Jack responded. The five-member Wolf family drove to their country farm located six miles southeast of Niland.

The Wolf family had arrived in the Imperial Valley in the mid-1930s. Jack's grandfather had come to this part of the country after water was redirected to the desert from the Colorado River, turning the area into a winter salad bowl. They started the farm with one hundred head of cattle and several hundred acres for farming. The Wolfs had always planted cotton and in the early 1950s began planting sugar beets to alternate their field crops.

As the expectation for California to feed many parts of the country became evident, their innovations paid off. In 1957, Jack's father was experimenting with relatively new arid land plants for long-term farming. He planted cotton and sugar beets as they also provided good income for next year's crop and revenue for the home.

In the lower Colorado basin, water was and had always been at a premium. Experimenting with low-water-use plants was important. Plants needing less water were going to be the plants of the future. Irrigation canals were part of everyday life in Imperial Valley. Ironically, the land in the valley contained much saline and the need for water was urgent. Not only did the plants need the water to thrive, but the water also served as a rinse for the plants. In the Imperial Valley, the water runoff created the fluctuating Salton Sea water levels.

Jack's father had also begun experimenting with the planting of jojoba seeds in his fields as a progressive future crop. He explained that the seeds from the jojoba plant would be used for oil. "In the future, jojoba seed oil will be important for this country, Jack. You, Katherine, and your offspring will

53

benefit from it." He wrote to Jack about this matter frequently. Jack had seen the tiny plants but they grew so slowly that any analysis of the plant's value was years ahead.

Jack's father could not stop talking about the changes that had recently occurred on the farm. Jack's mother was a bit more inquisitive about the child. She wanted to know more as they drove toward the farmhouse.

"Why didn't you tell us about the child?" she asked.

"Mom, Millie is going to be with us. She is ours. I'm sorry I didn't tell you sooner." Jack made every effort to explain only what was necessary. Katherine could not believe what she had heard but supported Jack's decision.

"She is our little bundle of surprising joy," affirmed Katherine. Katherine was very glad to hear Jack indicate that Millie would be with them. She felt a maternal tug in her womb that she had felt before only during very intimate moments with her husband. She loved her husband very much and this was just another example of his ability to read her needs and desires.

From a distance the farmhouse looked small compared to the giant cedar trees surrounding it. As the Wolfs drove closer to the farmhouse, Jack could not help but notice the beautiful Chocolate Mountains to the northeast side of the house. As sunset approached, his memories were vivid of the turquoise, blue, purple, and brown colors that settled on the slopes for a short time before the sun dropped behind the Salton Sea. He loved the contrast of the desert and the surrounding green fields. As a child he frequently climbed the salt cedar trees to take advantage of the surrounding view of the valley. The sun was the desert's best friend and had also been Jack's partner in many of his activities in the farm.

Katherine and Jack would be making their home in the guest house next to the main barn. The home had been vacated after the Mexican family living in it bought their own home in Niland. Jack's mom had then refurbished the small country-style house. Katherine welcomed the new paint inside and out, as she had seen the rundown place just a few years earlier. She had worried, knowing she would be moving to a home that needed so much work. It was a relief to see the modest house in better condition. Now, this would be the home of Jack, Katherine, and Millie.

As soon as their bags were moved into their new home, Jack and Katherine drove the child to a hospital in Brawley, 18 miles south, to have her arms and legs X-rayed. Jack provided advice to the technicians on which X-rays were needed. He was concerned about broken bones even though she seemed to be doing well.

Millie was very nervous about this experience and again, her confusion prevented her from verbalizing her emotions in Spanish. Besides, it seemed to her that no one would understand her words. Finally, the Wolfs took her home so that she could rest.

As Jack became involved with his part-time medical practice and with his father's farm, Millie's care fell, for the most part, to Katherine. Katherine was delighted to watch and help Millie fully recuperate. She was getting along very well with Millie, and learning more about the surprise of their lifetime.

"Me llamo Katherine. ¿Quíeres comer algo?" Katherine wanted her to eat something so that her young energy would return quickly. She followed the injured child's every move, making sure her needs were always met.

"Yo quiero mi amá y mi apá. ¿Dónde están?" I want my mom and my dad. Where are they? she asked. *"Yo quiero ir a Amapola y quiero mis gallinas."* Millie wanted to go back to Amapola and she wanted to see her chickens.

"Tu mamá se enfermó y tu papá te encargó con nosotros." Katherine tried desperately to tell her that her mother had become ill and her father had made Jack and Katherine responsible for her well-being. Millie was too young to understand.

Katherine worked tenaciously on the translations. She kept a small notebook with all the comments Millie made so that she could share them with Jack. Jack was better at the Spanish and he could understand what Millie was trying to say. It seemed to Katherine that her entire day was spent with Millie. The bond between mother and daughter was noticeable to Jack.

"Katherine, you're doing very well with Millie." Jack complemented Katherine's work. "She's responding well to you and she likes you, too." Jack's reassurance made Katherine extremely satisfied with her roles as mother and wife.

Katherine was having a rough time with the translations. She had learned limited Spanish during their stay in Ecuador but now regretted not paying more attention to the details of the language. Jack would always finish her sentences or end up translating for her on market days. But Katherine's limitation in Spanish was helping Millie become quickly acquainted with the English language. Both Millie and Katherine repeated after each other for the first six months of their relationship.

"*Agua*, water."

"*Vaso de agua*, glass of water." Katherine kept writing these phrases down so that she would not forget them the next time.

In the ensuing months, like any child, Millie grew a little more at ease. She finally began to eat full meals with the family. Katherine chuckled when Millie folded all the biscuits and slices of white bread into halves. She did not even know how to use a fork. Her traditional spoons in Mexico had been the cut-up tortillas folded to hold morsels of food. They served as the utensil for all Mexican meals in Amapola.

Katherine realized that Millie liked hot meals and ate them with more enthusiasm than the cold sandwiches she made for Jack. Katherine also noticed that Millie always saved food for the dog. Jack and Katherine realized that much of her behavior reflected her growing up in a village, although they weren't familiar with her homeland. They were more interested in observing and guiding than in forcing manners and expectations. That would come later.

Millie was overwhelmed by the new environment, different food, new language, and strange faces. She had never seen a home with such a pretty floor. The floors were covered with linoleum that reminded her of tile. Each section of the house had different patterns unfamiliar to her. The house also had tables and soft chairs. The bedrooms were separate from the living room. The two bathrooms had yet another floor pattern. Millie was used to having mud- and straw-packed floors in Amapola. Many times she watched her mother sprinkle the floor with water before the daily sweeping. The water helped to keep the dust from floating up and landing on the food and pottery dishes.

The kitchen was the gathering place in Amapola. There was always an open flame burning and clay pots resting on the adobe blocks. The fresh water was stored in huge clay containers. Millie's new family did not have to go far to get their water. She suspiciously watched water miraculously flowing from steel pipes protruding from the wall.

Her family took baths on the banks of the freshwater river. The men had constructed an adobe barrier to ensure the privacy of the women as they showered under the fresh stream of spring water. In Amapola, many green plants and large trees surrounded the open-air shower. In Imperial Valley, Katherine had carried Millie into the warm bathroom. Everything was white and clean with a huge towel waiting for drying. Things were so different in America. During the hot months, the use of water coolers kept the home comfortable but noisy. Millie observed all these new things but shared very few comparisons with her new family.

The people around her were very nice but deep down she missed her family. She missed being understood in simple Spanish. She had to say things two or three times before she was understood. She also learned to say things that made the Wolfs smile at her. "Yes" was the most frequent word at the edge of her lips. With so much on her mind, she would curl under the sheets in the evening and cry quietly to keep Jack and Katherine from hearing. In Mexico, her older brother and sister had taught her not to cry out loud so that the *lloróna* or weeping woman would not haunt their home. But in this new home she was too scared to hold back her tears.

At the Wolf farm, Millie made friends with the dogs, cows, and chickens. She watched many red-winged blackbirds eating the cattle feed. The noisy birds with their con-ke-ree sounds were always present. She formed a close relationship with the white-and-light-brown-spotted dog. The dog reminded her of her brother Antonio's friendship with the family dog, Tigre. She remembered the meals they shared with the animals. She followed the chickens and looked for their nesting grounds. She had fond memories of her favorite hen and her daily egg-seeking adventures. In Amapola, one egg was fried for the entire family, then mixed with chili and tortillas. Millie's new family had two eggs apiece in the morning.

The smells of an active kitchen were absent. The scents of Katherine's kitchen were not familiar to her. She missed the corn tortillas her mother made each day. She also missed playing with the corn dough and shaping little birds that were cooked for her father.

Millie also felt the absence of candles in the home. The Wolf family had funny lights with fancy white stiff hats as if protecting the light from the sun. She missed the candlelight at night and the games her brother played against the flame of the candles her mother made.

The Wolfs began to tell their friends and neighbors that Millie had been adopted in Ecuador during their two-year stay. She did not understand these conversations but was quickly adjusting to her own room filled with new toys. Her confusion surrounding the memories of her mother and father haunted her silently.

During her first Christmas in the United States, Millie finally met the white-haired, bearded man with the funny laugh and rosy cheeks. She had never seen presents wrapped in such pretty paper placed under a green tree. She had seen many similar trees in the mountains of her beloved homeland, but had never seen anybody place presents beneath them. More amazing for her was the belief that these trees were magic because more presents appeared each new morning just before Christmas Day. The pine tree was decorated with colorful breakable balls unlike anything she had ever seen. The Wolfs also had red, green, and white aluminum garlands hanging from the branches of the tree. To Millie, they looked like the ruffled collars on clowns. She was enthusiastic and helpful in placing many of the ornaments on the first Christmas tree she had ever seen. The red, green, and white colors were also those of Amapola.

In Mexico, presents were placed inside the children's shoes, which they set by the doors or in various rooms of the house. The Three Kings would bring goodies for the children on the morning of January sixth. Her last presents had included a rubber ball and a colorful paper doll with glitter trim painted on as a dress.

Her Christmases were more religious than those of her new family. In Amapola, the children dressed as angels to participate in a live nativity scene for the Catholic services. Her last year there, Millie's place on stage was right next to a real cow in the manger. She sneezed and needed a handkerchief. The entire congregation at church had snickered when she used her long satin skirt to wipe her running nose. Her brother and sister laughed so loud at home that the whole family shared the story over and over again. Millie missed her family so much.

The Wolf family was very devoted to the Catholic Church. They recognized that Millie had also been to mass because they did not have to teach her the sign of the cross. Going to church with Jack and Katherine meant taking a ride to town. In Amapola, everyone walked to the church when the bell announced services. The electric clock served as the notice for the Wolf family to leave for mass.

To hide her emotions, Millie began to spend many hours alone playing on the salt cedars and by the water canals. She played for hours with the house pets, and sat still to watch the wild birds. She always took any fallen baby birds to Katherine so they could nurse them back to health. Millie was grateful for the strong limbs of the trees that supported her while she climbed higher to see the distant lands from her desert dwelling. She often wondered if her family was on the other side of the sky. From her treetop cradle, the world was at her feet. Like Jack, she also enjoyed the sunsets and the glistening of the Salton Sea north of the farm. The desert sunsets cast brilliant colors against the lake.

In September 1958, Millie was enrolled in kindergarten. On the first day, Jack and Katherine personally drove her early in the morning to meet with her new schoolmates and teachers. Niland School included Anglo, Filipino, Chinese, Japanese, and Mexican families. The agricultural valley had brought many workers from the Philippines to plant and harvest tomatoes and grapes. The Chinese families came to Niland after the Pearl Harbor incident. They owned the small grocery store and the only Chinese food restaurant. Many of the Mexican families moved to Niland after the Bracero Program ended. The Mexican men worked as laborers in the fields of the Valley or with Southern Pacific Railroad. During the sweltering heat of Imperial Valley summers, many of the Filipino and Mexican families moved to other parts of California to help with the harvesting of grapes and other fruits.

During all of her elementary and high school education, Millie rode a huge yellow bus to school. It was on the bus that she made many friends she admired for their kindness and sincerity. Two little girls became her closest friends: Olivia, from Mexico, and red-haired, freckle-faced Thelma, whose parents came from Oklahoma. The three girls would eventually build a sincere, lasting friendship. On rainy days when the bus could not travel the muddy roads, Jack drove all three in his huge feed truck to the nearest paved road.

Jack and Katherine were proud that Millie was making great progress at school. Her English was much better than they had expected. In particular, her vocabulary about animals was advanced for her age. She liked animals a lot.

She liked to go with Jack to the feedlot to watch the animals and help feed them with silage the Wolfs prepared at the farm. Too small to reach the clutch, she enjoyed sitting on Jack's lap while he drove the noisy tractor across the cotton aisles. In the cotton fields, the white-tipped doves flew from their hidden nest between the small plants as the tractor approached their hideout. Millie convinced Jack to stop when the surprised birds flew from their nest so that she could jump off to look at the eggs or the new hatchlings. At times, she would take one of the eggs home to hatch, later bringing back a baby bird to the nest. She was keen at keeping track of all nest locations. The easy ones were the nests located at the top of the rusty poles holding the shades for the cattle at the feedlot.

Often she reflected on the past and wondered what had happened to the butterflies. In the Imperial Valley, monarchs were not abundant as they were in central Mexico. Nevertheless, the outdoors provided a bridge to her past life. The valuable connection kept her busy with daily activities at the farm or at school.

She seemed to adjust well in elementary school. By the end

of the first grade she, like all of her classmates, had a father and mother who attended school activities and functions. Her teachers were impressed with her determination to learn given her limitations in the new language.

The school administrators and teachers often commented on how lucky Millie was to have the Wolfs as her family. They also commented on how lucky the Wolfs were to have adopted the right Ecuadorian child.

Millie liked her peers in school and felt they liked her, too. Her teachers and classmates respected what she had to say. To improve her English-speaking abilities, she began participating in speech contests, encouraged by her teacher. In the third grade, the local Lions club sponsored a speech contest for students. In front of many parents and classmates, she won third place in the "My Country" speech.

In fifth grade she played sports, enjoying the competition with the boys more than they realized. During lunch hour, she played hardball with them, and played tether ball during the short recess. The school competed in President Kennedy's initiatives for physical fitness, and Millie was always in the running for many awards, to her parents' surprise and pride.

It was obvious to her that many students did not like the school food. She, too, only liked certain foods. She definitely did not like Monday lunches. Every first day of the week, the cafeteria served hot dogs and mustard, cottage cheese, and canned peaches or pear halves. In those days, pizza and enchiladas were not part of the school meals. On some days, she noticed the Mexican students with their sack lunches. They hid corn tacos behind their brown paper bags. They were embarrassed to eat Mexican food in front of their classmates.

Millie could no longer clearly define her few memories of the past. For example, the smell of cold beans seemed familiar to her. At the start of seventh grade, she volunteered to work in the cafeteria. This allowed her to eat only what she wanted and to help serve others. She also knew that her parents would not have to pay for her lunch on those days. Katherine and Jack were very proud of Millie, counting their blessing after that fateful night in Texas.

Not much was said about her past nor did she ask questions about it. As her life moved forward, she recalled few solid details of her early childhood. In a short time, she had become very fond of the farm. She worked on weekends to save money for college, helping Jack and his father brand new calves and cut horns. She enjoyed riding a horse to drive cattle from one corral to another and to direct cattle into loading shoots to trucks and trains that would haul them to the slaughter houses in Los Angeles.

She continued her interest in butterflies and birds, collecting the tiny wings and fancy plumage that fell from the sky. Most important to her was her collection of birds' nests. Her father and grandfather had also begun to help collect nests for her. There was scarcely a day that did not include the hatching of bird eggs of one kind or another.

She attended Calipatria High School. Niland was too small a

town to have a high school, and the district's secondary education was located eight miles south. She played sports for the Girls' Athletic Association. In those years, girls were not allowed to compete in sports with other schools, only within their own high school. She was also a cheerleader and a member of the school's student council, and continued to participate in debate and speech tournaments, too.

Her love of the farm led her to participate in many farm-related educational activities, including Future Farmers of America. Her interest in the use of plant oils instead of animal oils infused all her studies. She had learned much in conversations about this subject with her grandfather and father, and was very pleased to be part of a family that was concerned with environmental issues.

By her senior year in high school, she was writing most of her term papers on plant oils. Jack's father had begun the planting of jojoba in the 1950s, and now the Wolf family had several hundred acres of the crop growing in their arid desert lands. "Eventually," she told Jack, "the sperm whale and the seal will no longer be slaughtered because they will become extinct. According to research, the jojoba oil can replace the animal oils."

As usual, Millie spent her last summer before entering college working with her father on the farm. The irrigation of the cotton took most of her time. She helped Jack order the water and monitor the flow during the day. She also helped mix the silage for the cattle and took care of the sick animals during the hottest days in the Valley.

It was late that summer that Grandfather Wolf died in his sleep. The entire family was shocked and hurt by his death. Millie was heartbroken by the absence of his spirit. Grandfather Wolf had taught her many new and important things. He was a kind man with many fine attributes. Most of all, she admired the manner in which he took care of the underprivileged Mexican laborers who worked for the family. She attended school with many of the children of the laborers. Knowing that her grandfather and father treated her friends' parents with respect was very important to her.

Over the years, Grandfather Wolf had found the most beautiful nests to add to her collection. He would remain in her memories forever.

At his funeral, she reflected on the body, the mourners, the room, the smell, and the entire ambiance of the event. For whatever reason, funerals brought her childhood memories of the smell of wax and the strong aroma of the flowers. These childhood thoughts were foreign to her current life but seemed present in the heart. It was at this funeral that she began to mourn the loss of her past.

Grandfather Wolf looked at peace. As she stood next to the half of the casket opened for viewing, feelings of familiar surroundings descended on her. Her grandfather had encouraged her and had helped her build an unbreakable personal courage. He would be missed by all, and especially by Millie.

LUZ AL FUTURO
Light Toward the Future

In the autumn, Millie enrolled at Stanford University to pursue a bachelor's degree in international studies. From Imperial Valley to Palo Alto, she was forced to face new challenges and another new environment.

The flat irrigated farmlands and desert climate were traded for the mountains and hills of the Pacific Ocean region. Change for her was much easier than change for most other young adults. She had gone from brief memories of green mountain areas of Mexico to the desert arid lands of the Imperial Valley. She had gone from speaking Spanish to English in a matter of a few years. The move to the university would provide her with other new opportunities.

Once again, she said farewell to loved ones. Deep down in her soul she knew she had done this before. In a split second, her recollection of the pain attached to farewells was clear. As she boarded the Hughes aircraft to San Diego to catch a larger plane to San Francisco, her emotions were beyond confinement.

She was truly affected like no other time before. Perhaps she had grown and now understood human emotions better. She knew that the Wolf family had come into her life at a time she needed them most. They helped and protected her, and guided her to adulthood. From the small airplane window, she wanted to yell at her parents to tell them how much she loved them for all they had done. Tears flowed from her eyes. She could not help but feel sorry to leave the sweet farm surroundings of the Imperial Valley. She also felt she knew too much about things that were not so important and not enough of things relevant to her childhood memories of the family that began to raise her.

She realized how lucky she was to be part of the Wolf family. She knew she could not have selected a better set of parents and grandparents in the entire world. They dedicated all their energies to her upbringing. Her wet eyes were too blurry to stay focused on her parents as the airplane took her away from them.

The prop jet moved swiftly into a gliding mode and into the dusty air overlooking the valley. Over the green cotton fields and the occasional rows of palm trees, she recalled the day her fourth grade teacher asked her about Ecuador. The teacher's descriptions of the South American country did not match Millie's of her homeland. When Millie argued that the teacher knew nothing about Ecuador, she in turn questioned Millie's limited knowledge of her origins and background.

For the first time, she had felt a sense of humiliation and loneliness. At home she found out that her parents had told her teachers that she was adopted from Ecuador. Her parents spoke of her real father asking them to take care of her in America. "Your parents felt you could do better with us after they suffered an accident and we stopped to help." All these years, it had been difficult to understand the reason she had been left with the Wolfs. Millie really did not understand the reasons but did not want to ask too many questions.

More than anything, she wanted so much to learn about her real parents. Out of respect for Jack and Katherine, she placed her inquiries and bewilderment on hold. She did not want to hurt her American parents and therefore let her busy life keep her from any profound thinking about her past.

As the plane began to fly over the edge of the Salton Sea, her eyes tried to focus on the farm and cattle feedlot she had grown to love and appreciate. She could barely distinguish the salt cedars and the thin line of the water canal next to their home. As the small craft headed upwards, the clouds brought a melancholy feeling to her heart. She could not help but wonder what had happened to her past. On her way through clouds, she made a commitment to find out someday.

● ● ●

MILLIE ARRIVED AT STANFORD University on the type of sunny Silicon Valley day that attracts many students from the Midwest and the eastern states. Finding her way around campus, she was reminded of the many stories her mom and dad had shared with her about their own adventures there. Her parents had been inspirational in her selection of Stanford. Had she chosen another college, her parents would not have been upset, just a little disappointed.

Like many of her peers, she biked to classes from her freshman dorm. Her classes consisted primarily of general requirements. Just two focused on her major course of study. She adjusted well to her first semester of classes and to the different styles of instruction by the professors. University life was all she had expected and even better.

She did miss her family and not a week went by that she did not call her parents. In addition, she wrote frequently to tell her parents of her many experiences at the university. She had very few difficulties in finding new friends and learning the campus. But by the end of the first semester, she longed for a visit back home. She missed the little things she had treasured in the Imperial Valley — the open skies, the desert sunsets, and the occasional rattler sliding through the Russian tumbleweed. She especially missed the words of wisdom from her grandfather.

She went home for the winter break and helped her father move cotton trailers from the field to the gin. This part-time job also provided her with additional funds for her spring semester expenses. She hoped to depend less and less on her parents for economic support, believing they had already done more than enough for her.

During the second semester, she continued to enjoy the beautiful sights and moved more freely on campus. Leland Stanford named the university in honor of his young son, who died on a trip in England. That made her wonder what kinds of things her real parents had done to remember her.

Someday, she told herself, she would seek her roots and learn more about her past. The constant affirmation of wanting to learn more of her past was balanced by the many other questions she dealt with in the present. She surveyed the university and imagined the times her parents, the Wolfs, were students on the same campus. She wondered whether they had walked the same hallways and thought the same thoughts during their times. She would lose herself in those questions as she moved through different parts of the campus.

At Stanford, she began to make sense of the many conversations she had with her Grandfather Wolf about life and getting things done. He had pushed her to her limits and told her that if he did not push her, she would not survive in other situations. He taught her about courage to face adversity and courage to face reality. How right he had been in many perspectives he shared. He was a wise man. She had become very attached to him and his ways. He had taught her how to work hard with her hands and twice as hard with her brain to accomplish the task. Memories of her grandfather Wolf and the love she had for him were etched in her callused hands. She was so grateful to the Wolf family, her American parents. Stanford served an important role in helping Millie to gather all the thoughts and information together to make some sense from it and appreciate it more.

In the fall of 1975, she enrolled in her last year at the university. She was anxious to complete the degree and move back to help her father with the farm at the end of the academic year. However, her life began to take another tender turn of events that autumn.

One of the challenges she faced was a class in Latin American history. The reading requirements and written reports were demanding.

"Good morning class, I'm Dr. Ron Smith, professor for Latin American History, course number 2371. Please check to make sure you're in the right class." As Dr. Smith passed out the syllabus to the students, he walked around like an elementary-school teacher checking to make sure everyone had the proper paperwork.

"You'll be required to keep up with the readings and to write three term papers. Please make sure you choose topics that motivate you and challenge you to analyze all the elements surrounding those subjects. If you have any questions, you can reach me during my office hours, which are listed at the top right-hand side of the syllabus," the confident professor said. He also wrote his office phone number and weekly schedule on the chalkboard.

"We are going to begin with a brief history of Mexico. We will proceed to Central America and then to South America for the last nine weeks of the course. You will need to complete a research paper in each of the three areas of study." Dr. Smith continued to deliver the information with professional ease. "In addition, I will invite guest speakers to provide you with additional information on subjects related to Latin American countries."

Millie knew this class was going to be difficult but one she would greatly enjoy. She was looking forward to learning more about the United States' neighbors to the south. Growing up in the Imperial Valley, she had visited Mexicali, Mexico with her parents on a few occasions. She had many questions about the country and its people but did not want to bring any insecurities to the forefront of family conversations.

Being away from home gave Millie many opportunities to seek answers to the frequent questions squelched by her fear of what would be revealed. Deep down, she felt her Mexican roots. Since the fourth grade, she knew she wasn't Ecuadorian but Mexican. With apprehension she often stared at other Mexican children, seeking physical comparisons to herself.

More than anything, she wanted to learn more about Latin America so that she could help her parents in their business. She figured that she could help her father with the farm and with any international affairs.

The study of Latin America would also help her understand the increase in foreign immigrants coming to the United States. She was confident she would have more than enough topics to write about in Dr. Smith's class. In particular, writing about her interest in immigration policy and international business would play right into the class. She began to visualize how she would also write about Ecuador and learn more about the country where her parents lived for two years. Despite her uncertainty and apprehension, Mexico and Ecuador piqued her curiosity.

"The lectures by Dr. Smith were awesome," she told her
parents in a letter. "Our professor does a very good job in
describing the problems of the country of Mexico. Today we
studied the important natural resources of the country to
our south. Dad, Dr. Smith was able to share so much of his
knowledge of Mexico. I have not yet made up my mind
about the specific topic for my first research paper. I guess
I'd better hurry and make my decision. I am just so
enthused about learning more about our Mexican neighbors. I am also looking so much toward graduation. I will be
the happiest cowgirl from the Imperial Valley at this event.
Thank you so much for everything you have done for me,
Mom and Dad. I love you." Millie always closed her letters
with much appreciation and love.

The following week, Dr. Smith invited a graduate student
from the anthropology department to lecture the students
on the ruins of Mexico and the significance of their existence. "Allow me to welcome Hector Hill, graduate student
in anthropology studies with a focus on Mexico," Dr. Smith
began. "Mr. Hill will be graduating this May. He has just
recently been appointed as assistant professor at the
University of California at San Diego for the fall semester —
that is, pending his defense and graduation," Dr. Smith
quipped with pride as he introduced his graduate assistant.
"Please welcome Mr. Hill to our class." Dr. Smith extended
his hand to welcome the young speaker and then swiftly
gave him center stage.

The graduate student presented a well-organized program
to the class. He had prepared slides and handouts with
beautiful pictures of almost magical foreign sites. He was

poised and prepared like no other graduate student they had ever heard. Millie was impressed with his knowledge as well as his ability to engage their interest in volcanoes in such a short time.

Hector Hill was a distinguished young man whose dark hair and light brown eyes added to his good looks. His wire-rimmed glasses contributed to his credibility as a lecturer. His descriptions of the pyramids near Mexico City intrigued all the students most. The lecture on the Moon and Sun pyramids mesmerized Millie's spirit. She was amazed at the magnitude of the structures.

She had not known that these pyramids were the largest in Latin America. Mr. Hill explained that the Moon, or La Luna, and the Sun, or El Sol, pyramids have existed in Mexico since 500 A.D. He told the students that the Aztec Indian Empire was the most powerful within the region. At the end of his third and final lecture, the class acknowledged him with an enthusiastic round of applause. They truly enjoyed his presentation.

Millie left that last lecture wanting more. She had more questions than she had answers. His words had added color to the shadows of her dreams.

She took a last look at some of Mr. Hill's handouts. She stared at the rock-stacked columns holding the hallways of the buildings. She imagined the effort and the intelligence of the indigenous people necessary to build such major con-struction projects by hand. *Some day, I want to visit these places*, she thought to herself. She wound her way through the crowded halls until she reached her bicycle. She rode to her next class on an adrenaline high of excitement about the knowldge Hector Hill had provided her class.

As she rode her bike she noticed the change of weather in the air. The fall season at Stanford did not bring much visible difference in the look of the campus. There were no leaf color changes or major snowstorms. The only noticeable differences were the cool night temperatures and the frequent rain, a new natural phenomenon for Millie. Imperial Valley received very few inches of rain each year. By the end of her four years at Stanford, Millie had become enamored with the sound of rain.

She knew she would miss this weather once back in the hot Imperial Valley. There, the shadows of the large silos would not be enough to protect her from the scorching heat that took control of every inch of ground. At Stanford, shadows from the tall trees and stone buildings allowed a taste of colder air. Students rode their bikes with sweaters or coats tied around their waists in anticipation of the chilly breezes.

One day in the middle of November, she sat by the center fountain at the quad reading a Thanksgiving card her mother had sent her. Instead of going home for the holiday, she was staying on campus to finish papers and study for final exams. As she read, she felt the tiny tears wanting to leave the inside corners of her eyes. She was homesick and missed her family. Under the late autumn sun's rays she read with sadness. She disciplined her emotions as she felt the shadow of a body settle quietly a few feet away. The quad's circular fountain rim had ample room for many to sit and chat. The fountain provided a place to read recent mail since the campus post office was a stone's throw away.

Katherine had written her wishing the best and letting her know how much they missed their baby already. Katherine also wanted her to know that as painful as it might be, it was important for her to remain at school and complete her goals. Millie could feel the tender hug her mother gave her before she boarded the airplane to Palo Alto for the first time almost four years ago. The university had taught her so much but she had paid the price in pent-up emotions and profound loneliness.

She heard the person next to her laughing. As she turned, she realized a young man was also reading a letter. She folded her card and put it back into the envelope with much care. Her mother had sent her a twenty-dollar bill, which she placed in her wallet. As she turned to swing her back-pack over her left shoulder, she noticed the laughing young man next to her was the lecturer Dr. Smith had invited to class.

"Hey, aren't you Hector?" she asked.

"Yes, I am. Who are you?"

She politely extended her right hand. "I think you did a very good job in our class with Dr. Smith." She felt good shaking his hand. He had done an excellent job getting her more interested in Mexico.

Hector quickly folded his letter and stuffed it between some pages of a thick book. "Oh, thanks. What's your name?" he asked again.

"My name is Millie. See you around." She pulled the other strap of her backpack up before walking to her bike.

"Hey, what year are you?" he called out.

Raising her voice, she said, "I'm a senior. See you at graduation!" She headed on to her next class, peddling as fast as she could and checking her watch to assure herself of the time.

She felt lucky that she had the opportunity to meet Hector and shake his hand. She knew he was very intelligent. She wondered about the letter he was reading. He gave her the impression that he wanted to put his letter away as quickly as possible. She figured it was from his girlfriend, given the haste of his actions. As she peddled she wondered about him. She had never seen him before on campus. She assumed that, like most graduate students, he lived off-campus.

On Thanksgiving Day, Millie and a few friends spent part of the day feasting on cold cuts, sodas, and peanuts. She had never before been away from her family on such a special day, and the old feelings of deep loneliness filled her again. She had to remind herself that she had so much to be thankful for despite her hunger to know her past.

The following day, she dedicated herself to completing her research for all her term papers. She spent most of her time at Green Library looking up information in books and periodicals to verify her research notes. She had become well-versed in the use of the library and felt good about her ability to find important facts.

She sat quietly reading the reference books that she couldn't check out due to library policy. A passing shadow made her look up in time to see a vaguely familiar person. She was certain she had seen the guy before. She recognized the back of the neck of the clean-cut student assistant she had met ten days earlier at the fountain. Her eyes followed his handsome silhouette as he moved from the card catalogue to the reference desk. He was asking for information and pointing to the files, and she was curious to know what he was looking for.

What am I doing? she thought suddenly. *I have to get busy or else I won't finish.* She reminded herself of her responsibilities. She resumed reading and in a few moments forgot about the graduate student who had impressed her. The hours rolled by, and she grew tired of so much reading and note-taking. Mentally exhausted, she was ready for a break.

"Hello, Millie." Hector stood at her side as she stretched her tired limbs.

"Hector, you scared me!" She jumped from the chair when he tapped her on the shoulder.

"What are you working on?" he asked.

"I'm completing the final notes for my research paper for

English. This is one of the most difficult classes I've had."
She barely looked up at Hector as she closed the reference
book. Hector noticed that several of her fingers remained
between the pages in the middle of the thick book. He knew
her mind was still on the pages between her fingertips.

"How was your Thanksgiving Day?" he asked.

"I didn't get to go home. I stayed here to do research." Millie
smiled at Hector. "How about you? Did you get to go
home?" She looked closely at Hector, admiring his smooth
skin and handsome smile full of white, shiny teeth. He
seemed nicer up close than he did from a distance in the
lecture hall. Her fingers slowly removed themselves from the
smooth pages of her book.

"I stayed here on campus, too," he replied. "Millie, want to
take a break? Let's go to the student union for a Coke." She
didn't know what to say. For a split second she was ready to
go for another hour of study. On the other hand, a break
might be a good way to recharge her energy level.

"I only have a few minutes, Hector. I need to complete this
silly term paper on Faust." She quickly gathered her notebook and pens and stuffed them in her backpack, then followed Hector out of the library. They walked through the
center of campus to the student recreation hall. She wanted
to ask him so many questions about his lecture for Dr.
Smith's class, but knew this was not the right time.

Hector had other things in mind. He knew that Stanford did
not have many students like Millie. He wanted to find out

more about her and why she was there. Millie was a beautiful young lady with long, neatly trimmed dark hair. Her complexion was a constant light tan. It was obvious to him that she spent many hours in the sun. When she smiled, the corners of her eyes twinkled with small lines that were lighter than the rest of her skin.

He'd been wondering about the time he met her at the quad. He figured that Millie was reading a letter from a boyfriend. He was determined to learn more about her, but he didn't want to overwhelm her with question after question.

"When we saw each other at the quad, you said you'd see me at graduation. Are you graduating, Millie?" he asked.

"I'm very fortunate to be able to finish this May. My mother and father will be coming up for the special day. I know about you because Dr. Smith told us, remember?"

"Oh, yeah. He's a good professor. He cares a lot for the students he supervises. He's one of my advisors and he's helped me a lot. I'll be defending my dissertation the first of April." Hector was proud of his accomplishments. His five years at Stanford had been difficult and lonely. He was looking forward to completing his studies.

The student union did not have the usual Friday crowd. "Let's sit outside." Hector led Millie to a sunny table. He placed his books on the table next to the one he had selected. The few seats being used seemed to be occupied by older students who probably also stayed on campus to study instead of rushing home for the short break.

"What would you like to drink, Millie?"

"I think I'll just have a Coke. I'm actually a little hungry, to be honest with you."

"Do you want to share a tuna salad sandwich?"

She gave him a "you're kidding" look before responding. "That sounds good."

"Let me get this," Hector said as he walked off to the counter on the inside of the building. She waited patiently on a patio chair.

The pattern in the wrought-iron tables created many one-inch holes. Millie concluded that bird lovers had made the tables. She figured that the holes were big enough so the crumbs would tumble on the floor. The birds could eat the crumbs while the students hit the books. Her fascination with birds and butterflies was always strong and this setting was a great place to observe her feathered friends. Their hunger always reminded her of the tons of bird feed her father's farm had every day of the year.

The number of birds coming to every meal at the farm had always charmed and intrigued her. She remembered the many times she had tried to count the birds that would land on the pile of feed seed. She could never get an accurate count because they were constantly moving and jumping from one spot to another.

Her thoughts were interrupted when Hector graciously

placed a tray in front of her. He had brought more than she had expected. Potato chips, cookies, two sandwiches and two sodas along with plastic utensils. "Thank you, Hector," she said. She began to divide the tray contents in two.

They ate as if they had not eaten for days. For the first few minutes, potato chip crunching dominated the sounds of their conversation.

"What are you studying, Millie?"

"My major is international studies. I also want to be able to help my father with the farm so my minor is business. I'd like to learn about other cultures and places," she said. "How about you, Hector? How long have you been here?"

"I came to Stanford in 1972 from the University of Chicago. I'm majoring in anthropology with an emphasis in Latin America. I'll be leaving to teach at the University of San Diego at the end of August. Before that, I'll spend the summer with my family in Chicago. My parents are also coming to graduation. My mother has never been to California before. I think she'll like it very much."

They chatted about school and current challenges, but were both eager to hurry back to their work. They walked back to the library and began to focus on their assignments.

"Thanks, Hector. I really enjoyed the break. I'll see you soon. Next time, it will be my treat," she said gratefully.

"Hey, Millie, if you need help with Dr. Smith's class, give me a call. Or I can give you a call. What's your phone number?" She did not want to acknowledge that she liked the idea of hearing from him again, but immediately responded to his request. Hector wrote down the number and then disappeared into the stacks while Millie continued to study in the reference section. As usual, she remained there until very late in the evening.

Two evenings before the beginning of winter break, she and her dorm mates exchanged small gifts and greetings for the holiday season. They gathered in their pajamas to share the upcoming holidays before departing to their respective homes. They celebrated the completion of the semester and all the requirements for their classes. As they discussed their plans, the resident assistant came to tell Millie that she had a telephone call waiting. She jumped, because she knew her mother would be calling her before she left for home.

"Mom, I'm so happy you called."

"Millie, it's me, Hector." His voice surprised her.

"Hector! I am so sorry! I thought you were my mom. How are you?" She thanked God that Hector could not see her red face.

"I called you to wish you a Merry Christmas. I hope I didn't bother you."

"Oh, no. We're just having a little Christmas party before leaving for winter break. How about you?"

"I'll be staying here after all. I need to finish the final written draft of my dissertation. When are you leaving, Millie?"

"I'm flying home on Friday. My father needs help hauling the cotton trailers to the gin. Besides, the dorms will be closed for the break. I'm leaving the books behind in order to help my dad with farm chores," she said proudly.

"Listen, do you want to grab a tuna salad sandwich?"

Millie didn't hesitate. "When?"

"Tomorrow for lunch, Millie? I can pick you up and you won't have to ride your bike in the cold wind."

"OK. I'll see you around eleven-thirty. I'll meet you outside the front door of the dorm," she said. She paused a moment, and then thanked Hector for his call. "I'll see you tomorrow." She replaced the receiver on the telephone as if it were made from some breakable material. On her way back to the gathering she felt silly about the episode. All the girls could tell by the way Millie acted that it had been a guy on the phone. She didn't understand why Hector had called her, but was glad he did. She remained embarrassed by the fact that she had thought it was her mother on the line.

Hector was punctual the next day, arriving in an old, bright-red Plymouth Valiant. He gracefully opened the passenger door from his driver's seat. "Hi, Millie, how are you?"

"I'm fine. I'm sorry I mistook you for my mother last evening." Hector was unconcerned, and quickly headed the car across campus and onto the main roads on the west side of Palo Alto. "Where are we headed?" Millie assumed they would go to the student union for tuna sandwiches.

"I thought we'd go to a little seaside restaurant in Half Moon Bay. It's a beautiful place, right by the ocean. Some of my friends took me there for my birthday. I think you'll like it." The majestic redwoods lining the winding roads made the long drive to the restaurant worthwhile.

"How did you do in all your classes?" he asked.

"This was probably the most difficult semester I've had. But I hope to pass all my classes and be done with the degree." She responded with room for a range of outcomes. "How about you, Hector? How is your dissertation coming along?" She hoped that her questions would help to hide her surprise at his call.

It had been three weeks since they had spent a few minutes sharing a tuna sandwich. Both had so much to talk about. Their enthusiasm for each other's company was evident. "I read your term paper for Dr. Smith. I really enjoyed your topic and I thought I should call you."

"What! You read my paper?" She was not expecting to hear that Hector had read her term paper. Hector tried to reassure her that it was typical for graduate students to read research papers from undergraduates.

"Dr. Smith asked me to read the papers for your class, and I did. You have nothing to fear — you did a good job. It was well-researched and the topic was clearly developed. Good job, Millie," he said. "I didn't want to call you until you got your grade. Dr. Smith posted his grades yesterday, right?"

Millie was embarrassed again, her face blushing pink as the conversation focused on her. But she was glad Hector liked the paper, and glad she had received an "A" in the class. It was also kind of nice, in a way, that Hector seemed like such a caring guy.

As they approached the rustic beachfront restaurant, Hector and Millie marveled at the beauty of the scenery. The fresh saltwater air carried different memories for each of them. She missed the canals in Imperial Valley. He missed walking along Lake Michigan in the summer.

They sat by the window in a two-person booth overlooking the Pacific Ocean. The fishing boats bouncing playfully on the white-capped waves looked tiny from such a distance. The small, family-owned restaurant was the perfect place to chat and enjoy the beauty of the unpredictable ocean.

"Hector, this is a very pretty sight."

"I think so too, Millie. My mother will also like this place. When they come to visit me, I'll bring them here. My father loves seafood and his stomach will like this place, too." Hector laughed when he recalled his father's hearty appetite.

He paused for a moment, and then asked Millie what she was going to do after graduation. She thought he had already asked her that question before, but figured he had so many things on his mind that he did not remember. She did not hesitate to respond again.

"I'm going to help my father with the farm. My grandfather just passed away, and my father needs additional trustworthy help. My mom is so excited that I'm moving back. They have been so good to me."

"You love your parents very much, don't you?" Hector asked with a broad smile on his face. "You know, Millie, I love my parents too, but I don't think I've told them in recent years. I guess guys are different from girls. It's difficult for us to be emotional with our parents." Hector stared at the ocean waves breaking into their banners of blue and white. The endless cycle of the waves softened Millie's fears and she began to trust Hector, telling him things she otherwise would not have said.

When their soups were served, they spooned up the clam chowder politely, trying hard to keep its deliciousness from sounding as it entered their mouths. But the simple table setting and informal meal encouraged Millie to feel relaxed.

"What do you do when you defend your dissertation?" she asked Hector. She knew his current world revolved around the details of his research. His every waking moment was spent on perfecting the document.

"Well, you sit in front of a group of professors, some who may not be interested in your topic, and you respond to their questions. They ask you about your research to make sure you know your topic very well. They may ask you questions you haven't thought of or questions to which you should know the answers but don't. They might even ask you to do additional research. That's basically it," Hector explained with a sigh.

"Aren't you going to get nervous?" she asked, anticipating the answer.

"No." Hector surprised her.

"So what's your research on?" She had never before been so charged with curiosity as she was with Hector. His eyes and soft smile appealed to her more than she realized.

"I've researched two very important volcanoes of Mexico. I researched Paricutín and El Popo. Paricutín erupted less than thirty-five years ago and the other is expected to erupt sometime in the near future. The eruption of Paricutín created many difficult challenges and opportunities for the country," he said in a confident and knowledgeable manner. "I'll do OK in my defense. The chairman of my dissertation committee feels very good about my work." Hector let out another sigh. "Just pray for me on this day and I'll be all right." Goose bumps danced on Millie's skin.

For many years Millie had wondered about volcanoes. She knew that she had heard about such phenomenal occurrences somewhere else. She dug deep into her memory bank to recall the familiar topic, but digging clouded her thinking and confused her emotions. She really wanted to know more but felt too uneasy.

She wanted to pursue the topic of her past with Hector, but thought he probably wouldn't understand how she felt. She was determined that, given the right time, she would look things up herself and put things in perspective. The unknown pieces of her past bothered her a lot, more than she expected.

Even though Millie was outspoken and a risk-taker, she was afraid to bring the matter of her past forward with Hector. Her internal fortitude would not allow her to go past her current insecurities. The conversation with Jack and Katherine about her fourth-grade teacher's comments left Millie wondering what really had happened in her past. Every year, her curiosity became more complicated and intense but also more private. Her mind wandered while Hector enthused about the surrounding beauty of the romantic California coast.

"Volcanoes aren't of much interest to many people, Millie," Hector continued. In a split second, Millie returned from her thoughts and felt guilty that she had lost track of what Hector was saying. "I've had to keep my interests to myself because not everyone understands or knows about my area of interest and research. All I know is that I'm happy I'll be through very soon."

After dinner, Hector and Millie walked along the balcony facing the Pacific Ocean. From the edge of the wooden platform, they could see below them the waves crashing against huge rocks. A few seals perched on the rocks, waiting for just the right moment to jump in. Other large seals relaxed peacefully. Millie wished she could stand there all day and enjoy their serenity, but she knew she must get back to campus and finish packing.

Returning to Millie's dorm, Hector eased the car to the curb and reached across her to open the passenger door. He watched her intently as he made gracious small talk and thanked her for a delightful time, hoping for a kiss. But he could tell that she had other things on her mind. Millie could tell what he was thinking, and knew she would be sorry later for jumping from the car so quickly.

Hector hadn't had much time to dedicate himself to the opposite sex. His dissertation was more important. Millie was different, though. He knew it. But this farewell would have to suffice for now.

"Thank you, Hector, for a wonderful lunch and for very pretty scenery. I really enjoyed it."

"It was my pleasure, Millie. By the way, who's taking you to the airport tomorrow?"

"Several of us are getting a ride from the resident assistant."

"Well, why don't I give you a ride? It would be fun and it would give me a break from my work," Hector said. She thought about the offer and did not want to be rude or uncaring toward his kindness.

"All right. My plane leaves at four and I need to be there by three. You know how crowded the airport gets, so we would have to leave at — "

As she mentally calculated the timeline, Hector responded, "We need to leave no later than one-thirty. I'll pick you up then, right here. See you tomorrow."

"Thanks, Hector." She waved goodbye and turned toward the dorm.

What have I done? Hector thought. He had just committed himself to more time away from his studies. But Millie wasn't like the other Stanford girls he had met. Hector searched in his mind for the difference.

Hector thumped the steering wheel of his car as he drove off, questioning his actions. He had been so relaxed at lunch and enjoyed every bit of it, too. Millie was different, and his mind kept assuring his heart that he had made the right decisions.

Millie was eager to go the next day. She said farewell to her dorm friends who were also preparing to leave, and was ready for Hector to drive up so that she could load her matching baggage into his car.

She could not shake off the lunch conversation she had with Hector the day before. The information Hector had shared with her about his research interests had aroused her curiosity. She was still perplexed as Hector drove up. He opened his door and walked around to the small trunk to get it ready for her things. He was headed toward the dorm to help just as the door popped opened and Millie appeared with her hands and arms full of hanging bags and dragging suitcases.

"Hi, Millie. Please let me help you with your bags."

"Thanks, Hector," Millie said, noticing the many books and folders on the back seat. She had imagined her bags stacked there, ready to grab for a quick exit at the airport. "Hector, is all this your work?" Millie's interest in his research let her forget about her plan for a hasty exit.

"I'm going to Cal Berkeley's library to look for additional material. I'll go there after I drop you off," he said as they settled into their seats. "This works out well for me," he added with a broad smile directed straight at her eyes.

"Hector, you really didn't have to do this for me." Hector smiled again and headed north to the airport.

"Before we part, let me have your address so that I can at least mail you a Christmas card from the desert," she added in an effort to begin a casual conversation.

Hector was wondering again what the heck he was doing taking time away from his busy schedule. But he brightened at the thought of hearing from Millie during the holidays.

"Sure," he said. "Pull out a pencil and I'll tell you now before we forget." Millie copied down his address carefully and tucked it into her wallet.

At the airport, they waited together in the ticketing line. She was a little embarrassed that he had not allowed her to take her own bags into the airport, but instead had parked the car and carried the heaviest two himself.

"Millie, while we wait, could I have your address?"

"Get your pencil ready," she replied, surprising herself with her eagerness to hear from him soon.

As he copied down her address, Hector asked, "Is your last name Wolf?" Millie knew he had seen her name on Dr. Smith's class list. But then he added, "Do you have any other name?"

"My last name is Wolf." Millie knew what that was about. She knew that Hector was expecting her to attach a Spanish last name to her first name. He was curious about the origin of her name.

The ticketing agent checked Millie's suitcases and handed her the additional boarding pass needed for the connecting flight to Imperial Valley. Hector walked her to the gate to wait for boarding time.

"Millie, have a very Merry Christmas with your family. I know they'll be pleased to have you home for the holidays."

"Thank you for bringing me to the airport during such a busy time for you. Please have a good holiday in the midst of your research." She extended her right hand to clasp Hector's right hand in gratitude. Their eyes met over the handshake. With his free hand, Hector gently grasped her right elbow and pulled her toward his body. It wasn't a complete hug, but their cheeks brushed in a respectful farewell. In a split second they pulled apart, and Millie felt a strange void as she turned toward the departure gate.

Before reaching the boarding chute, she turned once more to Hector and waved a warm farewell. Hector waved back. He looked lonely.

The chute between the gate and the airplane reminded Millie of the many steers she had driven up a chute and into a truck for transporting to the slaughterhouse. The memories of the iron chute and the cattle rushing through momentarily made her forget her confused feelings toward Hector. But moving through the boarding chute like the cattle she had herded, she felt the loneliness return, and thought of flowers abandoned by the butterflies and bees after the pollen is gone. She could not understand why she felt so empty. The bittersweet feeling would last the entire trip home to Imperial Valley.

After takeoff, Millie watched from her window as the plane took a westerly turn and then headed south over the Pacific Ocean. It made her wonder how Hector had managed to drive so quickly across the Bay in heavy traffic. She realized she enjoyed his company so much that she had been unaware of the drive itself. She felt herself smile at the wonderful thoughts about Hector, and hoped no one would catch her grinning. *I'll get busy*, she thought, *and get a Christmas card to thank him for his generosity and time.*

As the airplane headed south to San Diego, Millie tried to figure out the meaning of her new friendship. She was enamored of Hector and wondered why the attraction had happened so quickly.

In San Diego, Millie boarded a small prop jet headed to

Imperial County. She welcomed another forty minutes to contemplate the skies and analyze the situation with Hector before meeting up with her parents.

Jack and Katherine were looking forward to having their baby girl spend some time with them. They had missed her so much these past four years. They were glad she had decided to return home every winter to help and spend time with them.

Katherine always cooked her favorite meals on winter breaks as a way of demonstrating how much she had been missed. Jack and Katherine knew that Millie's presence was not a lifetime commitment, but they welcomed the time she wanted to spend on the farm. It meant so much to them that she loved the farm.

It was a joy for Millie to spend time on the farm. She helped pull cotton trailers from her father's fields to the gin. The end of the year always meant it was time to harvest cotton in the Imperial Valley. The large cotton-picking machines moved through the fields, pulling the delicate buds from the plants. When full, the machines would empty their contents onto the trailers waiting at the end of the fields. Millie would hitch her pickup truck to the cotton-filled trailer and drive it to the gin. The gin would separate the seeds and debris from the cotton before bailing it and wrapping it with burlap. Millie's responsibilities were repetitive, but she liked knowing she was helping.

Though her love of the farm was enough to sustain her, Jack paid her handsomely for the work she performed. He was also financing her entire degree at Stanford. Millie knew she was very fortunate to have parents who could afford to send her there. Many students needed student government loans in order to keep up with the tuition costs. Millie knew how lucky she was.

Driving cotton trailers back and forth for twelve hours a day gave her many hours of thinking time. For the first few days, most of her thoughts were on Hector, wondering what he might be doing at particular times. She thought about the chance that he might also be thinking of her, but felt it was a remote possibility.

Over and over she mentally replayed the special last moments with Hector. She could not think of another time when she had felt like this before. It seemed ironic to her that she could spend so much of her time thinking about the simple expressions of friendship Hector had offered. She laughed at herself for repeating the scenes with Hector so often in her head.

A week before Christmas, she stopped in town and searched for the perfect combination Christmas and thank-you card for Hector. She hoped it would surprise him. She was getting home from the fields so late and was usually so tired that she had to do it now or miss the opportunity. She parked her big truck and trailer at the only grocery store in town to look for the perfect card for her new-found friend.

In the store, she read each card carefully until she found what she thought was just the right one with a simple Christmas and appreciation message for Hector. She made her purchase and drove home quickly because her parents were waiting for her.

"How was your day today?" her mother asked.

"It was just fine, Mom. And dinner smells great tonight. You know I love the way your pork roast always turns out. You are the best cook in the entire Imperial Valley." Katherine was very pleased to cook her daughter's favorite dish. She knew her daughter worked hard to help on the farm.

Besides, this might be the last winter that the family schedule would include Millie. Katherine and Jack wanted Millie to return to the farm but knew they should not count on it. After graduation, Millie might choose to seek professional employment elsewhere.

The Wolf family sat together to eat the delicious home-cooked meal. Dinner was always a special time for the family to talk about farm business and what was planned for the following day. Often Katherine would volunteer to help run errands in town while Jack and Millie worked in the fields.

After dinner Millie excused herself for the evening. "I'm really tired," she told her parents apologetically. "The cotton hauling was exhausting today." What she didn't say was that she was anxious to write her note to Hector.

Resting would be secondary that night for her. She wanted to have time to think about her note to him. If she didn't mail it the next day, he might not get it until after the first of the New Year. The card read:

"Friends Across the Miles are Dear
You are in my thoughts
For your kindness and warmth
Merry Christmas and a Happy New Year!

She chose a sheet of floral stationery and began to write a personal greeting to Hector:

December 22, 1975

Dear Hector:
Greetings from Imperial Valley. I hope you are doing well in your research. I have been thinking about you. I know the pressures of your work must be tremendous. I know that this task means a lot to you. I trust you will accomplish your goal before the New Year begins. I hope you are progressing in your research as you had anticipated.

I am very busy hauling cotton trailers to the gin for my father. The work is not difficult but it does require time and a lot of repetition of effort. Most of the fields are anywhere from four to seven miles away from the gin. Thank God for machines, they do most of the work. I just make sure they are in the right place and they don't run out of fuel. I enjoy the beauty of this part of the country. The shifting of gears on the trucks keeps me pretty alert most of the day.

I am sorry I have not written sooner. Life on the farm is hectic, as you can imagine. My day begins at 6:00 a.m. and ends at sundown. The heat is intense in the Imperial Valley this winter. I'll bet the summer is going to get super-hot.

By the time I get home, I am ready for a hot shower,

a meal, and then for bed. I get home so tired. This type of work requires a form of energy different from the one required at Stanford.

Really, I hope you have a wonderful Christmas and a very Happy New Year. I know your work will be completed. I will continue to pray for your dedication and your success. Thanks for the ride to the airport and the wonderful conversation. God bless you.

Sincerely,
Millie Wolf

She folded the note and placed it inside the envelope. She softly licked the flap with the tip of her tongue, hoping that Hector would see the detailed attention she gave the note. She heard the telephone ring as she pressed the envelope against her heart with the palm of her hand. Her high school friends, Thelma and Olivia, had been wanting her to join them at some of the many seasonal parties in town. If she got dressed again and went with them, she would have a chance to put Hector's card in the mail. Her father answered the phone and then knocked on Millie's door.

"Honey, you've got a phone call."

"I'll be right there, Dad." Millie knew that Thelma would be impatient to plan their evening out.

She wrapped herself in a terry-cloth robe to go to the phone in the living room. Katherine had often offered to install a phone in her daughter's room but Millie always preferred to have quiet there. Her father often spent many hours on the

phone with other farmers assessing the conditions for
planting so the phone was tied up most of the time anyway.

Millie laughed to herself, remembering when Thelma would
call her at 5:30 a.m. every morning to ask what she was
wearing to school. Thelma was a great source of amuse-
ment at the Wolf family dinner table because of her early
morning telephone consultations. She had to call early
because the school bus picked her up first. Even though the
bus was nearly full with many other students by the time it
reached the Wolfs', Thelma would always save Millie a spot
in their favorite seat in the back. Millie thought Thelma was
a real hoot.

"Hello, Thel— oh, hi!" Millie was surprised when she
answered the phone to hear Hector's voice. "Yeah, this is
unexpected," she told him. "I thought it was my friend
Thelma."

Hector was glad he had caught her unexpectedly. He had
surprised himself as well by calling Millie so soon. Now he
was nervous that he had interrupted dinner or some other
family activity.

"No, no. It's all right, I can talk," she assured him. "You are
always surprising me." Millie giggled with pleasure.

She composed herself to ask Hector how his research was
going. He was accomplishing much, he told her, but missed
their conversations. There was a long pause before she told
him that he was not going to believe her, but she had just
sealed a note for him.

Hector wanted her to tell him what she had written, but she told him he would have to wait. Instead, she described the wonderful weather in the Imperial Valley.

"We're enjoying a great winter here. It's especially nice at this time of night," she told him. "The thermometer hit 80 degrees today."

Hector asked her if hauling cotton was occupying all her time. He had never really spent time on an American farm. Stanford had been the closest he had been to living near any farms. He was curious about Millie's chores at the ranch.

"I've been helping my father with the sick animals on Saturdays and when the gin closes early. But I really appreciate your calling me, Hector. I kinda miss school." Millie was full of gratitude that he had phoned, but wondered how he had found her number. When Hector admitted he had had some help from Directory Assistance, Millie could not help but smile.

"Hector, I can't believe you would go to so much trouble to get my number." She rubbed her forehead as she questioned Hector in amazement. "I just wish you a very Merry Christmas I'll pray for you Hector," she added. "You'll do a good job, I know it."

Hector thanked her for support and told her how much it encouraged him to hear her voice.

"Thanks for calling me, Hector. It really means a lot to me that you called," Millie told him. "See you soon. Bye."

She could not believe that Hector would call her at home. It dawned on her that he seemed genuinely interested in how she was doing. What a nice gentleman!

He was a handsome man, too, Millie reflected. He was tall and eternally tan and had a beautiful smile that invited everyone around him to join him in his joy. She thought about the first time she saw him walk into the lecture hall with Professor Smith. His self-assurance was apparent in his demeanor. In many ways Hector reminded Millie of her reassuring grandfather, whom she missed very much.

Millie drifted back to her room with a mischievous smile and thoughts pleasant enough to keep her awake for a long time. She was exhausted but her adrenaline overflowed her blood vessels, rushing with the excitement of Hector's phone call. *He's crazy*, Millie decided before her tired body relaxed into a deep, peaceful sleep.

• • •

ON CHRISTMAS EVE, the Wolf family attended the midnight Catholic services as they had each year since their return from Ecuador. At mass, Millie found Hector taking up much room in her brain. The long services and the priest's soft voice allowed her thoughts to wander, and she could not keep them away from her new friend. At last Father Wayland closed with blessings and best wishes for a happy holiday, and invited the congregation to take the church's poinsettia plants home with them.

Millie approached the altar, made the sign of the cross and received a poinsettia plant from Father Waylan. She swallowed the urge to refer to him as she and her friends had in their catechism classes: Whispering Waylan. His voice was barely audible without the powerful microphone he used in church.

"Merry Christmas, Father Waylan!"

"Merry Christmas, Millie," the priest said softly.

The Wolf family embraced their friends warmly outside the small, quaint church before leaving to return home to a twinkling Christmas tree and many wrapped surprises.

For the first time that she could recall, Millie was not excited about Christmas. The rush to open presents and watch others open theirs was just not there. She agreed to help her father with the cattle in the early morning, and then she hoped to relax until lunchtime. In the afternoon, Thelma was going to pick her up, and they were going to visit Olivia.

Olivia was Millie's other special friend throughout her school years. She lived three miles north of Millie by the All American Canal. The three girls kept in contact now by letter-writing, and planned to be in each other's weddings. Thelma and Millie also visited Olivia every opportunity they had when they were home from college, and especially during holidays. Olivia had been very active in school until her freshman year, when she went diving by one of the main canals and hit a broken bamboo stalk barely visible from the edge of the canal. Olivia had injured her spinal cord. The tragic incident left her paralyzed from the waist down and confined to a wheelchair.

Thelma and Millie enjoyed reliving memories of elementary and junior high school with Olivia. In particular, stories about their daily bus rides seemed to be the funniest and most cheering to Olivia, whose accident had meant that she had to ride a different bus and attend a different school. Her mother told Millie and Thelma that their visits helped Olivia tremendously. Millie was surprised to realize that as time moved forward, she found her chats with Olivia increasingly rewarding.

After Grandfather Wolf passed away, Millie's visits to Olivia became even more meaningful to both young women. Olivia's large family did not have much. Olivia's father was a *zanjero* for the irrigation water district, driving from one canal to another to control and gauge water sold to farmers for crops and household use. Millie always made it a point to take Olivia some sort of surprise when she visited. On this Christmas day, she took Olivia some sweat pants and a Tom Jones record album. Millie felt rewarded every time Olivia smiled.

AMISTAD CARIÑOSA
A Dear Friendship

After a long day of farm work on New Year's Eve, Millie was exhausted and ready for a hot shower. She was relieved to get home and smell dinner cooking.

"Sweetheart, you have a letter waiting for you from Stanford," Katherine called as Millie removed her dirty, heavy shoes.

"Mom, have you paid the tuition for next semester?" Most letters from the university either wanted money or announced a change in schedules. Because she was a senior, much of Millie's school correspondence came from the alumni organization, inviting her future membership.

Her legs dragged her tired body to the living room as the aroma of fresh baked bread floated in front of her nose.

Approaching the small cherry antique desk that had been Grandfather Wolf's, Millie noticed the white envelope addressed to her. She practically tore the envelope apart when she recognized the handwriting — the same style as the grading notes on her term paper for Dr. Smith.

"Hector! I can't believe it." Millie's surprise and disbelief caused her to exclaim out loud.

"Of course I sent the tuition payment at the end of November." Katherine had not caught Millie's exclamation, but she could tell that her daughter wasn't listening to her.

"Mom, the letter is not requesting tuition. It's from a friend of mine at school," Millie revealed.

She hadn't said a word about her special friendship with a graduate student. Normally she confided in her mother about boys, but Hector was different from the other boys she had known. The way she felt about this young man made her nervous, and she hoped her mother couldn't see her excitement. She didn't know how her mom would react, so she didn't say much.

The one other time Millie was as thrilled about receiving mail was when her acceptance letter from Stanford arrived. Hector's letter brought a different acceptance notice important only to Millie. She had never paid much attention to the affection the boys tried to show her in high school, and in college had dedicated herself to studying. She figured that the cost of her education was too much for her parents to spend for her not to pay attention.

Katherine was curious but did not want to be nosy about the letter. Millie carried it into the bathroom to get the shower started. As she read the note, she began to take off her dusty work clothes for the much-needed hot-water splash.

December 30, 1975

Dear Millie:
I received your Christmas note this morning. First of all, I hope you aren't working too hard at the farm. I hope you can make some time for relaxation. Second, my work is coming along fine. I should complete the entire document before second semester begins. My professor has been working with me on some minor details. I'll be ready.

By the way, you spelled my last name wrong. It isn't Hill, but Gil. I'll forgive you this time! When are you returning to Stanford? I can pick you up at the airport if you don't have a ride.

The weather here hasn't been as nice as it has been at your place. We've had cold days and dreary afternoons. It will be nice when the sun shines a little more. I really don't have much time to enjoy the days anyway since I'm stuck on my project. I'm at the end of my patience with it. I'll be glad to finish and begin work in San Diego. By the way, I looked at the California map and found Imperial Valley. Your place is east of San Diego, right?

I hope you had a wonderful Christmas with your parents and friends. I'm sure your parents gave you nice gifts. Take care of yourself. See you when you get back, and if you need a ride, write me or leave me a message at the School of Education office. Happy New Year!

Hector Gil

Millie read the note over and over and over again. The water in the shower kept running as she read it once more. Katherine knocked on the bathroom door.

"Sweetheart, are you OK?" she asked.

"Yes, mother. I'm just jumping in for a shower," Millie answered through a cloud of warm mist.

"Please make sure you leave some hot water for your father," Katherine reminded her.

Millie knew that the water heater held only so much because when she was a small child and played for a long time in her bath, she would use up all the hot water. Her father would have to wait another half-hour before additional water was collected in the small water heater. This was not a problem during the hot summer days, when the outdoor reservoirs kept the water at desirable shower temperature. She hadn't realized that she'd stood without her clothes so long while reading Hector's letter.

As she jumped in the shower, Millie couldn't help but laugh out loud about what she had read. She was sure she had heard Professor Smith introduce Hector as Mr. Hill. Phonetically, Hill and Gil sounded alike. She chuckled at her mistake and realized how little she knew about him. They had met by accident, and now he was writing and calling her! She couldn't believe it. Her mind was filled with questions for Hector Gil.

Millie left the bathroom with foggy mirrors and dirty clothes on the floor, not her normal behavior. Katherine was meticulous about dirty clothes, demanding that they be placed in the hamper. There had been enough incidents of cow and horse ticks found in the bathroom and kitchen after Jack or Millie came in from the fields without taking the precaution of leaving their shoes by the door. This time, Millie just plain forgot. She had too many things on her mind. When her father came in for his shower, he picked up Millie's clothes before Katherine could find them. She had not grown up in a farm environment and was delicate about dirt and bugs. He was grateful for Katherine's love and dedication and the way she had adjusted to life in the country.

Millie sat cross-legged on her bed and read the letter once again. Hector's last name was intriguing; deep down it sounded so familiar. She had heard the name before but could not place it. By dinnertime, she had read the letter so many times she had every sentence memorized. She wished he were not so far away, so that they could talk in person.

It was time again to go through the difficult emotions of another farewell. Millie hoped it would be her last departure from the Imperial Valley. The beginning of her last semester would at least be the end of her plane trips to and from school. Both Jack and Katherine took time away from their chores to see her off at the airport. With each passing year, it became more difficult for the Wolfs to part with Millie. It was never easy for Millie to say *adios*.

It seemed to Millie that she had boarded the same airplane many times before. The short trip from Imperial Valley to Los Angeles would transport her emotionally to her university life. She knew she needed to make the transition in order to accomplish her academic goals. She loved her family and the Imperial Valley but knew that she needed to focus on her studies.

The view from 10,000 feet was the same view she had seen for the last four years, so her concentration was focused on Hector. She had left a message for him three days ago, taking him up on his offer of a ride from the San Jose airport. But she had not heard back from him and had planned an alternate route back to school. She told herself she did not need a ride and would take the train to the Palo Alto station. She figured that Hector had gone home for a few days' break. In a matter of minutes, the quick commuter airplane landed at LAX and Millie headed through the terminal for the flight to San Jose.

With her thoughts on Hector, the connecting flight arrived in San Jose before she knew it. The tiny airplane window presented a vast view of Silicon Valley. While she was sad to leave her family, she was also glad to return to the privacy of her small quarters at the university. She'd become used to the fast pace of studying and grabbing quick meals between classes. At the farm, Millie had always felt a special comfort and freedom. She had managed to help her family, earning her way through high school. College was a little different; she felt removed from her family responsibilities but depended on her parents for financial support. She looked forward to the day when she would complete her degree and return home to Mom and Dad.

She wore her backpack and carried a couple of shoe boxes

in her arms as she stepped into the terminal. She was glad she had tied the two boxes together. As she passed through the many friends and relatives waiting for other arriving passengers, she heard a familiar voice.

"Millie!"

The voice carried over the heads of the crowded airport. Hector was waiting for her at the gate. Millie's heart jumped when she realized whose warm, masculine voice she had heard. She was glad to know she'd have help with her boxes, but there was also another, unfamiliar feeling brewing within her.

"Hector, it's so good to see you! I wasn't sure you'd received my message," Millie said, putting her parcels down to greet her friend.

"It's good to see you, too." Hector smiled broadly.

Hector and Millie extended their right hands at the same time in greeting. They laughed at their simultaneous gesture and instead briefly embraced for their second and more personal greeting.

Hector wanted so much to kiss Millie on her forehead but instead restrained himself and welcomed her back to the Bay area. He was becoming fond of Millie, and he realized he had missed hearing her voice more than anything else. Millie's cheeks were rosy pink after the encounter. She'd received hugs from other friends, but they hadn't felt like this one.

Hector said, "Actually, I just got your message this morning. That's why you didn't hear from me. By the time I called your house, your mother said you had left already. Here, let me help you with your backpack." They walked to the baggage area to wait for the rest of her luggage. The faithful red Valiant was waiting for them in the parking lot. Millie was relieved to have Hector there.

As they drove from the airport to Palo Alto, Hector talked about his family. It was obvious to Millie that he was lonely.

"You know, Millie," Hector said, "when we were small children, it seemed to me we were always on the road for the holidays." Millie was intent on his words. He had not mentioned his childhood before and she was anxious to hear his stories.

"When we were kids, we would go to Mexico every Christmas to see our grandparents and family. My father would always drive with the car filled with kids and cardboard boxes full of presents for the relatives."

"Did you sleep most of the way?"

"As soon as I got old enough to drive, my father put me behind the wheel and we'd drive non-stop until we got to our home in Mexico," he said. "Our grandparents were always so glad to see us. The worst part was leaving them. My grandmothers would cry so much the night before we left. It was so sad."

It was evident to Millie that Hector loved his family very

much. He was describing the same pain of departure and farewell that she had always felt but could never explain. His stories of the trips to Mexico gave her goosebumps and she grew silent.

"Have you eaten?" he asked after a pause. "Let's go to Domingo's for dinner. It'll be my welcome-back celebration for you." He did not allow her much room to decline the invitation. She was taken by his gallantry and began to see that his respectful manner toward her came from his close family ties and strict upbringing.

The two had many questions for each other but polite small-talk dominated the meal. The informality of the pizza parlor provided Millie an opportunity to present Hector with a couple of simple but meaningful gifts. She offered the two shoe boxes to her friend.

"What is this?"

"This is a Christmas gift from me to you. I am thankful for your friendship even if I don't know much about you. Merry Christmas," Millie said.

Hector was stunned by her words. He carefully untied the twine knot holding the two boxes together. As he opened one, he saw a small envelope addressed to him. "You must read the note first," Millie told him.

Carefully, Hector read the note. His eyes moved from the note to Millie and back to the note as she sat patiently waiting.

December 25, 1975

Dear Hector,

Merry Christmas to you. I have chosen this gift for you to remember our friendship. There are three points of this friendship I want you to remember. Our friendship will continue by understanding our past, appreciating our present and believing in our future. I hope we can continue to be friends. I do hope you had a very nice Christmas.

Sincerely,
Millie

Hector folded the little note and reached for his wallet. He placed the note in one of the plastic credit card compartments in his wallet.

"What are you doing, Hector?"

"I like this message. I'm saving it as a reminder."

Millie was pleasantly impressed with the attention he gave her note. Hector removed the blue tissue paper from inside the first box. Under the layers of delicate covering, he found a very special surprise.

"Wow, this is beautiful!" Hector took the gift and placed it on the palm of his left hand. He looked at her with much appreciation in his eyes. "Millie, I love this." With little effort, Hector had already made the connection between the meaning of the Christmas note and the gift.

This gift had so much meaning for her, she had spent three days looking for it. But Millie had worried that he might not understand.

The dried cotton branch was no more than ten inches long. It had three smaller stems branching out from the center. The buds at the ends of the brown stems still had a tight hold on the beautiful cotton bolls.

"Am I responsible for spinning this cotton into our graduation robes?" Hector joked. It was obvious to Millie that he had liked her simple gift a lot. She knew that Hector loved the outdoors and anything that dealt with nature. The gift was perfect for him. "I really like this Millie! Thank you. I'm going to put it on my desk where it will remind me of the Imperial Valley."

"Open the next box." She nodded toward the unopened gift. Hector carefully placed the cotton bolls back in their box. He pulled the next box in front of him as if he were going to eat from it. Again he removed the tissue paper, but this time uncovered neatly stacked, one-inch-square, brown bars.

"What is this?"

"We made them." Millie pointed to the bars with pride. "My mother and I made them last Sunday. My friend Olivia has date palms growing on her property and her father gives our family a box of dates every Thanksgiving. We eat them or bake goodies with them."

Hector had never seen dates before. "At least not this kind," he joked. Their laughter reminded the waiter that their order for pizza wasn't in yet. "What would you two like?" The waiter could see that they weren't ready to order, but the restaurant was getting crowded and moving customers out was also part of his responsibility. Hector asked for one large pizza and two sodas.

He wanted to spend time with Millie rather than eat. His eyes were brimming with emotion and his heart was filled with excitement. He was so happy to have Millie in front of him.

The pizzas were delivered to the table but the pair barely touched the food. There was too much to talk about.

As the waiter removed their plates, Hector pulled a small square box from his jacket. The box was wrapped in light pink shiny paper and tied with a velvety white bow large enough to cover the five-inch package. A silk rosebud decorated the center of the bow.

Millie was caught off guard. She did not expect any gifts from Hector. She rarely received unexpected gifts since she had great skill in anticipating situations of a surprising nature. This one totally shocked her.

She carefully unwrapped the gift between glances at Hector. She pulled off the pretty ribbon and tied it to her ponytail, a ritual she followed every time she opened the first present of several.

"Hector, I have to put this ribbon in my hair, it's so gorgeous. Ever since I was small, I have tied ribbons in my hair from presents my grandfather gave me. He would tell me I was the best present he'd ever received in his life. I now do this in memory of him." She tied the ribbon as if her head were the top of a present under the Christmas tree.

As she pulled the box open, the delicate pink tissue paper parted to reveal a beautiful white handkerchief with a dainty lace lining. On one corner the letters MW were embroidered in a satin finish.

"Hector, this is too pretty for me!" Millie exclaimed. "I've never owned a handkerchief. This is beautiful! When do I get to use this?"

She lightly rubbed her cheek with the dainty material. It was soft and precious to her. Then she held the hanky from its center between her finger tips and fluttered it toward Hector's handsome nose. "Pardon me, mister, do I know you?" she teased.

Millie was full of questions about the neat gift. Hector explained that he had it made by his aunt who was a nun in Mexico. "My aunt visits us once every five years or so. The whole family admires the work she does for the poor people of the mountain villages in Mexico," he told Millie with pride.

"She visited my parents for Christmas and I asked her to do this for you. My mother finished it and sent it to me just three days ago." Hector was relieved that she liked the present so much. He had worried all day about this moment.

Now he felt satisfied with his decision to call his aunt for help with gift-giving. Hector's mother had always used handkerchiefs. When he watched his mother iron all the clothes, he got a kick out of seeing her press the tiny squares of cotton material. He told Millie of the many times he had teased his mother about her use of handkerchiefs. "Mom, if everyone else were like you, the Kleenex Company would not survive," he had once told her. Hector laughed out loud at his recollections.

"I know," Hector said. "You can use the hanky at gradua-tion. After all, you might need it with so much emotion in the air that day." They both laughed at the thought.

Hector drove Millie back to campus and politely carried her bags to her room. He was proud that she allowed him to escort her that far. He was pleasantly surprised to see farm-related posters on her walls — a huge John Deere tractor on the largest wall and a medium-sized picture of the desert Chocolate Mountains on another. A small Christ on a wood-en cross and a Virgin Mary statue sat next to her head-board. To each side were photos of Jack and Katherine and her grandparents. Hector took a second quick look at the pictures before she escorted him back to the dorm lobby.

She walked Hector to his car and thanked him for dinner and the lift to the dorm. She knew that he needed to focus on completing his dissertation. He knew that, too. But for the moment, both wished they could spend many more hours talking.

"Hector, thank you so much. I had a wonderful welcome-back evening," she told him. Again they extended their right hands, this time to say goodnight. Millie instinctively added her left hand around their grasp in a show of genuine affection. This was too much for Hector. He pulled her body toward him. She resisted at first but then allowed him to pull her sweetly close. In a matter of seconds, they were embraced in each other's arms. Hector wanted so much to kiss Millie's lips but stopped short.

Millie detected his reserved character and was glad he respected their friendship. And yet she wanted to kiss Hector, too. She hadn't kissed many boys before, just a few of her dates in high school, and those were friendly smooches, not romantic. She had never felt like this, ever.

Unlike most young women her age, Millie was very reserved. She recognized the same character in Hector, and that made her feel close to him. Both of them were in their twenties. By now, many others their age were engaged or married. But Millie was not in a hurry. She had so much to do and was so committed to helping her family that she had not given much thought to the opposite sex — until now.

"Hector, thanks. I'll see you soon."

She pulled away and turned quickly to walk toward the dorm. She turned one more time to wave goodbye and then disappeared into the dorm. Hector jumped into his car and drove off.

They were left with the same thoughts. Both wanted more time together, and both wanted to ask many questions.

Hector had told her a little about his family, and now Millie wondered about his aunt, the nun.

She took the Christmas gift Hector had given her and placed it under her pillow. She wanted to feel close to him by having the handkerchief close to her. Hector's stories of Mexico had brought up thoughts of the past. Millie wondered if her real mother had ever used handkerchiefs, since she was Mexican like Hector's mom. That made her wonder what part of Mexico her real parents were from and whether they were still living. She wondered if they would approve of her attraction to Hector.

He was tall and good-looking. He was gentle, warm, and caring. He seemed to be a good friend. But she did not want to interfere with his studies, and she did not want her own studies interrupted. Her parents had spent too much money on her education to have her studies brought to a halt due to a new friendship. She would have time after finals to become closer to Hector, she decided. She knew this would take some discipline.

Hector was working diligently to complete his research. One more week and he would submit his entire thesis to the chairman of his dissertation committee. He was looking forward more than ever to completing his work, because then he could pay more attention to his friendship with Millie.

In the meantime, Hector and Millie spoke on the phone once a week. It was a good way to keep in touch without the need for time away from studying. Millie learned more about Hector during the calls, and he learned a bit about her.

On Valentine's Day, Millie returned to the dorm after a full day of classes, and was pleasantly surprised to find a dozen miniature pink roses waiting for her. She hurried to take the roses from the dorm office to her room. The note attached by a thin red string wished her a Happy Valentine's Day in Hector's curly handwriting. The verse read: "Roses are Red, Violets are Blue, Millie you're sweet, and I want you. Will you please be mine? How about dinner tonight? I'll pick you up at 5:00 p.m. No regrets, my friend."

The surprising message brought tears to her eyes. She wanted so much to see him and be with him. She knew she liked Hector more than any other man she had ever met, and now she knew he liked her very much, too.

It had been a long time since they'd been together. Millie figured that Hector would be too busy to see her until he completed his dissertation. She was elated that he had thought about her on this special day just for couples. The flowers were fresh and fragrant. She was so full of joy that she threw herself on her small dorm bed and stared at the ceiling for a few minutes before realizing that five o'clock was just 55 minutes away. What would she wear? She was so overjoyed she could not think straight. She quickly grabbed a set of clean underclothes and rushed to the shower she shared with her roommates. She took two towels, since she had decided to wash her long, dark hair.

At a five o'clock sharp, the dorm office called Millie to say that she had a guest waiting. She grabbed her perfume bottle and quickly sprayed two spurts of the fragrance over her pink blouse and on her neck. She checked the mirror and was pleased with the final look. She had her mother to thank for ongoing advice on clothes and color combinations. She felt like the queen of the ball as she walked downstairs to greet her special date.

"Hector!" she exclaimed. "I missed seeing you!"

Hector rushed to embrace his energetic young friend. "I missed you, too, Millie." They hugged as if they were long-lost friends finally reunited. His broad smile was enough to excite all the other girls waiting for their dates in the reception area. Hector was freshly shaven and very neatly dressed. They made the perfect couple.

"Let's go, Millie. We have a reservation waiting for us." He didn't have much time to drive to Sausalito, a small bay town north of San Francisco. They hurried to his car.

"How's it going, Millie? How are your classes? Ready for graduation?" He was asking a million questions and Millie was trying to keep her thinking straight.

"First, I want to thank you for the wonderful pink roses. You're very thoughtful, Hector. You made me feel very special when I got in after classes today. Thanks!" she said. She was shy about sharing her feelings and her normally rapid rate of speech was slowed down to say the few words she had rehearsed while dressing.

Hector reached across the seat and took her hand in his. "I like you, Millie, and I want you to be my girl." Hector wanted to make sure he said the right thing. He knew he sounded old-fashioned, but his words made Millie felt like colorful confetti falling from the sky — millions of tiny paper dots that no one could gather quickly enough. She caught her breath and bowed her head to recover from the sweet words Hector had spoken. Her body was discreetly reacting to his words in a very personal way that was new to her. She knew she liked Hector very much, but she did not know how to respond.

"Hector, I, I — " She did not know what to say.

"You don't have to say anything, Millie. Just sit there and look pretty. By the way, you do look very beautiful. Actually, you look pretty all the time but tonight you look radiant."

His praise and relaxed attitude helped Millie to calm down. She asked questions about his research and Hector shared with her his recent progress as they drove northward.

The romantic restaurant was prepared for the many couples celebrating Valentine's Day. The tables were decorated in pink and red. Hector and Millie sat side by side at a table for two overlooking the bay. The evening lights were beginning to mirror themselves on the calm waters. Millie was impressed with the beautiful setting. Her parents rarely went out to eat, so her restaurant experiences were limited.

They began their evening with a glass of Napa Valley sparkling wine.

"I propose a toast." Hector raised his glass and waited while Millie joined her glass to his. "I propose that Millie become

my girl and that we get to know each other as time passes."
Millie was caught off guard. Most of the toasts her father
and grandfather had given were for health and happiness.
She immediately added her own words to the toast.

"Congratulations on submitting your work, my friend! I propose that good health and success follow you, and that after
graduation you do not forget about the farm girl," she said.
She touched her glass to his and her shaking hand caused
the goblets to make a tinkling sound. Millie was visibly nervous about Hector's toast. He had asked her to be his girl.
She had never been anybody's girl.

Hector put his arm around Millie while they waited for their
meal. She felt secure with his arm around her shoulders.
After the dinner and dessert, Hector invited Millie for a walk
on the pier. The night was perfect for a stroll under the
stars. As they walked along the ocean, Millie and Hector
joined hands. The moon was their only company as it was
still early for other lovers to be out. When he first heard
Millie's last name, he told her, it brought back memories of
his mother's stories of the old country where the wolves and
coyotes howled at the moon.

"Hector, do you remember the lecture you gave Dr. Smith's
class on the Mexican pyramids?" Millie asked. "I took in
every word you said. I really liked you from that time. And
you didn't even notice me." They both laughed. Hector
turned toward her and placed his hands on her shoulders.

"Millie, you haven't responded to my question. Will you be
my girl?" Millie froze and could only look up at Hector. He

slowly pulled her toward him to rest her head against his
shoulder.

The couple's silhouette resembled two affectionate love-
birds. The minute they spent in this position filled their
souls with anxiety. Hector was concerned that Millie was so
quiet. But she had not felt such a sense of belonging since
she was a little girl. Millie pulled her face away from
Hector's shoulder and, gazing into his eyes, began to
answer. His lips stopped her from speaking, and her words
melted in affirmation of her need. The moonlight shone a
silver lining on the shadow of the couple. The passion of
their wet kiss endured for what seemed to Millie like an
eternal commitment.

"We'd better go, Hector," she said, breaking from his
embrace. She didn't know how to say that she was nervous
about the deep kisses she enjoyed so much. Hector was also
a little embarrassed at the sudden depth of affection they
displayed for each other. He took Millie's hand and they
walked back to his car.

As he opened the door to help her in, Hector asked, "Would
you like to go to my place for a glass of wine?" Hector felt a
warm comfort with Millie, and wanted to show her that he
liked her and enjoyed her company.

"I really should get back to the dorm." Millie felt a little
uneasy about going to his home alone. She was curious
about where he lived but did not expect to visit there. But
more than anything else, she was really afraid of getting
closer to Hector and falling into a more emotional display of

affection. On this evening, however, she had her emotions under control. "All right, Hector, I'll visit your place for a glass of wine." He was pleased that she trusted his judgment.

Hector pulled up to a very fancy home on the Stanford campus. "Is this your place?" Millie asked doubtfully. She knew he couldn't possibly live in such luxury.

"Yes and no. You'll see."

Hector parked his car on the quiet street. He led Millie through the garden and the hinges screeched as he let the wooden gate swing back into place. They passed a lighted kitchen window, and Hector opened a side door leading to a long set of stairs to the lower level.

At the bottom of the stairs were humble surroundings belonging to a student. "Welcome to my Stanford dorm," Hector announced with a laugh. He was hopeful that she would not mind his plain dwelling. Quickly, she surveyed the one-room home with its simple shower and toilet covered only by a plastic curtain. All of the furnishings were neat and organized. There were more books than anything else. On an antique-looking nightstand, several photos were center-stage.

The cotton bolls she had given him were sitting against a wooden frame fitted for the branch. A brown-paper-covered card table and two chairs served as the dining area. A small refrigerator sat next to the card table. "Please make yourself at home," he said. Hector politely led Millie to one of the chairs and then opened the refrigerator to bring out a bottle of wine three-quarters full. He pulled out paper cups and poured the cold wine. "Please excuse the fine wine glasses. This crystal is the finest within these surroundings." Hector laughed at himself as he watched her body language for any potential signs of discomfort. He was glad she seemed happy.

"Miss Wolf, would you tell me about yourself?" Hector said. He pretended to be a counselor interviewing a client. "I want to know everything about you and more. You have ten seconds to start," he said. Millie could not help but laugh at Hector's strategy.

"OK. Tell me what you want me to tell you." She did not know where to start, did not know what he really wanted to hear.

"You have five seconds." Hector pretended to keep an eye on his watch. "Time out," he said. He got up and took his sports jacket off. He quickly walked to the opposite corner of the room where a makeshift closet waited with vacant hangers. "Your time is up!" Hector returned to his chair. "OK, beautiful girl, tell me about you." Millie could not stop laughing.

"Who lives here?" she finally asked. She wanted to know all the details, and she really didn't want to talk about herself because she felt she did not have all the facts. She tried to derail his questions and delay her answers.

"OK, I'll go first," Hector volunteered. "This is Dr. Smith's

house. I rent the lower floor from him. I've lived here for
three years. You are my first guest so I'm a little concerned
that you may not like it."

"Don't be silly, this is a great place to live," she assured
him. "I'd trade this for the dorm any day." She really was
pleasantly surprised to find out that Hector had such a nice
place.

Millie walked over to look at the pictures he had on his
nightstand. One was obviously an old photo and the other a
more recent one of Hector and his parents on graduation
day from the university. The older photo she guessed was
Hector and his family when he was a very young boy on
one of his trips to Mexico. "Are these your folks?"

"That is the first family portrait of us returning to Mexico
during Christmas," he said, smiling proudly. "Look at me
next to my grandmother. I was very chubby when I was a
kid."

The wine made Millie feel jealous of such a happy family in
the late '50s. At the same time she felt guilty to feel such
jealousy. The Wolf family had been everything to her and
were always there for her. *If only Hector knew the pain I feel
about family connections,* Millie thought. Her discomfort
weakened her knees.

Hector sensed her insecurity. He had never seen her body
sag with emotion the way it did as she held the old photo of
the Gil family. "Millie, what's wrong?" Hector asked with all
sincerity.

"Oh, nothing. I was just thinking," she responded with noticeable uncertainty.

Hector moved behind her and gently hugged her around the waist. As she turned to him he could not help but notice she had started to cry.

"Please, Millie, what's wrong?"

"I'm OK. I'm just so happy to have met you and I'm so happy today." She tried to convince Hector that nothing was bothering her. She did not want to spoil her time with him.

In a matter of seconds, he began to kiss away her tears. He pressed his lips to hers tenderly, and she could taste the salty residue. Hector politely sat Millie on the edge of the bed, knelt in front of her knees and began to kiss her hands as they rested on her lap.

"Millie, I want to hear it from your lips that you are my girl," Hector said between kisses. He had not heard it yet. He needed to hear it before he could feel confident. Millie knew she hadn't yet said anything about her feelings for him. She also worried that she hadn't discussed this situation with her mother. For once, she honestly did not have a specific direction in mind or a "Plan B" to follow. How could she be his girl when she didn't know whose girl she was to begin with?

Exhausted by her own thinking, Millie fell back on the bed with a deep sigh. Hector stood up and lifted Millie under the knees and turned her so that she could lie down. He sat next to her and began again to gently kiss her. She felt her heart being stolen, and she had never before been so aroused. Hector was also aroused. Gradually, he stretched out next to her and propped his head on the pillow so that he could keep his eyes on hers.

"Hector, we need to be careful. I don't want to hurt you or myself. I really have never been this close to anybody," she said. "I wouldn't want anything to happen that would disappoint my folks." Deep down, she knew she could easily let go. Katherine had warned her that she would face this moment someday. Millie had not thought the moment would be here so soon.

"Don't worry Millie, I would never hurt you. I can't help it, but I like you like I've never liked anyone else." Hector had been in this situation before but had never taken it so seriously. He wanted to handle Millie with so much care.

"Hector, I love you," she told him without reservation. She didn't know where the words came from but they were released from her heart without effort. He began to peck at her lips, and turned her on her side to face him. They embraced, and their kisses became passionate as Hector pressed his body against hers. She could feel that he was aroused. She wanted so much to please him and make him feel good, but also knew the dangers of proceeding. Hector did not want to hurt Millie in any way. He wanted to protect this woman ever so tenderly. But his hands were roaming on her back and buttocks, and then began to swim at the edges of her skirt. She immediately stopped kissing him and pushed his hands away.

"I'm sorry, Millie," he said. "I love you, too, and I can't keep my hands, eyes, and mind away from you. Let's be careful." They pulled apart a few inches to let their enthusiasm cool down.

"You are a beautiful woman, Millie. I am in love with you." Hector could not help himself.

"You're dreaming, Hector. Maybe you're seeing an illusion. Wake up! It's me, Millie." She was joking in hopes of getting him in a lighter mood.

"Oh, no, I'm not seeing an illusion. I'm seeing the woman I want and I love."

She laid her head against his chest and began to rub his back with tender, maternal strokes. He rubbed her shoulders, but then could not help himself and cupped his hands under her full breasts. He discreetly slid one hand under her pale pink sweater to feel the satin of her bra. The tips of her breasts were at perfect attention as if summoned for formal military review. How he loved this moment he was living!

Millie moved away quickly and sat up on the side of the bed. She smoothed her hair with her hands and stood by the card table. "I think I need to go to my dorm," she announced.

Hector got up and put his arms around her. "I'm sorry, Millie," he said. "I love you. Please don't feel hurt." Hector picked up his car keys from the small wooden desk full of papers. "Here, let's go."

At the dorm, Hector jumped out to open the car door for Millie. He walked her to the reception area and waited to say goodbye.

"Good night, Hector." Millie looked at him with some guilt. She had never let anyone touch her like he had, and she felt guilty because she enjoyed it so much. She gave Hector a kiss on the cheek. Hector responded quickly.

"Thank you so much for having dinner with me," he said. "I'm so grateful for your friendship. I'm sorry if I offended you in any way." Hector seemed genuinely apologetic.

"Give me a call when you have some time," Millie asked him, to reassure him of their friendship.

• • •

"MILLIE, YOU'VE GOT SOMETHING WAITING for you upstairs," the resident monitor said. Millie rushed to her room. She was expecting her yearly valentine from her parents. Since this was her senior year, she figured they had sent her something special. She was not surprised to find a box of dates and candy from them sitting next to Hector's beautiful pink roses on the ledge next to her bed.

The gifts made her feel melancholy and reminded her that she had left some unfinished business with Hector. She paced the small room and criticized herself for allowing her emotions to run in search of Hector's warmth. She wanted so much to be his girl. *Did I tell him that?* she wondered. *Did I ever respond to his question?* She could not remember what she had told him. Her mind was still following her hands feeling his skin. After twenty minutes of worry, she walked out to the public phone and called Hector.

"Hello?"

"Hello, Hector, it's me. Um —"

"What is it, Millie? Are you all right?

"Hector, I wanted to tell you that I want to be your girl forever."

A deep sigh of relief came over the phone. Millie could feel the relief as if it were hers, too. "Hector, I'm a little embarrassed about what happened tonight and I couldn't sleep without telling you that I'm sorry for getting carried away in your arms," she nervously admitted. She was worried she had done the wrong thing.

"Millie, I'm so happy to hear your voice. I'm so glad you called me. I'm embarrassed, too. I don't want you to feel bad. We didn't do anything wrong. I'll be more careful next time." Hector's reassurance made her feel better. "I love you, Millie, and I don't want anything to happen to you. I'm just very happy that you're willing to give me a chance to show you how much I love you. Get some sleep, baby. I'll call you tomorrow."

"Hector."

"Yeah?"

"I love you, too. See you tomorrow." Millie hung up the phone and smiled all the way to her room. She was relieved to have spoken to Hector, and was very happy that she told him she loved him. She meant her words.

Hector called daily to reassure her of his love. That gave her the strength to call her mother about her new friend. She even told Katherine that Hector had asked her to be his girl, although she knew that bit of information would worry her parents. They had often teased her about the day she would be swept off her feet by a prince charming. She always laughed at the end of the conversation, too busy to think seriously about any particular boy. But this was a different time. Now she was deeply involved in a purposeful and meaningful relationship with a man.

About a month before graduation, Hector defended his dissertation. Millie found herself like a parent waiting for the arrival of a son, pacing the hallway in anticipation of the end of that grueling academic process Hector had long worked for. She knew how hard he had worked to prepare himself for this final stage of his degree. She had felt the impact of his progress, too. Their contact had been limited to phone calls during the last two months.

Even afterwards, she would still have to wait to see Hector privately. His friends and professors had planned a gathering in celebration of the event.

She bought Hector an engraved pen-and-pencil set. The pen read "The Sun" and the pencil was inscribed "The Moon." She had first met and felt an attachment to Hector after his research presentation on the two pyramids in Dr. Smith's class. She planned to take Hector out to dinner and present him with the writing set at that time.

Hector emerged from the hallway that led to the conference room. His face showed stress but he was grinning broadly. He had worn a suit and a perfectly coordinated maroon tie. His hair was neatly combed. Millie was pleasantly surprised to see him in his professional attire.

"Millie, let's celebrate! We've made it! You and I will make it!" He picked her up around the waist and twirled her in the air. His elation was infectious. After he put her down, Millie embraced him and kissed him on the cheek.

"That's not the way you congratulate the man you love, is it?" Hector smiled at her and waited.

Embarrassed, she reached up to put her hand around the back of his neck. With a tender pull she brought his lips to hers for a brief kiss. "There. Congratulations!"

"Let's go to the party," he said. They left for a few well-deserved hours of celebration with friends and professors. Millie proposed a toast.

"To the man of the hour: May his dreams come true in San Diego and may he publish before we perish," she declared. Everyone laughed at her joke, including Hector, who had a toast of his own.

"Ladies and gentlemen, I want to introduce you to the

woman of my dreams. She's the woman who has inspired me to work hard and dedicate myself to the completion of my work during this last semester," he said. "I want you to know that while I'm proud of finishing, I'm more proud of having met this wonderful, beautiful woman. She's my dream girl. A toast to Millie Wolf, the love of my life."

Millie was shocked and humbled by his words and the sincerity in his eyes. She loved him all the more for including her in such an important event. She hadn't realized how much she meant to Hector during these crucial months of stressful dedication. When the celebration ended, she and Hector left for a quiet dinner alone.

In the car, she thanked Hector for saying such kind things about her to his friends. She told him how much she appreciated the fact that he had thought about her during such difficult times. Hector listened and drove, relieved that the hectic day had ended and a quiet evening with Millie lay ahead.

Downtown Palo Alto was the place to go for night atmosphere in the college town. She directed Hector to the natural food restaurant, her favorite for the past three years. The informal atmosphere brought little attention to a couple in love. The aromas of coffee and tea added to the relaxing ambiance.

"I have something for you." Millie pulled out a neatly wrapped box and a card. Hector opened the homemade card and smiled. The torn construction paper was in the form of a pyramid. As he opened the card, another pyramid appeared. At the bottom of the inside of the cover pyramid were the words "the sun" and written on the inside of the adjacent pyramid were the words "the moon." On the pyramids, she had written a symbolic message:

"To the sun that shines on my life and to the moon that loves me by night. I thank the heavens for the celestial gathering of planets that have brought you to me. You are the 'star' of my life. I love you today and will love you until the sun stops dressing in gold and the moon stops dressing in silver. Congratulations for your universal accomplishments. I knew you could do it!"

Hector reached for Millie's hands and brought them to his lips to kiss them. Then he opened the present.

"This is a great pen set, Millie. I've needed something like this. I'll treasure them forever." He read the inscriptions and looked at her with approval. "You're always making the right connections, Millie," he said. "Now I have something for you." He reached for his briefcase.

"For me?" Millie asked. "What did I do?"

Hector opened his briefcase on the table and pulled out a thick document held together by two crisscrossed rubber bands. "Here, this is for you. It's the first official copy of my completed dissertation. You can read the thesis later, but please read the acknowledgments now."

Millie took the document and pulled the rubber bands aside. She turned to the front matter and began to read.

This is dedicated to the love of my life. I just met her last semester, but have found that she has inspired me to a greater sense of accomplishment. I want to thank her for her kindness and her warmth. Millie Wolf, I dedicate this page to you. I want to continue to understand your past, to be part of your present and to believe in your tomorrow. Thanks for your endless inspiration and patience as I reached the final page of this chapter in my life.

The remainder of the page was dedicated to professors and friends, and the concluding paragraphs were written in Spanish for his parents. She was touched by his demonstration of affection in such an important document. She didn't think she was worthy of such praise, and made sure to pick up the dinner tab.

Although Hector had an exhausting day, he was also elated with the outcome of events. "Let's go have a celebratory glass of wine," he suggested. He knew that he could relax a little more now until graduation.

They drove to his apartment. Neither mentioned the last time they had been together there.

Millie had come to terms with her love for Hector, and felt confident that she would be wiser in handling any situation that might arise from another glass or two of wine. She also felt more at peace for having told her mother about Hector. And foremost in her mind was her goal of graduating.

They enjoyed reliving the day's events. After two glasses of wine, Millie needed to go to the ladies' room and asked

Hector for instructions on privacy in the one-room apartment. He directed her to the transparent plastic curtain, promising that he would look the other way while she did whatever she needed to do. She held the curtain closed with one hand while she lifted her skirt and pushed her panties down with the other. She was embarrassed; her father was a very private man and Millie had never had to be so open about her personal needs. When she was finished, Hector excused himself to use the toilet, too.

"Millie, would you please close your eyes? I need to use the bathroom and wouldn't want to be treated any different than you want me to treat you." Hector joked with her as he pulled the curtain closed. She could hear everything, including the zipper down and the zipper up.

Returning to the table, Hector moved behind her. He helped her up from the chair and wrapped his arms around her. Millie felt so tender with his strong arms around her. He kissed her passionately and she responded actively to his affection.

With their bodies glued together, they moved slowly onto the bed. Millie had promised herself she would not be caught in this situation, but for a moment her promise appeared to have been a passing thought.

Their hands sought each other's bodies in a desperate race for warmth and tender love. Hector's hands slid between her legs as her hands played with his hair and face. She war : d so much to please him. He wanted so much to be pleased and to please her. As he kissed her, Hector removed her blouse. Their desire was far beyond their expectations. Millie had never before been in this situation. She finally understood the advice Katherine had given her about going all the way. She had not known that feeling until tonight.

Hector pulled his hands away from the warmth of Millie's thighs and began to rub her back. He lowered his face to her breasts in search of security. She made no attempt to stop him until he tried to remove her skirt.

"Hector, please, let's slow down. I really want you but I don't want to do the wrong thing now," she pleaded. Millie was trembling with the newness of her desire. Hector stopped and stared lovingly into her eyes.

"Millie, I want you. If not today, I will wait until you are ready. I'll want you tomorrow and the next day and the next day. I don't want to hurt you in any way." They cuddled each other, speaking in the tender language of love they shared. "I want you to meet my father and mother. You'll like them and they'll fall in love with you," he said. Hector was so excited that his parents were coming for graduation. Introducing Millie to them would be the high point of their visit as far as he was concerned.

Millie's parents were also coming to Stanford for the cere-monies. She wanted them to meet Hector. She wasn't sure how they would feel about him, but they had never met anyone who meant so much to her. Millie encouraged Hector to focus on the upcoming special event so their bod-ies could refrain from more exciting things.

• • •

HECTOR AND MILLIE began to prepare for graduation and the visits from their relatives. It all would come to an end very soon. They agreed to split the graduation events as they shared their families and their time with each other. Hector's family would meet Millie the night before gradua- tion and Hector would have dinner with her family on com- mencement day. The ceremony itself would be chaos. They knew they would have to set a meeting place in order to congratulate each other.

His father's work schedule would not permit them to remain in Palo Alto for long. Her parents were arriving on the morn- ing of commencement and planned to help Millie pack her belongings. The Wolf family would then drive south togeth- er. The last trip away from Stanford was going to be a diffi- cult one.

Hector packed his apartment the week before graduation and stored his belongings for the two-week break in Chicago with his family. He was not expected to begin work in San Diego until August. Hector and Millie worried about the distance that would separate them for several months. She realized that for the first time in her life she was spend- ing lots of time on matters that were not here yet.

On the day she finished her classes and two days before graduation, Hector waited for Millie at the door of Dr. Smith's second-semester course. She was delighted to see him. The afternoon lecture was the last of her classes; she had successfully completed all the requirements for her degree. Hector took her hand and headed toward the student union.

"What are you doing here?" Millie was surprised to see him.

"You waited for me when I finished," Hector reminded her. "I thought I would do the same for you. Come on, let's go." He guided her quickly through the excited throng of students. They returned to the place where they had their first sit-down chat. The atmosphere was different this day, full of students and very sunny. The birds were out in force, picking up the crumbs that fell through the wrought-iron tables. For old time's sake, Hector ordered the tuna sandwich and potato chips. That memorable day around Thanksgiving when their friendship began seemed light years in the past. Hector felt he knew Millie from a long time ago.

She was touched by his manner towards her, how he always went out of his way to accommodate her and make her feel important. She was also high on the fact that she had just finished four years of schooling so far away from home. Tears ran down her cheeks as she waited for Hector to return with their food.

"What's wrong, Millie? What happened?" He put the tray of food on the table and squatted in front of her. He used his handkerchief to dry her tears. Millie just looked at him sadly.

"It's just such a happy but sad day for me," she tried to explain. "I've been here four years and today I finished my degree. I guess I'm crying because I'm happy. Heck, I don't know what's wrong with me. I'm sorry, Hector." She extended her arms to help him get up from his squat.

"I know how you feel, Millie. I felt the same way the other day after I defended my dissertation," Hector said. "I just didn't know how to handle it and I didn't have it in me to cry. I'm just glad we're both finished and I'm very happy we met."

They spent the rest of the day relaxing by the lake on campus, watching the sailboats and the seagulls. They reminisced about their years at Stanford. Millie realized how much Hector had sacrificed to get through his master's degree, and also how much she wished she had met him her first year of school. The lake at Stanford reminded Hector of the lake near his home in Mexico. He shared with Millie memories of the region where his family lived before moving to Chicago.

"Maybe one of these days you can visit Mexico with me?" Hector aroused Millie's interest in her past with his impromptu and unexpected invitation.

• • •

THE EVENING BEGAN in Millie's dorm room. Her roommate had already gone home for the summer, so Millie was using her side of the room to store packed boxes. She hoped Hector would help her move some of the heavier boxes out of the way so she would have more room to continue packing. She missed her father's help with that kind of thing. He had always helped her pack at the end of each school year, but this year the farm was too busy and she didn't want to wait until graduation day.

"Hector, would you please move these boxes over there?" she asked, pointing to where she wanted them.

He didn't mind helping Millie at all, other than that he couldn't keep his mind off of her and her beautiful eyes. As soon as the boxes were moved, Hector threw himself on the bed. "Help! Isn't there a Coke in this joint?" he teased.

"Shh, Hector, my neighbors are going to hear you," Millie said, placing her index finger in front of her lips to quiet him. "Let me run to the first floor and get you a Coke." While the rules of the dorm did not prevent Hector from being in her room, Millie felt a little self-conscious that he was there.

Before he could protest, Millie was out the door. Hector just relaxed and waited. He wondered what would happen to their relationship while they were many miles apart. He hated to think about it. Millie returned to find him with an empty look in his eyes.

"Here's your Coke. Now you can stop complaining," she joked. Hector sat on the edge of the bed to drink his pop; Millie sat on the floor facing him. "This is a good view, Hector." She teased him in hopes of lightening his mood. Hector took a long drink from the can and set it down before stretching out toward her.

"Come here, sweetheart." Hector pulled her to her knees.

"Now, this is better," Hector said in her ear. She had never heard him call her sweetheart, and it sounded good. She ran her fingertips in and out of his thick, black hair. He leaned back, enjoying the massage, and pulled her close in an embrace. "I'm going to miss you, Millie," he said. Hector could not keep his doubts to himself. "Will you miss me?" His brown eyes searched hers.

"Of course, I'll miss you, silly," she replied immediately, kissing him gently on his forehead. They stared at each other, filled with ambiguous notions of what life would be like without someone so loved. Millie had always missed her family very much, but those feelings did not reach the pit of her stomach like these she felt for Hector. He pulled her toward him and hugged her for a long time. They had never spent such quiet moments so close together before. They were not in a hurry, and for once did not have deadlines to meet.

After a few minutes, Hector began to hear sniffles. "What's wrong, Millie?" It gave him chills to hear her cry like that. He didn't know the reason and he didn't know how to help. "Hey, everything is going to be all right. You'll see," he said. "Nothing is going to come between us in the next few months. When I return to San Diego, I'll come see you in Imperial Valley." He tried to calm her down with words of endearment and encouragement.

Millie was so sad to think that she had met someone she liked so much and was going to have to say goodbye to in the next few days. She loved Hector and was sure she wouldn't see him for a long time.

"Hector, I don't want to be without you. I know I'm going to miss you more desperately than I have ever missed my family." She wiped her nose and dried her wet cheeks. "I don't know what you have done to me, but whatever it is, it has me so much in love with you." She snuggled in his arms.

Hector kissed her new tears ever so softly. He felt the same way but did not have the words to express his sentimental emotions. He tried to calm Millie down and make her happy. "Hey, how about going to dinner tonight? My parents are coming tomorrow and so are yours and we won't have another chance to be together for the next few months. Deal?" Millie's tears continued to create wet spots on his T-shirt.

Hector began to kiss her very dearly in hopes she would relax. In between kisses he told her how much he loved her. After awhile her sadness lifted and she began to return Hector's passionate kisses. Hector was intoxicated by the warmth of Millie in his arms.

His body was reacting to Millie's expressions of love. She knew exactly what was happening to her heart and liked the new feelings very much. Quivers of pleasure moved between her legs as Hector tenderly teased her to a height of excitement she had never before felt. She rubbed her hand over his groin to show him that she knew he was aroused and that she shared his passion.

Hector was a grown man in many ways. He was in great physical shape. Millie could almost close her eyes and see his body in front of her. She imagined all the outlines of his body, and knew she would remember every turn her fingers and palm made on this day. How could she forget? She had never before touched anyone like she was touching Hector.

Hector fumbled with the buttons on her blouse. Millie smiled at his clumsiness but Hector didn't care, focusing all his attention on touching her breasts. He turned her slightly from the waist, wrapping his lips around one protruding nipple as he sucked the honey from it.

Their passion was so natural and free, yet within minutes Millie felt the panic rising up in her again. Hector wanted more. He sensed her fear but hoped to show her how much he loved her. Slowly Millie pulled her hand from inside Hector's waistband. Hector kept his hand between her legs.

"Please, let's stop," she begged him.

"Millie, I love you. Let me show you how much I love you." He hoped he could convince her to relinquish her body to his heart. Hector was desperate for more, lost in his arousal. It was up to Millie to bring him back to reality. "Hector, please," she said more urgently.

She was embarrassed at their outpouring of physical expression. Her hand was wet with Hector's emotional release. She pulled back from Hector to grab a tissue and then turned away from him to button her blouse and pull up her pants.

"All right, Millie. I'll stop. I don't want you to be upset with me. I do love you, but I also need you." Millie did not know what kind of need Hector was talking about. She knew Hector loved her and that she loved him. To her that was all that mattered. Hector stood up, tucked in his shirt and zipped his pants. "Come here. Let me hold you," he said. Hector extended his arms to hold her and they stood quietly among the packed boxes.

Millie was embarrassed about having touched Hector so intimately, and questioned her own judgment in allowing him so much freedom. He, on the other hand, did not want her to regret their affection. Hector continued to reassure her of his love and held her close. Millie was sad to think about being without him. She knew the next few days would be a tangle of celebration and commiseration.

"Are you ready for what's ahead, Millie?"

"Are you kidding?" She shook her head. "I don't even know what to wear to dinner tomorrow night with your parents," she said as she walked over to her closet.

"My parents are going to love you as soon as they meet you," he reassured her. "You don't have to impress them with your clothes. Just remember that they don't speak much English. My father understands it and speaks a few words. My concern is meeting your parents, Millie. I want them to know that I care for you very much and wouldn't do anything to hurt you," he added. "I'm going to miss you, too, Millie," he said, hugging her again.

"Please, Hector, don't say anything about missing me," she

urged him. "My father is going to get very jealous of you if he knows that you'll miss me." She smiled to let him know she was sort of kidding him.

After dinner downtown, Hector asked Millie to come over for a glass of wine. "I propose that we stop and get a bottle of fine wine to celebrate your graduation."

"How about celebrating *your* graduation?" she countered.

"Well, I was hoping you'd want to celebrate my graduation in the same way I want to celebrate yours." He smiled broadly.

"Does that mean you're going to behave yourself?" she asked bashfully.

"Who me? I'm such a good boy. I'm obedient and kind," he joked. "I'll behave like a gentleman."

"All right, let's get a bottle and celebrate your successes," she agreed. Millie realized that his behavior would be her responsibility because Hector would follow her lead. With him, she felt comfortable and protected.

As they pulled up to the curve in front of Hector's place, she asked him, "Do you love me?"

"Of course I do," Hector responded without hesitation. He shut off the motor and turned to embrace her. He whispered in her ear, "You're really silly if you think I'd bring you to my place if I didn't love you. Lady, I adore you. You can't stop me from liking you more and more." Hector's sweet words made her giggle.

"Come on, let's go inside," Hector insisted. He walked around to open the car door for her, and extended his right hand to help her out. "My lady, please." Hector offered her his hand like a butler at a fancy home.

She graciously accepted the teasing and stepped forward without acknowledging his efforts. "Please unload the rest of my bags, sir," she teased back and walked briskly to the gate.

"Hey, wait for me," Hector laughed, hustling to catch up with her. Actually, he had purposely planned the wine and the visit to his apartment in order to surprise her with graduation presents he had carefully selected.

As he guided Millie inside, she was surprised to find his simple quarters decorated with colorful streamers, a Mexican piñata and several wrapped presents. Next to his bed was a vase with long gladiola flowers in white and pastel pink. A large hand-painted sign hung on the wall in her honor. It read: "Congratulations To My Girl on Her Graduation!" She stopped to catch her breath at the surprising scene.

"Miss Wolf, welcome to your graduation party!" Hector exclaimed. She turned to Hector and hugged him with the excitement of a little girl at Christmas.

She noticed a simple white envelope addressed to her resting against the vase. "May I open this?" she asked, picking it up from the table and waving it toward him.

"Please do." She removed her shoes to sit on the bed with her legs crossed. Hector was pleased to see how relaxed she was. He had spent a lot of time planning this surprise.

She opened the envelope to find a folded onion-skin note.

June 1976

My Dearest Millie,

Congratulations on finishing your degree. You should be very proud of yourself. I am so lucky to have found you at Stanford. So many nights of my life I've lived without knowing you. I knew you were in my dreams and in my heart. I was wondering when the time would come that I would bump into you. You are a beautiful woman.

I want and love you so very much. Please know that I will miss you during the next few months. However, be confident that I will think of you every day and every hour and minute of the day. Know that I will be in touch with you as frequently as you allow me to call you and write you.

I want to know you better and get closer to you. I am so glad to know that I'll be close to you very soon. Please know that I'll be next to you every moment of your day. God bless you.

My love and affection to you forever,
Hector

As she read the note, she could not keep the tears from running down her face. "You need to open your graduation presents, Millie," Hector said, directing her to the first one next to the bed.

"Wow!" she exclaimed, unwrapping a copy of *War and Peace*. "I've been wanting to read this." On the inside cover, Hector had written a dedication to her. Millie took the pretty ribbon and tied it to her hair as she looked at him with a broad smile.

Next, Hector pointed to the sink. On top of the old sink was a tiny box wrapped in shiny blue paper and a white bow. The gift was a small bottle of perfume.

"Hector, this is really nice," she said as sprayed the floral scent under her chin. He was happy to see that Millie was enjoying herself.

On the small study desk, she found a large, flat box wrapped in newspaper. The box was tied with a navy-blue seersucker ribbon. "Go on, open that one, too," Hector said. Millie was getting nervous about the number of presents he had given her.

In the box was stationery with her initials embossed in gold at the top of the sheets and matching envelopes with gold trim all around. "This is beautiful! I really like it," she said. "I guess I have no choice but to write to you in Chicago on a daily basis." Hector liked what he had just heard.

A smaller box inside the larger one held stamps ready to be

used on the embossed envelopes. "Hector, I don't know what to say. This is truly a surprise," she added, blushing.

The last gift was located under the bed. Without words, he merely pointed underneath Millie. She rushed to get on her knees and look. "Another present!" Hector nodded his head in agreement.

She pulled out a beautifully wrapped gift with a huge pink ribbon. Before opening it, Millie turned to Hector and hugged him for the many gifts she had already received. "Thank you. You are a sweetie."

Millie cautiously removed a gold seal that held the tissue paper together inside the box, then pulled out a pink terry cloth robe and matching house slippers. Her initials were embroidered on the robe in fancy white satin letters. "Oh my God! This is gorgeous, Hector!" She held the soft material up to her body. "I love it! Thank you, thank you, thank you!" Her face was radiant.

She reached for Hector's hand and he helped her from the floor. She stood on the tips of her toes to reach his lips, and gently placed her hand on the back of his neck to pull him closer. "You've surprised me like I've never been surprised before. I love you very much for all you do and for your caring approach toward me," she added with a wide smile. Hector was glad the surprise worked out just as he had planned it. He pulled away to pour their wine.

"All right, I propose a toast to my beautiful Millie," he said, lifting his plastic cup toward her. "¡Salud!"

"*¡Salud!*" Millie touched her cup to Hector's. "I propose a toast, too. I toast to your success as a college professor and to our friendship," she said as she raised her cup in the air. "I thank the good Lord for giving us the opportunity to meet. And one more thing. I propose that you stay in contact with me, otherwise I'm going to shrivel up like a dry plant without water." Again she touched her cup to Hector's. They held their glasses in the air as they sought each other's lips. Millie made sure that the pecks were short but loving.

After a few glasses of wine, she began to feel lightheaded. Hector laughed at her silly jokes but maintained a respectable distance, adhering to her request to be good.

"Why did you spend so much money on me, Hector?" Millie asked, emboldened by the wine. "I know you don't make lots of money as a graduate assistant. You didn't have to buy me so many gifts."

"Millie, you shouldn't worry about that. I wanted to do this for you. It was my pleasure. Besides, you are the only girlfriend I have," he joked. "I'm very happy that you graduated and I'm happy that I finished, too, so this is my celebration for many reasons. The most important reason is that I found you." Hector reassured her with his response.

"How about some music?" he asked. "I can play some oldies but goodies. How about it?" Hector moved to his record player and placed an album under the fine needle. Then he lit candles in three corners of the room.

Millie thought the lighted candles, hanging decorations, and soft music really made the small room seem magical. "Wow! This place looks great!"

"May I have this dance?" Hector extended his right hand to help Millie up. She curtsied in front of him. "It'll be my pleasure, Mr. Gil." They danced to the slow beat, a flicker of candlelight the only distance between them. Hector was deeply attracted to the woman he held in his arms, and had never felt so much in love before. Every part of his body reacted to her in ways no other woman had ever inspired.

Millie's love for Hector was so strong that it scared her. She could feel his love reaching to every inch of her body. She liked the way his thigh moved slowly between her legs as they danced. It was strange how his legs and hands could make her inner self react so much. They smiled at each other knowing they were meant to be.

The evening was so generous with affection that Millie could not help it as her tears flowed silently on Hector's chest. "What's wrong?" he asked with concern.

"These moments are so happy and so sad at the same time. Soon we'll be so far away from each other. I'm truly going to miss you," she added sorrowfully.

"You shouldn't worry, Millie. I'll call you and write you and think of you all the time. Pretty soon I'll be in San Diego and then we can visit each other." Hector made every effort to reassure her of his determination to keep in touch. But deep in his heart, he felt the very same sadness that she was voicing.

"Come on, you need to be happy and ready for tomorrow and then for graduation," he said. "I don't want your parents or mine to think you're unhappy with me. I'll never let go of you, Millie." Hector meant every word. "Let's take you home. It's late and you need to get some rest," he said. "Tomorrow I'll pick my parents up at the airport and then I'll come by to pick you up at five o'clock. My parents eat earlier than we normally do because of the time change. We'll eat early to suit their hours." He helped Millie collect her gifts and carried the boxes to his car.

At Millie's dorm, Hector walked her to her room to say goodnight. His arms were filled with boxes that she needed to pack to take home. He wished the night hadn't ended so soon but understood her fears about getting too close too fast. They had just met seven months ago yet it seemed they had known each other all their lives. Meeting each other's parents would give them the opportunity to learn more about each other, to find answers to some of their many questions.

"Good night, Millie." Hector held her in his arms and kissed her with eternal patience. "I love you. Get some rest. I'll see you tomorrow."

"Hector, this has been a beautiful night," she said. She also wished it did not have to end so soon. "I'll be ready for tomorrow's dinner," she added. "I love you very much." Hector kissed her on the forehead and closed the dorm door as he left.

For the first time, Millie was grieving her departure to the desert. She really was going to be lonely without Hector. She spent the rest of the evening packing her clothes, but also spent an hour creating a special letter for Hector. She had looked up his home address in the student directory. Her thank-you letter would be waiting for him by the time he arrived in Chicago.

OJOS DEL RECUERDO
Memorable Eyes

The day before graduation, Hector picked up his parents at the airport and took them to their hotel. They were thrilled to visit California on such a special occasion. Hector's parents were as proud as peacocks of their son's success and looked forward to meeting his girlfriend. This was the first time he had been so open to them about a relationship, so they suspected that he really liked this woman. When Hector told them that Millie was graduating also, they planned an appropriate celebration.

On the other hand, Millie's parents were nervous about meeting her beau. To their knowledge, Millie had never had a serious relationship before, and this one seemed to be more serious than they expected. Their concern did not dampen their overwhelming pride for her accomplishments, however. Millie had worked hard for her diploma, and they were especially pleased that she had achieved so much at their own alma mater. They also looked forward to the drive back to the Imperial Valley, when they would be able to enjoy the coast in the only family outing they had had together in several years.

Hector called at half past four to see if Millie was ready for dinner. She hadn't heard his voice all day and was glad to hear it again. She knew it had been a busy day for Hector, and that she would be faced with the same the following day when her own parents arrived. "Millie, are you all right?" he asked.

"Yes, I'm ready to meet your parents," she said. "Did they have a pleasant flight?"

"They've been resting at their hotel for the last four hours. They were tired when they got in," he told her. "I'll be by in just a few minutes to pick you up."

He arrived at Millie's dorm carrying a clear plastic box that held three miniature roses. "This is for you," he said, handing her the corsage. "I ordered one for my mother, too. I chose three roses to symbolize our friendship and love for today, tomorrow and forever."

"Please, help me pin it on. I'm nervous about meeting your parents."

"Don't worry, baby. My parents will like you very much." He pinned the velvety white flowers to her blouse. Then he placed one hand on each of her arms. "I love you very much, Millie," he said. "I've told my parents that you are my special girl. As a matter of fact, I told them that last week. So you have nothing to worry about. Besides, you look gorgeous." Millie had decided to be conservative in her appearance for this first meeting with Hector's parents. She wore a simple light blue blouse and navy blue slacks. Her long, dark hair was neatly parted down the middle and held in place by a simple gold barrette.

Hector's parents were sitting in the hotel lobby when Hector walked in with Millie's hand in his. Millie recognized them from the photos she had seen in Hector's apartment. Though nearly sixty, Hector's father was still tall and dark-haired like his son. Hector's mother, a pretty woman herself, sat quietly and watched her son and his girlfriend.

"*Apá, aquí le presento a Millie Wolf, mi amiga y mi novia,*" Hector said. (Dad, I would like you to meet Millie Wolf, my friend and girlfriend.)

"My pleasure, Mr. Gil," Millie ventured, extending her hand.

"*Señorita Wolf, mucho gusto. Mi hijo me habla de usted con mucho cariño.*" (Miss Wolf, my pleasure. My son has spoken to me about you with much affection.) Millie tried not to stare at his beautiful deep eyes and long eyelashes. He reminded her so much of her childhood, and his skin was a bronze color like hers.

Hector put his arm around Millie and gently turned her to face his mom. "*Amá, esta es Millie. La muchacha de la cual le hablé.*" (Mom, this is Millie, the girl I spoke to you about.) Both women were wearing the small corsages pinned to their blouses.

"*Señora Gil, bienvenida a Stanford y California. Hector también me habló de usted.*" Hector was glad Millie had spoken Spanish to his mom.

"Ay Millie, usted que sí es una muchacha muy bonita. Hector me dijo que usted era muy guapa pero veo que él se sacó la lotería." (Oh, Millie, you are a very pretty girl. Hector had told me you were attractive but I can see he has won the lottery.) The two couples walked in to their reserved table for dinner.

"Millie, cuéntenos en dónde vive. ¿Y sus padres conocen a Hector?" (Millie, tell us where you live. And your parents, have they met Hector?) Hector's dad had many questions for her. Millie was still nervous, wanting so much to please Hector's parents, but to her surprise, she was charmed by Mr. Gil's personality.

Millie talked about her father's farm, her grandfather Wolf and her parents. She also bragged on Hector, recounting the story of how they met and how much she appreciated his friendship. Hector's parents did not speak much about their life in Chicago, but Millie was mesmerized by the kindness in Mr. Gil's eyes.

After dessert, Hector's mom pulled a small box from her purse and handed it to Millie. *"Aquí está Señorita Millie,"* she said. *"Mi esposo y yo queremos felicitarla por su graduación de la universidad. Es un humilde regalo para usted. ¡Felicidades!"* (Here it is, Miss Millie. My husband and I want to congratulate you on your graduation from the university. It is a humble gift for you. Congratulations!) Hector's mom smiled with affection as she spoke to Millie.

Millie did not expect a gift from Hector's parents. *"Gracias, Señora y Señor Gil,"* she said as she looked at them with appreciation. Inside the small box was a colorful set of hair ornaments made out of bread dough. The headband was the prettiest, made to look like tiny, delicate flowers adorned with small, white citrus tree buds scattered between the colorful blooms. Two hair clips decorated with the same flowers were also in the box. "These are so beautiful! I'm afraid to wear them for fear I may break them," Millie said as she put on the headband to show everyone. "Thank you very much for the gift."

Hector's parents said goodnight to the young couple and retired to their room for the night. Hector drove Millie back to her dorm.

"This was a wonderful evening," Millie told him. "You are one heck of a lucky man. Your father and mother are kind people. And your dad's eyes are very powerful," she added as they walked to her room.

"Yeah, they are. When we were kids, all we needed to see was my father's eyes to know when we were in trouble," Hector said, laughing. "I told you my parents were going to like you very much," he added. "I could tell they really enjoyed meeting you."

"How do you know, silly?" Millie asked. They entered her room and closed the door behind them.

"Because I love you very much," he said. "You're the girl I've been looking for a long time," he added. "I want to get very close to you and learn everything about you that there is to learn." He looked into her eyes and slowly got an assertive hold on her around her waist. He pulled her close and kissed her for a long time. Millie held Hector as if she did not ever want him to stop.

"Oh, Hector, I don't know what I'm going to do without you this summer." Millie was already feeling sad. "It's going to be awfully sad for me. The company of my parents will only meet the surface of my needs. You're able to reach deep into my feelings." She began to shed huge tears and slumped on the edge of the bed.

"Hector, I've never met anyone like you, ever. I'm so much in love with you. I've always felt lonely even with my parents present. My life has always had some missing pieces. I never knew my real parents, my real family. Only in my dreams do I see scenes of my past memories. Hector, you make me feel better for the person I am today."

His heart was so touched by her sweet words that his eyes were wet, too. He kissed her again and whispered words of love and encouragement in her ear. He realized that he could spend the entire night with her, just holding her and loving her.

"Hey, I need to go," he finally said. "We have a long day tomorrow," he added. "I see you have your gown ready to go. I took mine to my mother for her to get it ironed at the hotel." Millie's black regalia hung from the window. Her mortarboard and tassel waited on one of the dorm chairs.

As they said goodnight, Millie held Hector in her arms as tenderly as a mother holding a newborn. Hector felt so wanted it was difficult for him to let go. When the dorm door closed, she carefully removed the corsage and placed it in a wooden pencil box her grandfather had meticulously carved. She would keep the memory of this evening along with Hector's notes to hold him near to her heart. As she jumped into bed she grabbed her pillow and fit it next to her as if Hector were lying close.

Early in the morning the traffic was triple its usual volume and Millie worried that her parents were caught in the commencement frenzy. At least they would be rested and dressed for the occasion after their overnight stay in Monterey.

Millie's mother had sent her a new tailored suit for the special occasion. Millie felt important yet somewhat melancholy. Finishing the degree from Stanford was very important — a milestone as far as she was concerned. Yet she would be leaving the home she had known for the last four years, too. And she would miss Hector even more than the university. Shortly after nine o'clock, her parents interrupted her bittersweet thoughts with a knock on the door.

She rushed to embrace them in gratitude and love. "Dad, I'm so glad to see you. Mom, I missed you so much."

"We're so happy for you today. You look wonderful, honey," Katherine said.

"Where's Grandma?"

"She couldn't make this trip, Millie," Jack answered. "But she did send her love." He handed her a bag filled with wrapped goodies. "Thelma and Olivia sent you a gift. Also, there's something you need for graduation," he said. "Boy, we have lots of boxes to carry back home. How much did I pay for all these books?" he joked as he surveyed the crowded room.

Millie pulled the tiny boxes from the bag her father had handed her. In one she found a small card and a wrist corsage. The note was from Katherine, congratulating her on this special day. The other boxes were from Thelma and Olivia. Thelma sent her a fancy dictionary. She had written a congratulatory note inside its hard cover. Olivia sent a pair of earrings, small flowers with a tiny pink pearl in the middle. Her card said, "Looking forward to seeing you soon." Millie's fondness for her friends back home was rekindled. She could depend on them to help ease the pain of his absence.

The Wolf family walked to the Stanford Stadium among thousands of other people headed for the commencement ceremonies. They agreed on a place to meet afterwards, and Millie rushed to her assigned gate with robe and mortarboard in hand.

She wondered about Hector as she rushed through the crowds. His graduation robe was more colorful and decorated than hers. The mantle for his doctorate degree added dignity to the upgraded design of the robe. *He probably looks really handsome*, Millie thought.

"Millie! Millie!" Hector's voice came from deep in the crowds. She looked around until she spotted her sweetheart moving in her direction. They reached for each other and embraced. "I'm so happy for you, baby," he said. "You look very pretty, too."

"I'm so glad to see you." She was all smiles with her Prince Charming. She was right; he did look handsome.

"I'll see you tonight," he said. "I love you, and graduation is not going to keep us apart," he told her before he disappeared into the crowd.

The warm sun lighted the stadium and heated the graduating students and spectators. Everyone stood to be acknowledged during his or her turn at graduation. With so many students, the different departments were having smaller ceremonies in their respective areas. Hector and Millie had made sure that their parents would have seats at the individual and more personal graduation ceremonies later in the day.

At seven that evening, Millie and her parents arrived at the Italian restaurant where Hector was patiently waiting in his suit and tie. Millie anticipated that he would be dressed in a way that would not disappoint her father. He stood at attention as they walked through the outer doors of the restaurant. Hector open the inside doors to greet them.

"Millie," Hector greeted her formally. "Dr. Wolf, Mrs. Wolf, I am Hector." He extended his right hand to shake Jack's hand.

"Nice to meet you, Hector," Jack responded. "I have heard a

lot of you from Millie. She is impressed with you," Jack
added, much to Hector's surprise.

"Millie has told us about you," Katherine said with a smile.
"It's good to finally meet you. I understand congratulations
are in order today?"

"Yes, ma'am. Thank you."

"Let's get to our table," Jack led the way to the reception
desk. "Reservation for Jack Wolf for four people," he
informed the attendant. They were shown to a corner table
next to the window facing downtown Palo Alto.

"Hector, tell us, where is your home?" Jack asked.

"I was born in Mexico. My father brought us to the United
States in 1954," Hector said. "I was almost five years old,"
he added.

Memories of the first time she saw Millie flashed in
Katherine's mind as Hector spoke of Mexico. She and Jack
had never shared the details of finding Millie with anyone,
and guarded their secret carefully.

"My father worked as a laborer in Chicago before retiring a
few years ago. My mother is a housewife. I'll be teaching in
San Diego beginning this fall," he added with a broad smile.
"My parents flew back to Chicago today." Hector tried to
anticipate the next question from Jack or Katherine. He felt
he was talking too much but knew they would want to know
all about their daughter's boyfriend.

"Millie has told me how much she loves the farm," Hector offered. Jack was grateful for an opportunity to discuss the farming business as well as politics and geology with such a knowledgeable person. As the foursome ate dinner, Jack realized he felt a little jealous of the intelligent man sitting across from him — a man he suspected might be stealing his daughter's young heart and innocent soul.

As the plates were cleared away, Katherine said, "Millie, we thought this would be a good opportunity to give you your graduation present." She pulled a business-sized envelope with Millie's name typed on the front of it. Millie was not expecting a present from her parents. They had already sent her the new suit and some money for graduation. She carefully opened the envelope with a dinner knife and pulled a note out. Inside the folded paper was a Polaroid picture of a small Ford pickup truck.

"What is this?"

"Dear, it's your new vehicle. It's your graduation present from both of us," Jack told her.

"Wow! A pickup for me?" Millie jumped from her seat to kiss her parents. "Thank you so much, Dad and Mom. I can't believe this." She was stunned by such an important surprise. Hector, thinking ahead already, was glad that Millie would have her own vehicle. She would be able to travel to San Diego to see him!

The dinner ended with a toast to the graduates. "This was a very nice dinner, Dr. and Mrs. Wolf," Hector said. "Thank

you. It's been a pleasure meeting both of you. I really need
to finish packing now because I'm leaving tomorrow."
Hector's farewell was formal because he worried that
Millie's parents would be watching every second for any
exchange of affection.

"Millie, I'll write you from Chicago," Hector said, and kissed
her on the cheek. He shook hands with her parents and left
for his apartment. Immediately he felt guilty that he had left
Millie without showing more affection toward her. He worried that he had given her parents the impression that he
wasn't serious about their daughter.

Millie was left empty. She recognized that Hector was con-
trolling himself tightly, unlike the numerous times he had
shared his love with her privately. But this time, his farewell
was cool, and that made Millie very sad. She hated for them
to part that way.

Her parents drove her to her dorm and returned to their
hotel for the evening. Millie began to prepare a small bag for
the trip home; everything else was already packed. She was
getting ready for bed when a knock on the door took her by
surprise. "Hector, what in the world are you doing here?"
She looked as if she had seen a ghost. "I didn't think I'd see
you any more."

"Are you kidding?" He feigned amazement. "Did you think I
would let my pretty Millie leave without saying goodbye?"
he added. "I couldn't leave you that way. I'm in love with
you and if I had it my way, we would not be parting." She
hugged Hector as hard as she could and kissed his cheeks.

"Millie, let's sit down, please," Hector politely requested. He had had a very long day and was ready for a few calm minutes. Millie was also exhausted.

"Sitting down is a good idea," she agreed.

Hector knelt down in front of her as soon as she sat on the bed and gently massaged her tired feet. Millie was a little embarrassed; no one had ever rubbed her feet like that before. "Please, Hector, you're going to relax me so much that I'll want more."

"Precisely. I want to be asked for more," he said. "I'd be happy to comply." Hector rubbed her calves and kneaded the strong muscles of her legs. She ran her fingers through his hair, and that seemed to relax him, too.

Hector stopped rubbing her feet and stood up. Carefully he lifted her with one strong arm under her buttocks and the other behind her back. He turned her as he sat on the bed and placed her in his lap. "Come here, honey," he said. She curled like a child against Hector's chest. Hector kissed and rocked her, feeling as nurtured as she did.

Millie suddenly had a strong sense of déjà vu. She was sure she could remember when someone, a long time ago, had held her in the same way. It made her feel so loved. Hector was overcome by an urge to protect her and watch over her. For twenty minutes the couple maintained the tender pose.

"I'm going to miss you so much," Millie said when their eyes met.

"I know. This isn't going to be easy for me either." There was a note of desperation in his voice.

Millie unfurled her body and lay back on the bed. Hector pressed tightly against her, his arms around her and his hands massaging her shoulders. She felt so happy and relaxed — she belonged to Hector and finally realized what that meant. She gave in to her emotions since this was the last time she would see him for awhile.

Hector's arousal was obvious as she ran her hands along his chest from the hollow of his throat to his navel. He unbuttoned her blouse and lightly touched her exposed flesh. He whispered sweet nonsense in her ear, teasing her with the sounds. The movements of his body against hers called her sexual senses to attention. She unbuckled his belt as quickly as she could and pulled his zipper down, reaching to touch him over his undershorts. Hector's kisses on her breasts sent her flying through the clouds. His body seemed to scream for more from her as his pleasure grew to an uncontrollable level. The gentle caresses from his lips teased emotions from her that were tender and new. The light tugs in her belly as he sucked her breasts reminded her of baby calves tugging at their mothers for more.

"Hector, we need to stop," She sat up and pulled her blouse closed. Hector sighed and righted his own clothing.

"Millie, you turn me on so much." But again he allowed her to set the pace. *One day*, he thought to himself, *I'll take charge of directing our love to a peak. The right time and right approach are just around the corner.*

• • •

THE WOLF FAMILY returned to the farm. Millie spent most of the trip thinking about Hector and wondering about his trip to Chicago. She wrote postcards every time they stopped at a rest stop or diner. Waiting for her at the farm were Grandmother Wolf and her new pickup truck, but the excitement of returning home had been dulled by Hector's affection. Things were not the same for Millie.

The Imperial Valley was the same. The May weather was typically hot. She spent her first day unpacking clothes and memories of the past four years at Stanford. She felt lonely in her room, and the emptiness was compounded by her grandfather's absence. The dried nests on the shelves near the ceiling looked forlorn. That spark of motivation she was used to had flown the coop.

She took her time looking at every little object while she unpacked. When she took out the robe Hector had given her, she sat on the bed and held it close to her. It made her think of the last moments she'd spent with Hector in her dorm. She wondered about her womanly feelings. Just to recall those last moments with Hector aroused her again.

Katherine and Jack knew that something was up with Millie. She wasn't as talkative and not as involved in family life. They figured she just needed time to regain her place in the Imperial Valley after four years away.

She tried to keep her mind occupied by concentrating on work. Olivia and Thelma visited the first night Millie was home. She was glad to see them but wished she could share the news with her buddies. After the girls had gone home and her parents were in bed, Millie answered the phone to hear Hector at the other end.

"I miss you, Millie. I miss you very much," Hector told her, lamenting the distance. "I'm a very lonely man."

He thanked her for the card she sent, and told her that his parents had also received her thank-you note. "They really like you. They know how much I love you."

"I don't know if I can wait until August to see you," she whispered to Hector. Hector was glad to hear her say that; he didn't think he could wait until August, either.

Meanwhile, Millie stayed busy working with her father. While he served as a part-time doctor in the local clinic, she managed the cattle and took other farm responsibilities.

Every day she drove her shiny blue pickup to check her post office box for letters from Hector. One day she met Thelma for lunch first, and revealed to her that she had a boyfriend. Thelma hadn't changed. She wanted to know everything about this guy that Millie seemed to like so much. She rolled her eyes in amazement as Millie tried to describe Hector's many attributes.

After lunch she ran in the post office to retrieve the day's mail. Besides the usual business mail for her parents, there was a large envelope postmarked from Chicago. Millie rushed to her truck and tore open the seal. Inside was a long letter and another sealed business envelope. She laid the envelopes on the dashboard and hungrily read the letter.

Dearest Millie:

My life is lonely without you. I miss you so very much. Only God and the sun know how much I love you. I cannot live without you, and that's a fact. I'll be traveling to Mexico soon to see my relatives. My parents and sisters and brothers are going as well. We'll be leaving July 1 and will return on July 20. My parents make this trip every year to see my grandmother and relatives.

I want you to join us in Mexico. My parents also think it would be a great idea. They are very happy to include you. You'll have your own room and you'll be with family all the time. How about it? I really don't want to go unless you can go, too.

To make your travel easier, I have enclosed your airplane tickets from Mexicali to Guadalajara, Mexico. I had to look at a map to figure out the closest connection to Mexico from your home. I'll pick you up at the airport in Guadalajara, and from there we'll drive to our home. Please, please, consider this important invitation for both of us.

I love you very much and I miss you too much. I'll call you soon.

Love,
Hector

Astonished, Millie read the letter several times. She rested her head on the steering wheel to catch her breath. Inside the second envelope were the tickets from Mexicali to Guadalajara. Her heart was already soaring in the clouds as she read the message.

But how could she leave her father in the middle of the summer with so much work? How would she break the news to her parents? She didn't have to think twice about wanting to go, and hoped her parents would consent to the trip.

She worried for the rest of the day about the best way to approach the subject with her parents. Should it be at dinner, lunch, or when? Several days passed before she had built the internal fortitude to mention it. She loved her parents very much and didn't want to hurt their feelings. Yet her excitement kept her reading and rereading Hector's letter.

Finally she decided to tell her mother, going home early for lunch in order to beat her father there. She tried hard to appear casual, but her nervous voice gave away her fears. "Mom, Hector has written to invite me to visit him and his family in Mexico. What do you think?" Katherine immediately shared a sweet smile with her daughter.

"Do you want to go?" Katherine asked her. "Do you feel that it's necessary to maintain your friendship?" Before Millie could answer, Jack walked in the kitchen for lunch. "What are you girls gossiping about today?" he asked without noticing their sudden frozen body language.

"Millie is going to Mexico for a visit," Katherine responded

nonchalantly. Millie elbowed her mother gently and
mouthed a silent thank-you when Jack wasn't looking.

"When are you leaving, Millie?" her father asked with obvious concern.

"I don't even know if I'm going, Dad," Millie said. "I've been
invited and I want to go but I haven't said that I would yet,"
she added. "But I am really interested in the country and
wouldn't mind getting to know the real Mexico."

"It's important that you make up your mind soon so you
can take the necessary precautions," Jack insisted, always
thinking like a doctor. Although he knew Millie would fit
naturally into the Mexican culture, he wanted to make sure
she had the right documents for travel. He had heard many
stories about Americans who had been jailed in Mexico
after crossing the border. He also wanted her to watch what
she ate to avoid the so-called Montezuma's Revenge.
Millie was thrilled to hear her father speak of the trip as
though it were already planned. She ate her lunch without
saying much more, but Jack and Katherine could tell that
she was really enthused about going.

• • •

MILLIE BOARDED AN AIRPLANE in Mexicali for her first trip by
air south of the border. The flight would take about three
hours, and then Hector would be waiting for her at the airport. Hector and his family had already been in Mexico for a
week. Millie would stay with them during their second week

there. Katherine had helped her select several gifts for
Hector and his parents.

Her stomach was tied in knots all the way to Guadalajara.
Other passengers were bursting with excitement about traveling south. She had never seen so many cowboy hats on an
airplane before. As they descended into the valley, she could
see the huge city to the north. She was confident that Hector
would be waiting for her just outside the gate.

As the plane touched the ground, the loud speakers played
Mexican music, exciting the passengers even more.
Everyone began to clap in appreciation for a great flight.
The airport was a small one, but the plane parked at least a
quarter of a mile away from the terminal. Millie was confused. In her experience, passengers walked to and from the
terminal to unload and board. This time, she saw buses
waiting to take passengers to the terminal. She joined the
others on a crowded bus and within five minutes was at the
main terminal. Her legs shook and her heart pumped faster.
The cool weather in Guadalajara was surprising. Clouds
high above the valley threatened a shower or two. The
Imperial Valley heat was now far to the north.

As she entered the terminal she immediately searched the
crowd for her prince. With so many people, hats and bags,
it was difficult to focus in any one direction.

"Millie, Millie!" shouted Hector from a distance. He was
making his way against the traffic of the incoming passengers. Millie breathed a sigh of relief at his familiar voice.
"Welcome to Mexico, Millie. I'm so glad to have you here

with me," he said. "Thank you for coming to this part of the world!" Hector could not hide his joy at having her visit him in Mexico.

She could only hold onto him in a long embrace. "I've missed you too much," she said as tears of joy flowed down her cheeks. "I don't want to be away from you, Hector."

"Come on, let's get your bags." Hector took her by the hand and led her to the moving belt filled with boxes and suitcases.

"Why are there so many boxes, Hector?" she asked.

"Many Mexican people do not have money to spend on suitcases so they pack their things in boxes," Hector told her as he grabbed her familiar suitcase.

"I have a couple of others coming," she said, reminding him of her packing habits. As they chatted, they gazed in each other's eyes affectionately. Hector held her hand as if he would never let go.

When all the suitcases were retrieved, Hector escorted her to the taxi stand. "We'll take a cab to Zamora, Michoacán," he said. "It'll be faster this way. Zamora is about thirty minutes or less to our home." Millie was glad she was with someone who knew the land and understood the people.

As they rode she stared at the cacti, stone fences, corn milpas, and adobe houses and had many unspoken questions. She wished she could be alone with Hector. She had missed his tender affection, his sweet smile, and his kisses. In the cab, she made a point of sitting close to him and holding his hand. He put his other arm around her shoulders and squeezed her toward his body. He was feeling lonely, too, and would have preferred to have her to himself.

From the city of Zamora the couple took a bus to Tangancicuaro. The mountainous area was green and fresh. Many of the flat areas were planted with corn. Hector's town rested on top of one of the mountains near a lake.

The bus stopped at the main plaza to load and unload passengers. The surrounding wooden pillars holding the adobe buildings together showed so much of the Spanish influence. The brightly painted adobe homes added to the ambiance of the town. The green, yellow, white, and pink colors stood out in the bright sun against the reddish-brown earth.

"We live on the outskirts of town, Millie. Do you have comfortable shoes?" Hector asked.

"I'm fine, Hector," she said. "Let's go."

The late afternoon sun was calling it quits for the day as they walked. Hector had hired some young boys to help with the luggage. Toward the center of town, the houses were connected. Many of the homes were painted in two colors, a light one covering three-quarters toward the roof and a darker one at the bottom part of the home. The stone fences, guayaba and orange trees, and cacti provided natural boundaries for the people. Millie noticed very poor adobe homes with chickens, pigs, and donkeys waiting on the front porch. A picture began to develop in front of her eyes that brought clear memories of this scene. She did not know where she had seen them before, but she could not stop staring at the adobe homes.

"Millie, welcome to our home." Hector stopped in front of a wooden gate in the middle of a stone fence. Many stones formed the typical Mexican fence. Tiny lizards were visible crawling from stone to stone in search of insects.

From the wooden gate, a cobblestone path led to a beautiful white adobe home surrounded by flowers, trees, and vines. The blooming laurels, bougainvilleas, calla lilies and gladiolas cheerfully showed off their brightest colors. In the courtyard, the chickens looked for seeds and corn in between the cobblestones. Large pottery jugs rested on wooden stalls on one side of the house. On the other, colorful clothes were drying on a rope tied from two trees. The roof's red clay tile gave the house a hacienda atmosphere. A large eucalyptus tree's gorgeous trunk grew on the west side of the home. The sun had been generous to the tree and its huge limbs demonstrated its strength and age. One branch held a big swing, waiting for the children to arrive.

An old bell attached to a rope dangled from the gate. Hector swung the clapper back and forth. "What are you doing, Hector?" Millie wondered.

"I'm ringing the bell to let them know we're here."

"Do you do that all the time?"

"No, only when special people like you arrive," he said,

laughing. "My parents are waiting for us," he added. "They'll be very happy to see you." Hector seemed concerned that his parents had not come out to greet them. But he placed his hand on Millie's back and gave her a soft push up the path. He figured they might be in the back orchard looking at the trees or gathering wood for a nighttime bonfire. Hector, Millie, and the three young boys walked the sixty yards or so to the home. She found it strange that there were no people to be seen.

"Are your parents home?" she finally asked.

"Yes, they should be waiting for us, Millie," he answered wistfully. "They must be inside doing something."

On the patio Millie could see birds in bamboo cages hung against the white walls. There were at least five small cages with different types of birds singing beautiful notes.

As the couple and their young helpers approached the first step to the home, all the doors popped opened suddenly, and the air filled with mariachi music. A group of strolling musicians stepped out to the patio. Hector's parents came from another direction and the rest of the family emerged from yet another door.

"Wow! What's happening here?" Hector asked.

"*¡Felicidades hijo! ¡Felicidades Señorita Millie!*" (Congratulations, son! Congratulations, Miss Millie!). His father yelled at the top of his lungs over the music as he hugged both of them. His mother and entire family rushed to hug Hector and then Millie. As the music played, Hector introduced her to the rest of his family and especially to his grandmother.

Hector and Millie had not expected this type of welcome. His family had planned the celebration for a while, and when they found out Millie would be visiting, too, decided to prepare the festivities in honor of both the graduates.

His family had immediately recognized that Hector had met a woman he loved, and that a fiesta for him would be more meaningful with her presence. Hector's parents had kept the party a total secret. He was so engulfed in Millie's upcoming visit that he hadn't paid attention to all the things that had happened in the last few days. Yesterday his father had killed a pig and told Hector he was donating it to a compadre's fiesta. Hector had even helped shave the pig's hair from its skin. It had been an arduous endeavor with minimal fanfare. With the some of the pork meat and lard, his mother had made more than three hundred tamales. His brothers and sisters had cleaned the house and the yard, saying they wanted everything ready for Millie.

How could I have been so blind not to catch on? he thought to himself. He was just glad Millie was by his side. He didn't like parties for himself or celebrations in his honor. But because he wanted Millie to feel comfort and happiness in his home, he handled the surprise with grace.

As the mariachi music flowed in the air, many friends began to show up for the party. In the back of the house, Hector's father had a cook tending the frying of the pig. As the sun set, so the cooking was completed. Several of the aunts and uncles brought large clay pots of beans, rice, and cactus salad. Hector's mother had prepared a large pot of hot salsa. His brothers opened big tins of jalapeños.

The family pulled tables and chairs together for visiting relatives. Bottles of liquor and soda pop were opened. The zinzontles and canaries accompanied the music with their own happy tunes to welcome everyone to the Gil home.

Hector's family had left for the United States many years ago with education at the forefront of their goals. To have a son graduate from a university was a major accomplishment. Hector had fulfilled his father's dreams — a son who would be able to use his mind and get compensated for it instead of toiling like an animal in the agricultural fields or cleaning other's peoples messes in the urban centers. Hector was an inspiration to all his family.

Millie saw Hector's grandmother hug him joyfully many times. Petra also hugged her and placed her soft wrinkled hands on Millie's cheeks. *"Eres una muchacha muy bonita,"* she told her. (You are a pretty girl.) Millie closed her eyes as the old woman's hands touched her tenderly. Childhood memories tugged at her consciousness.

"Como el jefe de esta familia, un brindis para mis hijos y hijas y para la Señorita Millie," Mr. Gil announced. (As head of this family, a toast to my sons and daughters and to Miss Millie). Everyone scrambled to get a glass for one last toast. Once everyone was settled again, Hector's father stood up.

"Queridos amigos, aquí les presento a mis hijos y a la Señorita Millie. Ellos son buenos hijos con su madre y con eso me consuelo. Que el Gran Dios les dé muchos triunfos en sus vidas y que les traiga la paz en su muerte. Brindo por los buenos hijos que Dios nos díó a mí y a mi querida esposa." (Dear friends, I present you my children and Miss Millie. They are good children with their mother and with that I am satisfied. May the great God bring them many successes in their lives and in death may peace be with them. I toast to the good children God has given my beloved wife and me.)

The party went on into the night, the mariachi playing songs everyone liked and the guests offering toasts to the couple and their successes. Family and friends were delighted to congratulate one of their own, and many pointed to Hector, advising their children to be like him in the future.

As the moon danced with the dark clouds in the sky above, the Gil family enjoyed the fiesta below. The party ended when the heavy rains began to pour. No one was sorry: The rainy season was here and everyone understood the importance of water from heaven.

As friends and neighbors left for their own homes, Hector's immediate family gathered in the kitchen. The rain clattered on the clay tile roof. The large kitchen had recently been modernized. A gas stove stood in one corner of the room. Mexican rock tile had replaced the old clay floor. Colorful pottery pots and pans hung from the ceiling next to large wooden spoons and spatulas. Several candles burned at the table while the family spoke of the day's event.

Hector and Millie thanked his father for the fiesta. His family was glad that Hector, after so many years away from home at the university, was finally spending time with them during their annual trip to the homeland.

Hector felt so proud to be part of this family. And more so, he felt like a complete man with his woman at his side. The woman he dreamed about all of his life had finally appeared, to his great surprise.

Millie was not missing a beat. Her heart was full of appreciation for the love and respect she immediately felt for Hector's family. She had never seen such a close-knit family before. Jack and Katherine were close to her but not as affectionate as Hector's family was toward him. She envied Hector and wondered what her real family would have been like had she grown up with them.

Millie was the second most-talked-about topic of discussion around the table. Everyone wanted to know how the two of them had met and what she had studied at the university. They wanted to hear about her life on the farm with the animals, and they wanted to learn about her parents and her family in general. She was glad to share as much as possible. As Millie spoke, Hector's sister took many photos from different angles around the table. Once again, Hector's father contributed with a warm, family-oriented toast over a shot of tequila. All the family joined the head of the house with different beverages around the table.

"*¡Salud! ¡Salud! ¡Salud!*" All the children raised their glasses to join the toast.

Hector escorted Millie to one of many rooms facing the patio of the humble home. The rain continued to pour, and the birds had placed their songs on hold for the following morning. The little bedroom was well-organized. In the candlelight, Millie's eye immediately caught the numerous small statues of saints and crosses hanging on the wall. One side of the room had been made into a bookcase. "This is my aunt's room," Hector said. "She lives in the convent but visits my grandmother periodically."

The single bed was carefully arranged. The white crocheted spread was smoothed over a pink sheet. A vase filled with fresh gladiolas rested on a small wooden table next to the bed. A large yellow candle spattered soft light on the adobe walls. A pitcher of water was next to the vase, and a clean glass was turned upside down on a starched white napkin.

"There's no electricity in this room," Hector told her. "You'll need to use additional candles if you want to read tonight," he added. "A bedpan is under here." He pointed under the bed. The family's two bathrooms and shower were outdoors.

"Hector, this is so beautiful. I'll be all right here. Please wake me up early in case I oversleep," she requested. She placed her hand on his face to thank him for the day. "I love you so much."

Hector gave her a sweet kiss. "Good night, my love," he said. "I'll wake you up. Get some rest because we have a busy day tomorrow. We're going to see something very special." She returned his kiss and began to close the door behind him. He added some slight resistance to keep the door open a little longer as he poked his head inside the room. "Oh, by the way, don't let the mice bother you. They run around the attic chasing each other and rustling the corn," he told her with a big smile.

Millie spent what seemed a long time just looking around the room. She had first latched the unusual twisted lock on the door. Then she noticed all the books. Many religious titles were on the shelves nearest to the bed. The rest of the books looked like picture albums, yearbooks, and English readers. Pottery bookends and several of the small saint statues divided the books by topic.

The floor of the room was covered with *petates* (reed and weed woven mats). The dried yellow mats were comfortable on her feet. Next to the bed was a small altar with a Virgin of Guadalupe statue, patron saint of Mexico. An old bible sat next to the statue with several rosaries waiting to be used. Small vases of flowers adorned the altar and red, green, and while satin drapes hung from the ceiling. In front of the altar was a one-person kneeling bench. She assumed that this was Hector's aunt's prayer area.

The structure of the piece was all too familiar to her. She had knelt on one before. Church memories flashed vividly in her mind as she stared at the wooden cross. In the next second she found herself kneeling and looking up to the Mexican saint. She felt very lonely and began to cry. Somehow, she thought, she would have to surrender her doubts about her past to Hector. She would not be honest otherwise.

Tears ran down her cheeks as she looked up to the saint and prayed silently in her own way, seeking comfort in the unknown. *Please, my lady of Mexico, don't let me live bearing the cross of my past.*

She got up from the altar and looked again at the bookshelves. She pulled out an old album filled with crumpled, yellowing photos, and guessed that they were Hector's baby pictures. The album was dusty. She carefully pulled the cover open and was surprised to see pictures from the early 1900s. Women in long skirts and men in peasant pants and shirts were photographed in front of some type of curtain. She cautiously closed the album and returned it to its place.

Then she pulled one of the English books from the shelves. It was a fifth grade language arts book with a stamp inside the cover that identified it as property of the Chicago Public Schools. This must have been one of the books the children would bring to study during Christmas vacation, Millie speculated. As she flipped through the pages she recognized the book as one she had used in grade school. She returned it to its location and was about to go to bed when she decided to return to the set of albums on the adobe shelves.

She moved her fingers over the albums and counted. Her favorite number had always been five, so she counted across four albums and pulled the fifth one in hopes of finding baby pictures of the man she loved so much. By her numbers game, she ended up choosing an older, more fragile volume, bound in leather.

Pictures of Hector's father, mother and siblings were abundant in the dusty album. She turned the pages to find more photos of what she presumed were family friends. The more she looked, the more the pictures became familiar to her. She was astounded by her own magnetic interest in the old photos. At last, she found one of Hector's father and mother with a tiny baby. The picture looked so real and was so familiar to her. Then she found photos of Hector's father with another man in front of a smoking volcano. A profound feeling overtook her, and her skin prickled with goose bumps. The two men looked so familiar to her. Their smiles were warm and full of hope. Carefully, she closed the album and sat awhile with it on her lap.

Millie finally changed out of her travel clothes and laid out casual clothes for the next day. She was tired; her body knew it but not her mind. She lay awake in bed for another half-hour listening to the rain on the tile roof. The thick adobe walls kept the other night sounds outside. As Hector had warned, the mice were active. She could hear their little feet run across the ceiling, and imagined them feasting on the dry corn stored in the attic. She always enjoyed the sounds of nature. On this night, the rain showers and the festive mice kept her company until her eyes closed for the night.

• • •

MILLIE WOKE UP to the noise of the donkeys and roosters as they welcomed the early morning sun. The rain had stopped and the mice had disappeared. She guessed that the cows were getting milked by the distant sounds of noisy calves.

Thinking of their hunger took her back to the time Hector had tasted her breasts. She smiled as the pleasant thought awakened her with open arms.

She realized that she might have slept longer than she wanted. Underneath the door and window she could see bright light peeking through the slivers in the uneven carved wood. She rolled out of bed to open the small window facing east. Lazily, she smoothed the bedspread back to perfection and then threw her arms wide. She wanted to touch both sides of the room as she stretched her wings to the new morning. She put on her robe and picked up the small bag containing soap, a toothbrush and her makeup.

Unhooking the silly crooked-fork lock, Millie could hear Hector and his family in the kitchen. The birds were singing their happy tunes again. The aroma of corn tortillas cooking was so enticing. The familiar smell coaxed her eyes closed for an instant as she inhaled a long, deep breath of flavored air. "Good morning, Millie," Hector called from the kitchen. He walked out to her room to guide her to the wash area. He had already taken a shower and was dressed for the day.

"Good morning," she responded with a smile. "Why didn't you wake me up earlier?"

"I knew you were tired and needed to get some rest," he said in a satisfied manner. "Yesterday was a long day for you. Besides, we're going to do lots of walking today, so resting was essential," he continued in a paternal tone. He tried to take her bag to help her as he guided her toward the shower.

Millie was nervous that Hector was seeing her right out of bed for the first time. "You look just as pretty as always," he assured her. "I'll be in the kitchen when you're finished." He returned to the kitchen as he spoke, not wanting to embarrass her further. "Remember, there's no hot water," he called back to her. She thanked him as she quickly walked into the red brick shower area. She knew that each member of the family should use only a small amount of water, not so different from the rule at home in the United States. Hector had offered to heat some water for her but she did not want to be treated differently from the rest of the family.

She noticed several hollowed-out gourds used for soap containers and to hold small rocks. These must be the rocks from the volcano Hector spoke about, she thought. He had spoken of people using rocks to wash their skin clean. After Millie undressed, she inhaled the fragrance of the large yellow bar of soap and then carefully placed it back in the hanging gourd. Then she gently rubbed her cheek with one of the rocks, noting its texture against her soft skin.

The cool water chilled her naked body. The sun wanted to peek inside but it was still too early. She imagined the pleasure of warm water after the sun's rays had penetrated the water tank for a few hours. The sun needed to rise a little more before the bricks would permit it to enter.

While she washed, Millie heard people on the cobblestone streets herding cows. She could make out the clip-clop of the horseshoes on the rough road. It reminded her of her duties left behind on the farm. She wondered how her parents were getting on without her help. Jack and Katherine had said that Millie's trip to Mexico would be a great vacation for her, but she could see their trepidation as she had boarded the plane. She had tried to reassure them that she would be all right.

The odor of fresh cow dung seeped into the shower area. From the roofless stall, Millie could look up at the blue sky. The day would be a beautiful one. As she finished bathing, a monarch butterfly alighted briefly at the top of the brick. *How strange*, she thought to herself. She hadn't seen many of this type of butterfly in Imperial Valley. With the exception of the little white butterfly that appeared during onion season, not many others were seen back home.

She dressed quickly and joined the family in the kitchen. *"Buenos días, Señorita Millie."* Several of the family members welcomed her at once. She froze for a second in the doorway at the initial familiar smell. *This is probably like my childhood home*, she thought. She would never have imagined that her sense of smell could lead her to forgotten memories.

The family was eating a breakfast of eggs mixed with tortillas, chiles, and beans for what they called *chilaquiles*. The corn tortillas they were eating were almost blue in color. "What kind of tortillas are these?" Millie asked, pointing.

"Those are made from blue corn," Hector replied as he seated her next to himself at the table. Hector's grandmother was working quickly to make as many as possible so that the family could enjoy the delicious tortillas while they were hot.

From the ceiling of the kitchen, Hector's grandmother had strung chiles and plants from a thin rope to dry upside down. Millie began to recall helping her mother as she hung plants for drying. She could clearly remember the floating spider webs like the ones in this kitchen. But where was this past? She blocked the kitchen sounds for a moment while she searched her mind for the answers. Jack and Katherine had said very little to her about her childhood prior to becoming part of the Wolf family.

Returning her thoughts to the present, she offered the gifts she had brought for the family. She placed a bottle of fine California wine in front of Hector's father. For his mother, she had brought a small perfume. *"No tenia que hacer esto, señorita,"* Hector's mother remarked. (You did not have to do this, Miss.)

Hector's father had a great sense of humor. In English he joked, "Why didn't you give me this last night? I could have used it in one hour." Millie gave the family a box filled with white chocolate candies, date bars, and nut bread. Mr. Gil continued to tease her. *"Este es pan gringo. Asegúrate de llevarla a ver a los panaderos de aquí, Hector."* (This is gringo bread. Make sure you take her to see our breadmakers, Hector.) "Thank you, Miss Millie, and welcome home again," he added genuinely.

After breakfast, Hector took Millie on a tour of the humble hacienda-type house. With the surprise party going on, she had not had an opportunity to look around. He also took her to the main plaza in the center of the town. He showed her the church and the different municipal quarters for government business. Millie took it all in. She had never been south of Mexicali, so this was all new to her.

In the afternoon they visited the famous Camecuaro Lake. "We have many picnics here, Millie," Hector said proudly. "The name comes from the Tarascan Indians, and it means water." They rented one of the available canoes, knowing that they were fortunate to be there on a weekday when they could be alone on the clear lake.

Large trees surrounded the edge of the water. The lion-claw tree limbs fascinated Millie. She was particularly impressed with the clarity of the lake, which allowed them to see the roots of the trunks reaching deep into the water. They could both see twelve feet below the bottom of the canoe. "This is a gorgeous place, Hector," Millie said. She couldn't help but fall in love with the splendor of the emerald view.

"I'm going to take you to a special place on the lake, Millie," Hector said, pointing to a far corner. Hector directed the canoeist in the direction he was pointing. The guide moved his paddles swiftly without splashing, an expert at moving on the lake with little effort and very little noise. The bright green canoe floated over the clear waters like a magic carpet gliding through the air.

Not far was a huge tree providing generous shade on a tiny island. The trunk of the tree covered a large area and its many big roots extended in all direction into the water. The tiny island was not larger than a merry-go-round canopy.

"This is the place my father proposed to my mother many

years ago," Hector said. "My father has always pointed it out to us ever since I can remember." He laughed at himself for doing the very same thing.

"Your father is very creative." Millie smiled as she realized Hector would someday look and act just like his father. "Your mother had no option but to say yes to such a romantic proposal from a handsome man in a beautiful place."

Hector asked the canoeist to leave them on the tiny island for a couple of hours. They jumped out of the hand-carved canoe, and walked to rest themselves against the large tree. The grass around the tree was tall and Millie recognized it as a nesting area for ducks.

"*Que se venga el Mariachi.*" Hector asked the canoeist to bring the mariachi as the young man turned the boat around to depart.

Hector sat with his back to the trunk of the tree and helped Millie sit between his legs with her back against his chest. They gazed at the hundreds of lilies in bloom all around them. The silence of the remote location touched Millie. "Hector, this is so beautiful." She sighed deeply.

"I'm glad you like this place," he said, sounding content.

"Do you think the way we feel now is the way your mom and dad felt?" Millie asked, her eyes twinkling with love.

"Those days were very strict. I don't think that they ever

were this close until after they were married. My father proposed to my mother at a family picnic on a Sunday afternoon. He was probably lucky if he spoke to her a minute or
two alone," he said as he kissed her on her neck. "Most
people didn't even hold hands before marriage.

"Have your parents ever told you what happened to your
real parents?" Hector dared to ask a question that Millie had
wanted him to ask for a long time. Her eyes swelled with
tears in anticipation of the sensitive topic.

Her awkwardness and uncertainty brought such pain that
she had purposely concealed her doubts for many, many
years. "Hector, how do you get over things you don't understand?" she asked, her fingers fiddling nervously in his
hands. She bent her knees to her chest and held them tightly with her arms. Hector continued to hold her closely from
behind like a shepherd protecting a frail sheep. He knew
this was a delicate subject because she never spoke about
it, but he was curious and wanted to help.

"My parents told me that my real parents wanted me to
have a better life in the United States, and therefore, they
asked the Wolf family to care for me," Millie said. Her tears
and sniffles poured over the cotton sleeves of her blouse. "I
don't remember much about my childhood. I did find a box
hidden in the closet with small clothes covered with dried
blood.

"My mother, Katherine, had put a note in the box dated
September 1957. The note said that the clothes were mine,"
she added. "I guess they were mine," she said, and began to

cry harder. "When I was in grade school, they told me that my real parents had an accident.

"I remember that I had brothers and my father and mother were very nice," she said sorrowfully. "I wish I knew more." She accepted a handkerchief from Hector and wiped her nose.

"I've been afraid to ask my mom and dad questions because they've been so good to me," she admitted. "They've given me everything I needed and more. They love me and I love them," Millie said. "I just wish I knew more so that I wouldn't have to think about it so much."

"What else do you remember from your childhood?"

"Well, I remember houses like your dad's and trees as tall as the Stanford tower. I remember many flowers and butterflies. As a matter of fact, when I was a freshman I wrote a research paper on monarch butterflies, but the insect scientist I interviewed did not know where they migrated in the winters." She strained to remember the few things she had saved from her past.

"Millie, when we get back to the United States, let's speak to your dad and mom about your past," he suggested. "Let's tell them how much discomfort this matter brings to you. I don't think it's healthy for you to feel the way you do," he said with concern. "Perhaps they don't know about your past either. Or maybe they know a lot about your past but have a valid reason for not telling you." He did not want to have this special day stained by Millie's sadness.

Soon, the canoe returned for them. From their seats in the boat they could see the blue clouds reflected on the quiet lake. Millie felt so relaxed leaning back in Hector's arms that she did not want the moment to disappear. "Can we come back here again someday?"

"I'll do anything for you, baby," he said with satisfaction. He was so glad that this lake had brought a special fascination to her eyes.

They glided along the shore filled with blooming lilies until they were joined by another canoe filled with musicians. The men, dressed in black suits with many silver decorations, played for the couple as the boats headed back to the dock.

"¡Toquen 'Dos Arbolitos' para mi novia, muchachos!" Hector shouted to the lead musician. "Millie, I want them to play for you. In our own ways, Mexican men show admiration and love by playing songs that have a strong meaning to us." He spoke into her ear so she could hear him over the loud music. "This is one of my favorite songs. It's about two little trees that grow, loving each other and providing shade for each other." Millie could not contain her tears as the emotional music and her love for Hector gave way to a sentimental feeling. The musicians played every song that Hector asked for until the two boats reached their original starting point. Hector helped Millie from the canoe and they walked back home holding each other around the waist.

As they approached the plaza, the smell of fresh bread baking caught their attention. "Let's stop by the bakery and take some home," Hector said. He remembered his father's direction to show Millie the local bakery. The aroma of baking bread came strongly through the screen door of the humble home. The patio was filled with flowers and large lemon trees grew in the center. Many large sacks filled with flour rested patiently against the walls, waiting their turn.

"Hector!" Several men dressed in white stepped forward to greet the couple. *"¿Cómo está usted? Felicidades por sus triunfos universitarios,"* one of the men added with a big smile absent two front teeth. *"Su apá nos contó."* (Congratulations on your university successes. Your father told us.)

"Esta es mi novia, Millie." Hector politely introduced Millie to the three round-bellied men. Their large aprons were covered with grease stains and flour.

"Pasen." The man with the most flour on his face invited the couple to another screen-enclosed room. Millie was amazed at the wonderful odors and the simplicity of the business.

Many different gourds hung on the wall. A rope tied to the necks of the gourds held them all together. Corks set in place at the tops of the necks covered the openings of the natural water containers. Just like at Hector's home, the bakers had several bamboo cages full of singing birds. As Millie walked past the bamboo containers, she stood on tiptoe to watch the birds as they sang their welcome to the bakery's visitors.

"This family has owned the bakery for many generations," Hector told her. "The families in this town continue to do

the things their great-grandfathers did in the late 1800s."
She was appreciative of Hector's description and of a culture where fancy mixing machines were not yet known.

The three large ovens were made out of adobe bricks. Each
of the ovens had a long spatula waiting by the opening,
used to retrieve the bread from the oven or to place the
uncooked dough over the heat. Large pieces of wood burned
under the ovens. The bakers showed Millie the large masses
of dough waiting to be rolled into bread. In one of the ovens,
French brioches were already cooking. Uncooked rounds of
dough were going into the middle oven, and one of the bakers pulled cooked bread from the third.

The bread resembled turtle shells decorated with white
sugar. After the loaves of fancy bread were cooked, the
baker placed them in a large basket that resembled a straw
hat. Young boys were waiting to carry the baskets on their
heads to sell the bread out in the streets of the town. The
sides of the hat held the bread in place. Hector and Millie
were handed pieces of the hot and fresh Mexican bread. The
steaming treat was the perfect end to a long yet wonderful
trip. They walked home as the sun began its descent for the
day.

"¿Le gustó el paseo?" Hector's mother was preparing the
evening meal when they returned and wondered if Millie
had enjoyed the trip. Hector helped his mother place the sil-
verware on the table as he told her of the sights he had
shown Millie. Mrs. Gil had already cut up flank steak into
tiny pieces for tacos. The family ate heated corn tortillas
folded in half and filled with the different ingredients

Hector's mother had set on the table. There was fried left-over pig chitterlings, cactus, rice, beans, and cut-up beef tongue. Millie had never seen so many ingredients for an evening meal as Hector's family served. But the meal was just a minor part of the gathering as conversation dominated the ambiance of the kitchen.

After the meal, Millie and Hector helped his father remove the dishes from the table. The family had used several clay pots and wooden forks that needed washing. Hector's mother had used a special tablecloth for the occasion. As she pulled it away from the wooden table, Millie moved over to assist her, grabbing a corner to help fold the large rectangle. The naked table displayed its many years of use. She politely took the broom away from Mrs. Gil to begin sweeping under the kitchen furniture. She could tell Hector's mom appreciated her help.

Millie bent under the table to scoot the broom into the far corners and pull the crumbs from the center. As she swept she noticed carvings on the head of the table where Hector's father sat. Tiny flowers decorated a message. *"Para mi padrino, Teófilo Gil, 1952."* (For my godfather, Teófilo Gil, 1952).

"What is this message doing here?" she asked.

Hector's father came to the table and knelt on one knee. He rubbed his right hand over the message in a form of endearment. *"Esta mesa fué un regalo especial de una niñita."* (This table was a special gift from a special little girl.)

"What little girl?"

"Millie, you're going to get Dad started on a long, long story he frequently tells," Hector warned her. "Maybe tomorrow, Dad, please?" Hector hoped to persuade his father to tell the details another time. "Perhaps when we aren't so tired," he said carefully.

"Señorita Millie, mañana le platicó de la niña Milagro, mi ahijada." (Miss Millie, tomorrow I will tell you about the little girl Miracle, my godchild.) He got up from the floor, shaking his head at having to wait until the following day. He tried to strike a compromise: *"¿Si quieren ir a visitar a mi compadre en Amapola? Manaña será un buen día, hijo."* (Do you want to visit my compadre in Amapola? Tomorrow will be a good day, son.)

"Do you want to visit the town of my father's friend, Millie?" Hector asked. She was busy cleaning and picking up the trash, taking direction from Hector's mom.

"Sure," she responded, without much thought.

"All right, we go tomorrow morning at ten o'clock after breakfast," Hector's father said in his stilted English. He was delighted that Millie was willing to drive to Amapola with them. The family went in different directions after the kitchen was set for the following morning. Hector and Millie stepped out to seek the comfort of the silver moon.

The romantic couple spent several hours in the dark shadows of the fruit trees. Several hand-made wicker benches had been placed under the trees to protect them from the bright Mexican sun. Hector's grandmother and grandfather had sat on the benches frequently to watch their grandchildren play while the adults worked around the house. The night was cool as the clouds again threatened the peaceful darkness. A light from the patio shined toward the couple but reached only a short distance from the doors. Hector and Millie were alone with their kisses.

"Millie, why don't you come to live in San Diego with me?" Hector asked in a pleading manner.

"What?" She was shocked by his request. "You know I can't do that," she told him, caressing his face.

"When we get back, I don't want to be without you. Please think about it," he insisted.

"Hector, you are one crazy guy." Millie shook her head in amazement. "If your parents could hear you they would think you were crazy for asking me all these things," she added.

"Oh, no, they wouldn't," he responded quickly. "They would say that I really love you and want you and that you should move to San Diego to please me," he joked.

"One day when you get married, do you want to have kids?" Hector tried a different line of questioning.

"I want to have lots of children," Millie responded by raising both hands in the air and showing seven fingers.

"Wow! That's too many to support," Hector shook his head

at her the way she had at him, and they both laughed. Their laughter melted into a passionate embrace and they kissed again under the Mexican sky.

EL MILAGRO
The Miracle

The following morning, Millie woke up to a light sprinkle. The birds in the bamboo cages greeted her with their lovely songs. Hector and his parents were in the kitchen conversing about their plans for the day. She paid little attention to their words as she slipped by to the shower. *The water will be a little cold today,* she thought. As she brushed through the garden, she noticed huge rain drops on the leaves and flowers. Some of the flowers had bent petals from the evening rains. The calla lilies still held moisture in the cups of their spiraled white petals.

The kitchen was filled with a new set of aromas. Hector's mom had prepared menudo for breakfast. The red soup was already being savored as Millie entered the room. "Come sit down and have some soup, Millie." Hector stood while she sat next to him.

"¿Le gusta el menudo, Señorita Millie?" Hector's father asked as he cleaned his mouth with a white paper towel stained with the red soup. Everyone else laughed at the idea that Millie might like menudo.

"What's so funny?" Millie smiled, assuming the teasing was meant for her.

"We laugh because not many Americans like menudo," Hector explained. "It's made with tripe or cow stomach lining," he said, raising a spoon filled with tiny pieces of honeycomb-patterned meat. "My mother also adds cow hooves for flavor," he added, pointing to his father, who was chewing on a bony-looking piece of meat. Millie had no experience with such a soup, but reluctantly tried it.

"*Está muy bueno, señorita.*" Hector's father praised the soup as he chewed on a piece of cow hoof. In English, Hector's father explained, "When men and young boys get drunk, the Mexican women know that the menudo will get them out of their misery. The menudo cures their ills," he advised in a faithful tone.

"It works," Hector affirmed.

"*Si no quiere comer menudo le preparo unos frijoles con queso,*" Hector's mom offered maternally. (If you do not want to eat menudo, I'll prepare some beans with cheese.) She served Millie a small bowl of the rich, red soup. Following their lead, Millie added onion, oregano, and crumbled red hot chiles. The addition of a generous amount of lemon changed the flavor to a taste she found more reasonable.

"I've been around many cow hooves before," she said, "but I've never seen cow hooves in soups or in people's mouths." She giggled politely. Her comment brought a burst of laughter from the entire family.

The family prepared their "Land of Lincoln" van for a trip to visit Teófilo's compadre. Hector's mother cut all the calla lilies from her garden to take to the family. While the others loaded the large tin cans filled with water and crowded flowers in the rear of the van, she also cut pink gladiolas and white roses. Millie was helping with minor chores in preparation for the short trip across the mountains. She knew it would be filled with the wonderful company of Hector and his parents and the aroma of fresh-cut flowers. She did not realize that they had made this traditional and very serious visit since the late 1950s.

The family traveled an hour northwest to the small village of Amapola. Hector rested his arm around Millie against the leather seat. The radio was playing Mr. Gil's favorite Mexican songs of love and revolution. The music must have brought him many melancholy memories of growing up in Mexico, because as they drove, he told many stories. Hector had heard them many times before, and made hand signals to Millie asking for her patience with his father.

They traveled on a government-paved road until they came to a small wooden frame indicating they had reached the road that would lead them to Amapola. The Chevy turned onto the dusty, rocky trail leading to another set of smaller hills and valleys. "Hector, have you explained to Millie about my compadre?" Mr. Gil asked as he looked at Hector in the rear view mirror.

"Who are we visiting?" Millie asked.

"My father's compadre, Octavio," Hector responded nonchalantly. "This man and my father were very good friends until tragedy struck the whole family," he added with an indifferent look. Millie's skin exploded into thousands of goose bumps. She could feel her palms perspire as the radio played the Mexican mariachi folk songs.

She had no idea why the story of Mr. Gil's friend made her so nervous. "Was this family very close to your family?" she asked Hector in hopes of getting more specific information.

"My father and Octavio had a very close friendship. So close that my father and mother became compadres with Octavio and his wife by baptizing a daughter," he added, tilting his head downward in a sign of respect.

"My father believes that this man's spirit still lives," Hector whispered so his father would not hear. "My father sometimes wakes up in the middle of the night because he says Octavio woke him up. He lights a candle every first Friday of the month to the Virgin of Guadalupe on Octavio's behalf," Hector told Millie quietly. "You should visit our house in Chicago. My father has an altar and on the Day of the Dead, he lights more candles for all of Octavio's family.

"In the Mexican culture," Hector went on, "we honor the dead in many ways. Besides going to church and lighting candles, my father believes that it's his duty to visit the gravesite of his compadre so that his compadre can rest in peace," Hector told Millie as the van reached a hill where the village of Amapola could be seen. "My father visits this place every year," he added. *No wonder they're bringing flowers*, Millie thought.

In 1957, Teófilo had offered a *manda* on behalf of his compadre. In Mexico, Hector explained, a *manda* serves as a religious offering to a saint. In return, the offering would grant Teófilo some favor or miracle. Teófilo asked the Virgin of Guadalupe to help him find his compadre's missing child, and committed himself to walk on his knees from his home to the church if his *manda* were granted.

Millie turned her attention to a distant village filled with white adobe homes. The red color of the clay tile roofs complemented the green trees surrounding the homes. The sun played peekaboo with the clouds as they blew over the mountainside village. At the very top of the mountain a tiny white cross was visible from the road. Hector's words kept resonating in Millie's mind.

"That's a pretty little village," Millie said. "Which one is it?" She was trying to keep her many thoughts in order.

"That's Amapola," he responded casually.

"Hector — " she began, unsure of herself.

"Yeah?"

"Amapola sounds very familiar to me." Her voice was shaky. This whole trip was starting to make her feel very peculiar.

"What do you mean? Maybe because we saw a lot of amapola flowers near Stanford?"

"I don't know." She tried to reconstruct Amapola in a world

215

in her mind. *Where did I hear this before?* she wondered. The van turned once more and the cacti and mesquite trees concealed the view of the village.

The van came to a halt on the side of the clay road by the lonely site of the village's remote cemetery. Newly unearthed burial sites could be seen among age-encrusted graves. Some of the wooden crosses were bent in the direction of the constant, silent wind. The grass was lush and green from the rainy season. Many wildflowers grew around the perimeters of the rectangular graves. The cemetery was surrounded by generously built cacti, and two large eucalyptus trees marked the east and west boundaries near the stone fence. Corn crops surrounded the other sides. Millie could see several men working in the corn *milpas* around the cemetery. Their donkeys were waiting at the edge of the crops, tied to a skinny mesquite tree.

The annual visit to this place was an emotional time for Hector's father. His family knew that the few minutes spent at this place must be solemn. Teófilo walked ahead to the gravesites while the others helped with the flowers. A shadow of loneliness gradually occupied the small area where the graves were located. The shade of a large eucalyptus tree provided welcome relief from the late morning sun.

Millie carefully carried a large tin can filled with white calla lilies. The long green stems limited her view so she poked her way through them with her head. The peaks of the single-petal flowers brushed her skin. The soft petals caressed her face the same way Hector had done many times before. For a brief moment, the white flowers aroused her senses.

Hector carried a basket full of roses ready to be inserted into the empty tin canisters waiting at the burial sites, and also several umbrellas in case of rain.

From a distance, Millie could see Hector's father kneeling in front a tall wooden cross that leaned toward the large limbs of the eucalyptus tree. Several other crosses stood next to each other waiting for the sunsets, the rains, and the infrequent visitors.

Her first glimpse of the resting-place caused Millie to remember her grandfather Wolf, who had influenced and inspired her so much. The memory of him gave her internal strength. She hoped that his spirit would enlighten her own recollection of names and places she had known as a small child but could not remember yet. *How wonderful it would be to learn about my ancestors someday,* she thought. "Come this way," Hector called as he walked ahead of her.

Hector helped the women climb the stone fence to enter the cemetery on the northeast side. With puddles from the recent rains remaining, climbing over the fence was simpler than walking to the wooden gate at the far end. Millie handed over the tin can filled with flowers. Hector received them on the other side and placed them on a wet grassy area in order to extend his arms to help her over.

Millie knew instantly that she had climbed this type of rock before. She remembered the holes between the rocks through which she often watched the animals when she was small. She hated for her thoughts to leave her without fuller explanation. As she straddled the rocks, Hector's warm hand grabbed hers to help her reach the ground. Gallantly, he lifted her from the waist to boost her from a small rock she had landed on to a larger dry area next to one of the gravesites. Millie could have climbed over the fence by herself but welcomed the chance to be held in Hector's strong arms.

Hector's mother, Natalia, climbed the stone structure with the help of her husband. Both of them walked over to the tall cross and sat on a large volcanic rock next to the grave. She held on to her husband silently as he removed his hat and bowed his head. Hector's father repeated this ritual year after year, remaining in front of Octavio's grave for about thirty minutes. He felt spiritually relieved after visiting the cemetery.

Hector and Millie carried the homemade planters to the corners of the graves. *"No dejen de arreglar las flores para mi compadre y para los niños,"* Mr. Gil called toward the young couple. (Don't forget the arrangement of flowers for my compadre and the children.)

"Está bien, Papá," Hector replied as he began to fill other empty cans with roses and calla lilies. "He wants us to make sure that we place flowers on the other gravesites," Hector told Millie.

Millie had not realized that the tall cross stood for one of the family members. Hector had not explained the situation very well and the others did not talk about it either. "Who are the rest of the family members?" she asked Hector as they moved to the smaller crosses.

"The family was killed many years ago," he explained. "As I told you, my father was very close to his friend," Hector added. "His family died with him in a tragic accident."

"How did they die?" She followed Hector from one gravesite to another, placing the flower-filled cans on the edges. Before Hector could respond, she noticed a gap between the burial sites. "Why did they leave a space here?" Millie wanted to know all the details. Teófilo eavesdropped on her questions, curious to hear how his son would answer. Teófilo was ready to respond himself.

"A little girl was lost in the tragedy and this is the symbol of her place," Hector said as he held her hand and guided her a few steps back to where his parents were peacefully tending the gravesites. They still could not understand how in one instant the entire Luna family could leave this world so tragically. The quiet daylight vigil was very important for them. Hector noticed that his father seemed sadder during this visit than he had in recent years.

It had been four years since Hector had traveled to Mexico with his parents. University work on his degree had kept him away. *Maybe Papá is getting older and more sentimental,* Hector thought as he noticed the anguish on his father's face. He knew that his father continued to feel responsible for the accident. Many times, Teófilo's children tried to explain to him that he had no control over the fate of the family or the circumstances of the accident. The loving advice did not help Teófilo overcome his despair.

Teófilo had suffered much guilt over the death of Octavio

and his family. The immigration service had contacted him in Chicago seeking knowledge about the deceased. Besides cooperating with the authorities, he had mustered enough money to finance the cost of having a private mortuary prepare the bodies for the trip back home. He knew that if he did not, the family would be sent by train; by the time the bodies arrives in Amapola, the decomposed humans would be considered wasted and the families would not be able to say farewell to the deceased. That September day in 1957 still haunted him. He could not get over the devastating outcome of the noble family's failed trip to Chicago, which he had initiated. He could not help that his tears still flowed.

Teófilo recalled his trip to Texas to identify the bodies of Octavio and his family. Afterwards he had also traveled to the Mexican state of Tamaulipas to search fruitlessly for his missing godchild, Milagro. He had returned to Chicago filled with guilt, and became a worrywart toward his own children. It seemed to him that the least he could do was pay this yearly visit to the graves and in his own quiet way reflect on the pain he continued to feel even after nineteen years.

Hector held on to Millie as they watched the calm tears flowing from his parents' eyes. His father took his handkerchief out of his back pocket and wiped the salty wet drops before they fell on the edges of Octavio's grave. His mother had already dampened her cotton lace hanky. Hector could feel their pain deep in the pit of his stomach.

Hector was only eight years when the accident happened, so his memory of the event was distant. His mother had remained with the family in Chicago while his father traveled to take care of the matter. Hector knew the details after hearing them from his father so often. For many years, the entire family helped to pay off the debt that their father had accepted on behalf of his best friend. Teófilo's personal commitment eased some of their pain.

Millie grew quiet as she realized the grief behind their visit to the cemetery. She knew the best thing to do was to follow Hector's lead on this trip.

Eventually Hector's parents gathered their composure and Mr. Gil began to relate the details of the tragic event. A very light drizzle started falling into the aromatic country air. The young corn leaves swished and tapped each other in the wind.

"¿Señorita Millie, usted conoce el dolor profundo?" Do you know about profound pain, Teófilo somberly asked. Millie did not know how to respond. Out of respect, she just shook her head softly. "He was my best friend," he added sentimentally. As he spoke, he turned his hatband on his finger like a tiny hula-hoop. *"Yo me siento muy mal en estos días por lo que le pasó a mi compadre y a su familia,"* he added as he watched his sombrero go around and around. (I still feel very bad these days for what happened to my friend and his family.)

He got up and helped his wife from the volcanic rock. He signaled to Hector to do the same for Millie as he moved to the vacant gravesite. Millie was nervous; she didn't like sad stories and she knew she was about to hear one. The two couples stood in front of the empty gravesite where a tin can was filled with the prettiest flowers.

"¡Ésto es lo que me duele más!" (This is what hurts me the most!) Teófilo pointed at the empty space where wild poppies and tall grass grew. Hector sensed Millie's discomfort and hoped that she would not be bothered by the grim story.

"Mi ahijada, Milagro, desapareció en un cerrar de ojos," Teófilo said as he bent his head to stare at the cause of his pain. My goddaughter disappeared in a brief closing of the eyes, he said. Millie's knees weakened and shook at his words. Hector noticed her tight grip on his arms. She leaned more on him than she ever had in the presence of his parents.

"Honey, what's wrong?" he asked, looking at her with concern.

Teófilo continued his story. *"Milagro era una muchachita muy bonita y muy especial para su papá y para nosotros."* (Milagro was a pretty little girl and very special to her father and to us.) He bent downward to pull out some of the loose weeds softened by the rains.

"What happened to the family?" Millie had to ask again. She felt a strong need to know the details.

"Octavio took his family to the United States but a train ran into the vehicle and killed them all," Teófilo sadly related. "We could not find Milagro," he added. "We looked all over Mexico and Texas with no luck," he explained to Millie in English.

She vaguely remembered the name Milagro. The story of the lost child reminded her of her own lost childhood, and her silent tears began to fall on the unoccupied lot. *"Señorita Millie, no llore."* (Miss Millie, don't cry.) Hector's mother tried to console her with her own words. She patted Millie on her shoulders in appreciation for what she thought was attentiveness to Teófilo's pain.

Millie turned to face the tall wooden cross standing behind them. The pain of her past cried inside her. For many moons she had strained to recall the words of her childhood. Amapola's cemetery renewed her passionate desire to remember her father and mother. She placed her hands on the cross. *Maybe by praying to the soul of this man, his spirits will guide me to mine,* she thought to herself. Hector and his parents were surprised at her distress. It was evident to them that she was in pain.

The raindrops were a blessing in disguise for Millie, camouflaging her tears as she silently debated what to say.

Hector embraced her as his parents looked on. "I remember little things that mean so much to me," she finally said as she cried on his shoulder. He could not understand what she was trying to say. "Hector!" she sobbed out loud.

"¿Qué le pasa?" Natalia stepped toward her, wondering what was wrong.

"The picture in the album — " she spoke in Hector's ear. "The picture with your father and the baby with the parents. I think I remember that." The emotional release made her fall to her knees. Hector and his parents tried to hold on to her but the pull to kneel before Octavio's grave overpowered her. "I think my name was Milagro when I was a small child." Her voice was heavy with emotion. She looked up to the heavens hoping to find the answer to her questions. She could not explain her sorrow in words, but her brimming eyes told the whole story. Hector felt helpless; he had never heard a woman in such delicate pain.

Teófilo and his wife looked at each other in silent alarm, not knowing what to say to each other or to Millie. After they met Millie at Stanford, Teófilo had pointed out to his wife the similarities to Octavio that he saw in Millie's face. Natalia agreed, but they did not mention it to Hector. They were just happy to know that he had met someone so nice who was bringing them fond memories of their goddaughter.

Hector's parents knew that Millie had been adopted. They did not fully understand all the meaning behind her sorrow, but they tried to show her that they understood her pain. "Let's go to visit Octavio's mother," Teófilo decided, feeling a need to break away from the cemetery. He had not visited Octavio's home for the last ten years, but would just go to the cemetery and return home to Tangancicuaro without driving to Amapola. "I don't even know if she is still living," he said as he placed his hat on his full head of hair.

Millie was feeling better even though she was embarrassed for crying over what might have seemed like nothing to the others. She was relieved that they could quietly leave the cemetery, although she knew she would need to return on her own. The location ignited more inner emotions and childhood memories than any place she had ever been. The two couples returned to the van and headed for Amapola. Millie was curious about the village that looked so pretty from the distant hill. "Amapola," she said just loud enough for all to hear, "is a beautiful name for a small village." The little town looked even prettier as a rainbow appeared behind the distant adobe homes. Hector and Millie admired the colors of the gorgeous phenomenon. "Do you think we can find the pot of gold?" she asked Hector.

"We might find more than gold," he replied optimistically.

Mr. Gil guided the van onto the riverbed. The village had plastered the bottom of the river with rocks so that vehicles could reach Amapola. During the rainy season, cars often had to wait until the current was low enough to allow passage. The van drove through a foot of clay-colored water gushing from the recent rains. Two very tall oak trees welcomed the visitors to Amapola as they left the river behind. The villagers stared, wondering if a family was returning from the United States. No one recognized the people driving the van with Illinois plates. Most visitors were immigrants returning to Amapola from California or Florida, where they had worked in the agricultural fields.

The van passed adobe homes and newly built brick homes. Colorful clothes hung on drying lines and over bushes. Amapola had made some changes since the last time Teófilo and Natalia visited. The trees were taller and the number of brick homes had increased. As they passed by the main plaza Millie noticed the white adobe church facing west. She could see pigeons perched on top of the Spanish tile roof.

A bright flash of memory showed Millie the same birds from another vantage point. She could see the pigeons going in and out of the adobe holes at the very highest level of the outside walls, and she was watching from inside the church.

The large vacant lot next to the church reminded Millie of a place where silent movies were shown. She remembered carrying a small stool made with cowhide and wood to the lot. And she remembered chewing off a long string of hide that held together one of the stool legs.

Mr. Gil stopped the van at a large, white adobe home. On its large double doors was a picture of the Lady of Guadalupe. At the very top, a very large, old, withered black ribbon hung by threads from a nail. Millie was nervous about who they were going to meet, but was comforted by the many birds singing beautifully on the other side of the wall. An olive-skinned woman in her sixties greeted them in a dark *rebozo* and long skirt.

"Señor Teófilo, que gusto de verlo por estos rumbos," the woman immediately opened the door wide to allow the visitors in. (Mr. Teófilo, how happy I am to see you around this area.) She had recognized the guests. *"Señora Natalia, hacía mucho que no pasaba por acá,"* she added with a wide grin showing a few missing teeth. (Lady Natalia, it has been long since you passed through here.) *"Pasen, pasen."* She welcomed them in the house.

"Muchas gracias, Blanca," Hector's mother replied. *"¿Y tu mamá, Baleria, cómo está?"* Natalia added, looking around the patio. (Thank you very much, Blanca. And your mother,

Baleria, how is she?) The patio was tiled in a red and cream pattern. The kitchen was on one side. The home was similar to the Gils' with different rooms staged around the patio. Several wood posts decoratively carved at the bottom and top held the large outdoor beams.

Millie noticed the swallows building their nests on the sides of the beams. She was always appreciative of the engineering skills of the birds and could not help but stop to watch. A fresh mud nest still black with moisture was evident right above her head. As a mother swallow arrived, tiny beaks with yellow linings stretched out for the airborne morsels of food. The birds entertained Millie but she needed to follow the family into the house.

Teófilo could smell the boiling pinto beans on the stove. *"¿Están cociendo frijoles y calabaza?"* (Are you cooking beans and squash?) He raised his nose in the air to get a sniff of the seasonal squash.

"Son las primeras calabazas del ecuaro." They are the first squash of the small field, Blanca told him with much satisfaction and pride.

"Mi mamá está en el solecito," Blanca pointed toward the outside patio about a hundred feet ahead. *"Se le acabo la vista hace tres años."* (My mother is out in the sun. She lost her sight three years ago). Blanca led the others through the house. Large pictures hung on the walls. An outdated calendar advertising mercantile supplies for the home hung close to the corner of the patio. Millie felt she knew the place. The hundreds of plants in clay pots warmed her spirits. Some of

the smaller plants were in empty jalapeño cans. She noticed a familiar type of pot made from pieces of cut glass plastered on half-opened clay containers. She was glad to be able to recall so many simple things, but frustrated that she could not shape all her memories into some order.

Blanca led them to the outside patio. The rain had stopped and the sun was shining over the garden full of azaleas, zinnias, gladiolas, pansies, calla lilies, roses and snapdragons. Large Mexican poinsettia bushes grew all around. Blanca's mother was sitting in a brown wicker chair under a tangle of flowering, fruiting vines. On her lap was an open basket filled with dry corn that she was tossing to the hens and chicks and two large roosters. At arm's reach, her wooden cane rested against the thin trunk of a bougainvillea vine.

A massive interweaving of morning glories covered most of the area around and above the elderly woman. The sun still managed to warm her legs and her face. "What are those green things?" Millie asked Hector, pointing to the larger-than-prickly-pear fruits dangling from the confusion of vines.

"Those are chayotes, a vegetable used in soups and salads and I don't know for what else," he replied as they walked toward the old woman. "Why don't you ask my mother," he suggested in a whisper. "She knows about all that stuff."

"*¿Quién viene, hija?*" the old woman asked as she tossed another handful of corn to the chickens.

"*Mamá, es una sorpresa,*" Blanca said. (It's a surprise).

"Pues dime, ¿quién es, hija? Sabes que ya no puedo ver," she said in a loving voice. (Well, tell me who it is, daughter. You know I cannot see.)

"Es don Teófilo y doña Natalia y sus hijos." Blanca bent over to say the words into her mother's ear. (It is Teófilo and Natalia and their children.) The grandmother handed her daughter the basket of corn and raised her wrinkled hands in the air to welcome the visitors. Her broad smile showed only two dark teeth.

"¡Vengan para acá!" The elderly woman reacted with joy, asking them to come to her. No one would have guessed she was blind until they drew close enough to see the white clouds that had formed over her green eyes.

Teófilo took his hat off and knelt in front of her. He had not known she was blind, and felt additional guilt for not visiting her more frequently. She took his aging face in her hands. *"Ay, Don Teófilo, ya lo estrañabamos por Amapola,"* the woman said to him, first feeling his cheeks and then shaking his hand in appreciation for the visit. (Oh, Mr. Teófilo, we have missed you in Amapola.) Teófilo's eyes were watery. The last time he had seen her she was in much better physical condition. As he lifted his own weathered bones from the floor, he realized that time was slipping away.

"Señora Luna, se ve muy bien a sus años," (Mrs. Luna, you look very good for your age.) Teófilo touched her hands to let her know how much he appreciated her.

Next the older woman took Natalia by the hand and felt her

shoulders. *"Usted, muy elegante como siempre, Natalia,"*
Baleria remarked, smiling at the air perfumed by the recent
rains and the flowers above her. (You are elegant as always,
Natalia). The woman fixed her old battered *rebozo.* Her long
gray braids fell long on her baggy blouse. Colorful tiny ribbons tied the ends of the braids. *"¿Y los niños, dónde están?"*
She extended her hands to greet the children. Time had
passed by her so fast that she still assumed Teófilo's children were young.

"Ya no son niños, Señora Baleria. Son hombres bigotones,"
Teófilo told her with a laugh. (They are no longer children,
Señora Baleria. They are men with large mustaches.)

Hector moved forward and copied his father's gestures. *"Yo
soy Hector,"* he said as he placed his hand on hers. The
sweet woman placed her hand on his head as she spoke.
"Esta calabaza es igual a la de tu papá," she said as she ruffled
Hector's thick head of hair. (This squash is the same as your
father's.) Baleria broke into a smile and everyone else followed in a contagious hearty laugh.

"Le presento a mi novia," Hector said bashfully as he looked
at Millie. (I present my girlfriend.) Hector extended his arm
to bring Millie to the blind grandmother.

Millie noticed the deep lines of endless time etched in
Baleria's face. She was a happy woman who regretted her
lack of vision but had mastered the use of her hands to
speak and to feel the things that were important to her.
Millie was a little nervous to meet her yet felt a strong desire
to greet the loving woman with a hug.

"Yo soy Millie." She spoke into Baleria's left ear as she had observed everyone else do. The old woman reached out to hug Millie after she heard her voice. Then she took Millie's hand and pulled her close. The aging woman ran her wrinkled fingers over her face, following the lines of Millie's nose and cheekbones. She pulled Millie's long black hair close to her nose and smelled the ends as if recognizing a familiar fragrance.

Millie willingly allowed the woman to feel her hair without pulling away. She was very nervous, feeling immediately that the old woman was more perceptive than everyone else put together. Baleria smiled as she caressed Millie's smooth skin. With her index fingers she traced the edges of Millie's ear lobes. Millie knew right away that the blind woman remembered her face just as she remembered the elderly woman's soft hands.

Tears began to fall from the woman's sightless eyes. She pulled Millie forward and hugged her again in a very tight hold. The familiar smell of dried corn on her *rebozo* made Millie smile at the same time a stream of innocent tears ran down her cheeks. Baleria did not let go of Millie's hands. Teófilo and Natalia knew that Millie was about the same age as the lost granddaughter and felt that Baleria was remembering the past.

"Esta muchachita es mi niña." This young lady is my girl, the blind woman said. *"Esta es Milagro,"* she said as she wiped her tears with her *rebozo*. Everyone got very quiet. *"Esta niña tiene la misma nariz y los oídos de mi hija Milagro."* This young girl has the same nose and ears as my granddaughter

Milagro, Baleria added with great satisfaction. She could not see the frozen statues of the adults watching the curtain rise in such a dramatic way. Millie bent over to hug the woman again. *"Ésta niña tiene los oidos y la nariz de mi niña Milagro,"* grandmother Baleria repeated to herself when the others stayed silent. *"Si no es, no me digan,"* she added as she wiped her tears with the edges of the dark blue *rebozo.* (If she is not, don't tell me.) *"Hemos sufrido mucho por no saber de esta niña."* (We have suffered a great deal not knowing about this girl.) Millie knelt before Baleria and placed her head on the old woman's lap. Millie's heart was heavy. So many things in her past were beginning to make sense. She didn't understand everything but was emotionally sure that she knew Baleria from her childhood. She cried in pain on the woman's lap. *"Esta niña es mi nieta Milagro."* This girl is my granddaughter Milagro, Baleria insisted.

How could Doña Baleria be wrong? She had helped bring this child into the world. She remembered her every detail. When Milagro disappeared she kept going over and over the details she did not want to forget. *"Mi hija, hemos resado por ti tanto."* My child, we have prayed for you so much, Baleria cried as she caressed Millie's head over and over again.

Blanca ran inside the house to get photos of the young child Milagro. She wanted to compare, she wanted to believe. They had worked so hard to find the child for many years and could never determine what had happened to her. *"¿Natalia, será o no será?"* Teófilo finally asked his wife with tears of confusion in his eyes. (Natalia, is she or isn't she?) Watching the elderly Baleria insist on the identity of the girl was convincing enough for him.

Hector helped Millie from the floor where she knelt before Baleria. Under the bright sun and lovely flowers, she hugged Hector and cried. Hector cried, too, as he watched his father and mother huddle over Baleria to comfort her. Teófilo hugged his wife as they cried. *"¡Es ella, te lo dije que ella era especial, viejita! Vamos a pagar la manda pronto, Natalia,"* Teófilo smiled at Natalia through his tears. He had asked a saint to grant him this miracle and it had happened. Now he would comply with his promise in return.

"¡Este es un Milagro de Dios!" Doña Baleria cried with her hands over her face. *"Blanca, ve por el padre."* The elderly woman told her daughter to run for the priest.

Teófilo went over to hug his long lost goddaughter. He was crying like a baby, but he cried from relief. *"Hijo, me has traído más que orgullo. Esta muchacha es mi ahijada. A la que tanto he llorado."* (Son, you have brought me more than pride. This young woman is my goddaughter. I have cried for her so much.) Teófilo reached out to hug his son.

Hector's parents were nervously holding hands as they began to understand Millie's confusion. Blanca returned with the pictures of Milagro as a child. She also sent a young boy to get the priest. Hector walked to the kitchen to bring out the red and green chairs for the rest of the family. Then, Teófilo and Hector compared photos of Octavio's young daughter with the woman sitting with them. It was obvious to them that Millie was indeed Milagro. Her smile and face had not changed much. She had long skinny braids in the old pictures. "How could this have happened?" Hector asked himself as he took his handkerchief to wipe his tears.

Padre Angel hurried to Baleria's home as soon as he heard the news that Milagro had returned. Now a white-haired man in his seventies, Padre Angel still had vivid memories of the child they could not find. He had also prayed for many years that a miracle would happen. His frail body was uplifted by the possibility that his prayers had come true.

"*¿Milagro, eres tú?*" Is that you, Milagro? Padre Angel asked with tears streaming down his cheeks. He immediately saw the resemblance to Octavio and Dolores Luna. He knelt in front of grandmother Baleria and kissed the earth for the miracle that had occurred in Amapola. Millie asked the priest about her mother's relatives. But the family had been devastated by the tragic accident and immigrated afterwards to the state of Washington to pick apples and cherries. They had visited Amapola only a few times since the 1960s.

"We will say mass on Sunday in honor of the good Lord who has brought Milagro back," Padre Angel said with gusto. He and the others patiently heard Millie's story of being raised on a California cattle farm. She could not tell them how she had survived the accident nor how she got to California, and at the moment they weren't really interested. They were just happy she had returned to her homeland. Millie felt that a tremendous load had been lifted off her shoulders. She listened with fascination to the stories about the lost little girl. Teófilo told her many things Octavio, her father, said about her when she was just a toddler. She felt blessed with this information of her past, and realized how lucky she had been to live with the Wolf family in California. If all of her family had died in the tragedy, she reasoned, then she must have been the sole survivor.

She worked hard to fit all the pieces of the puzzle together. She searched for some familiarity in the house, the patio, and the yard. Baleria pointed to the chicken coop and told stories of how her little granddaughter got on her knees to look for the recently laid eggs. She also recalled Milagro's love for butterflies and birds. Millie knew she was at home as so many things about her life began to make sense. She was glad that her grandmother's maternal instincts were strong and that her blindness had not kept her from pursuing her dream of finding her granddaughter. Millie felt guilty that she had not had the same determination to look for her grandmother.

Millie excused herself to use the bathroom. The outdoor shack was old and dilapidated. Aunt Blanca asked her if she remembered when her father built the outhouse. Inside, three holes of different sizes had been carved out so that the family could have a choice when relieving themselves. Millie barely remembered the outhouse until several pigs chased each other into its pit. They reminded her of how she used to wait for the pigs to leave before she would go in. *How could she have forgotten so many little things?* Millie wondered. She sat in the middle between the large and small holes. An old basket filled with multicolored cobs was still in the place she remembered. The cobs were used instead of the soft paper she learned to use in California. She was elated to have these memories of her childhood. *Can this really be happening to me?* she asked herself over and over again.

Occasionally she wondered about her father and mother in California. What would they say about this? How would she tell them? Did they know about her family? Did they know that Amapola existed? So many questions were circling in her mind.

By late afternoon, the entire village of Amapola was exchanging exaggerated news about the child lost in 1957 returning in 1976. Many of the people were shocked at the news that she had been raised by Americans in California, but were also very pleased that she was an educated woman. Millie was the talk of the entire village, and everyone wanted a glimpse of her.

Blanca had busied herself preparing a traditional late lunch for the guests. The families celebrated the miracle by eating the squash and beans along with albondigas soup, guacamole, cactus, and chicken tacos. They drank fresh watermelon juice. For dessert, Blanca cooked sweet guayabas draped with fresh green mint leaves.

Millie's grandmother was very pleased that the miracle had occurred in her lifetime. She was so happy she barely touched her food. She spent the two hours talking so everyone could hear her stories of the family. While everyone enjoyed the meal, Millie surveyed her surroundings in an effort to take mental pictures of her childhood home. She wanted to have sure memories of this place so that she could share it with her parents in California.

She noticed old things made of bamboo hanging from the ceiling. The bamboo had collected dust and weathered spider webs hung loosely from the structures. Several bundles of dried manzanilla tea leaves waited to be thrown into hot boiling water. Millie remembered her Mexican mother and the plants they would gather together. Her heart was relieved but new pressures began to sink in. Solving one problem had created others. How would she handle the matter with Jack and Katherine? She was grateful that Hector had been present as all of this unfolded; she knew that he would help her.

The Gil family and Millie bid a tearful but happy farewell to the village of Amapola. Millie was sorry to leave her aunt and grandmother so soon. She promised to visit again and to bring with her the people who had taken such good care of her. She also committed herself to writing and sending photos of herself and her American family. Grandmother Baleria cried as she touched the face that brought back so many memories of her son and his family. *"Esta será la última ves que te veo, mi nieta,"* the elderly woman told Millie when she asked for her blessing. (This will be the last time I see you, my granddaughter.) Baleria raised her hand to make the sign of the cross before her granddaughter.

"Señorita Millie, ahijada, esa bendicíon es hecha de milagro," Teófilo added. (Miss Millie, goddaughter, that blessing is made of miracle.) Blanca made sure that Teófilo's family left with gunny sacks filled with corn, squash, and tea leaves.

Millie convinced the Gil family to stop at the cemetery so that she could bid farewell to her family. Hector held her hand the entire brief way back to the cemetery. He was still in shock over how the trip had turned out. Millie politely asked to be left alone for a short time. Hector and his family waited in the van while she retraced the steps to the Tame Cactus.

She began to cry her heart out once again. She felt she had missed something by not knowing the mother who carried her or the father who loved her as a child. She could not think how to bid farewell to the cemetery other than to pay her respects to her family. More than ever, she wanted to know everything about her father and mother. She was also eager to speak to her parents in California.

The Gils kept the once-in-a-lifetime story alive by talking about it over and over again while driving back. For Octavio's blind mother to figure out that the lost child might be present was a miracle to the family. "You will always be part of the family, Millie," Teófilo told her as they arrived back home in the dark hours of the night.

Millie kissed Hector goodnight and excused herself for the evening. She retreated to the silence of the room that waited for her tired spirit and emotionally drained body. There had never been a day like this before in her life. She looked again at the picture albums containing memories of Teófilo and Octavio, inserting tiny pieces of brown paper to mark the pages for future reference. She finally blew out the candles and fell into the deepest and most peaceful sleep ever.

• • •

THE FOLLOWING MORNING, she woke to the smell of fresh *toqueras* being baked outdoors in a small clay oven. The sweet corn bread smelled delicious to Millie. She was very hungry as she had not felt like eating much the last day or so. Hector welcomed her into the kitchen with a warm embrace and a tender kiss on the cheek. "Only two more days in Mexico," Hector said as he escorted her to her chair. "I squeezed some fresh orange juice for my favorite girl." Millie welcomed the familiar drink. Mexico had introduced her to unfamiliar foods but orange juice was well known. She enjoyed trying all the Mexican foods but found herself missing the hamburger with fries on the side.

Hector brought her a plate filled with fresh pineapple cut in round slices and some of the hot cornbread. He also gave her a hot tortilla folded over a melting bright-orange squash blossom. He wanted to make her feel all right about what had happened yesterday. To her surprise and delight, the squash-blossom quesadilla was very good.

"Millie, estamos muy contentós de saber mucho más de usted," Natalia said as she poured her more orange juice. She hoped to reassure Millie that they were very comfortable in knowing more about her.

"Tememos pendiente de sus padres, Señorita Millie," Teófilo said as he ate. He and Natalia were worried about her parents.

"I'll call them today," Millie promised them.

Hector and Millie went out into the cobblestone streets for an early morning walk. They strolled hand in hand alongside the horses toward the center of the small town. She was hoping the telephone office would be open so that she could call her mom. In the rural parts of Mexico, telephones were not installed in homes. Only one line was available for the townspeople to use. In Tangancicuaro, the mercantile store operated the telephone line and distributed fresh milk.

Many horses stood patiently outside the adobe homes waiting for the large milk cans to be loaded on their sides. Men and women were milking a few cows at a time in the back yards. The milk was then transported to the mercantile store. Liter by liter, the store owners measured the contents of the cans and paid the people for their share.

Seeing the hard-working people starting their busy day reminded Millie of helping her father on the California farm. As young as eight, she was always up at the crack of dawn because going to work with her father was a very important event. As Millie and Hector passed other adobe homes, women dressed in dark skirts and *rebozos* swept the streets of leftover fruit peelings. They also swept away cow and horse manure that had been dropped near the entrances of the humble dwellings. Their brooms were long with straight stiff bristles at the end.

Other women carried their lime-soaked corn to the grinding mill in shiny tin buckets filled higher than the rims with yellowish kernels. They carried the ground corn back in the same buckets to start the tortilla-making process. Young girls moved quickly with clay jugs filled with water on their shoulders. Other girls carried fresh flowers to the church.

Millie could not believe the number of people conducting business on the street. A vendor had set up a small, portable wooden stand. Naked white- and yellow-skin chickens hung by one skinny foot. The chickens were sold as one or in pieces. Prospective buyers were inspecting the dangling necks of the poor animals. Hector caught her expression and politely tried to provide an explanation of the featherless friends. "You know that the chicken is used for soup and everything else," he said. "My favorite parts of the soup are the feet and the neck and those are also the favorite parts for many people," he added. The butcher had a whole steer hanging upside down. People purchased different parts cut to order out of the lifeless animal. Millie was used to seeing upside-down, butchered steers. Back at the farm, whenever a steer broke a bone, the men at the farm would butcher the animal and Jack would share the meat with the men who helped with the chore.

Under large oak trees, many Tarascan Indian women had set up bundles and piles of fruits and vegetables for the townspeople to purchase. In addition to the fruits and vegetables, they carried flowers, pottery, cheese, and tamales from their homes in the mountains every morning. They brought a supply of banana leaves to wrap the cheese in so that buyers could carry it home. Millie watched closely as they wrapped a small, round cheese in the leaves. They used tiny strings from the same leaves to tie the cheese into a safe bundle. Young children walked with flat tin pans filled with multicolored gelatins for sale.

The women spread bright red and green thin blankets on the ground on which to display their products so that the townspeople could point to what they wanted. Millie watched the women pull their money from their skirts. They had wrapped the coins in a handkerchief. Their hand-stitched, embroidered blouses complemented the vivid products they sold.

On the plaza, another man was selling freshly killed doves.

He had shot them early in the morning and was offering them for sale by raising his hand filled with the grey and white animals hanging like bananas from a tree. Millie could almost feel the warm feathers in her hand. Watching the people she knew so little about was enjoyable and relaxing after yesterday's exhausting surprise.

The hours passed quickly as Hector and Millie inspected every vendor's products. Hector offered to buy things for her, but she was more interested in the conversation than in buying the product. Hector was glad she was happy.

"Hector, do you think we can go the mercantile store to see if the telephone line is available?" she finally asked. Hector knew the call would be a difficult one for her. He did not know how to help except to offer his support.

"Sure, I think they should be ready for us, Millie." He took her hand and led her in the direction of the telephone.

Besides the small phone booth in the corner, the mercantile store offered many services for the town. Reams of cloth awaited inspection. Large tin cans filled with lard, sugar, and salt were located right behind the counter. A big plastic container contained petroleum for lamps.

Millie requested a call to the United States. Hector gave the lady at the counter the necessary instructions. He paid for the call so that Jack and Katherine would not be shocked by the voice of an emergency operator.

"Hello, mom?" Millie began to rub her forehead nervously.

She had gone alone into the small wooden booth, while Hector waited outside the store. "Yes, I'm all right. How's Dad?" She was glad she had called her mother while her father was out in the fields.

"Mom, I need to talk to you." Millie interrupted her mother's description of events on the farm. Her eyes were beginning to water in anticipation of the story she had to tell. "Mom, we went to this little town that seems to be the town where I was born.

"No, no, it's true." Millie was painfully sorry for having to say it. "They even showed me pictures, Mom," she added as she began to cry harder. Millie felt the 1,500 miles between them but this was the only way to communicate for now. Hector had asked her if she wanted to return home early, but she did not. She was in love with Hector more than ever and leaving him early was not an option.

Katherine had begun to cry also. "Mom, I still love you, you don't have to worry about that. You and Dad are the only ones I know," Millie told her. "No one knew. It was by accident and luck." She tried to explain what had happened but it was difficult even without the tears.

The woman in charge of the phone line signaled Millie to end her call because other people were waiting. Millie called out to Hector.

"My mother wants to know how to call me back. What number should she use?" She continued to sob as Hector came to her rescue.

"Here, let me speak to your mom and give her the information," he suggested. Hector crowded into the small booth with Millie and suggested to Katherine that she call back in two hours when the line was not so busy.

After the call, Hector and Millie went for a walk in the hills. The green fields and growing corn crops relaxed Millie, and the time passed quickly. They returned to the mercantile store to wait for the call. Millie knew that Katherine had called Jack immediately to give him the news. She was sad she was not there to tell him in person.

The call came in for Millie and she moved into the booth again. She knew her father would be on the other end of the line. "Hello, Dad," she answered. Jack launched into the many questions he had.

"I'm fine, Dad," Millie assured him. "It was difficult at first, but I'm all right now. I do want to know more, Dad," she said as her eyes began to fill again with tears. "The grandmother recognized me, and she's blind. But I saw pictures.

"I told them that I'd bring you to meet them one of these days. I love you very much, Dad." Millie could hear that Jack had begun to cry, and he handed the phone to Katherine.

"Mom, please know that I still love you," Millie said again. "Please tell Daddy that he's my father more than ever. I want you to meet these nice people," she added. "I'll be home in two days," she said as the conversation neared the end. "I love you, Mom and Dad," she added in a last whisper of emotion, and slowly hung the receiver back in place.

"Hector, that was the most difficult conversation I've ever had with my parents," Millie said. "They were concerned that I was upset and angry," she added as they walked back home. "My father told me he didn't know any of this. I believe him." Millie had regained her composure and spoke to Hector with great relief.

"He said that he checked my whole family and they were gone instantly," Millie told him. "He said that I survived by luck. I'm sure we'll have a long conversation when I get back home." She was pleased that her parents were not mad but just concerned.

"Your father probably did find you after he had seen the death of your family," Hector suggested, trying to provide bridges between the known and the unknown. "Remember you said that you found a little dress covered with dried blood?

"Maybe you were seriously hurt and your father took care of you," he added to comfort her. "I'll bet if your family had survived the accident, your father would have helped everyone." Hector wanted her to feel comfortable with the situation. He knew Millie's parents were not to be blamed for anything, and so did she. They walked back holding each other around the waist. Hector was so much in love with Millie, he did not want anything to hurt her.

The pair arrived in time for the late lunch meal. *"¿Cómo está tu mamá?"* How is your mother? Natalia asked.

"Todo está bien, mamá," Hector interjected, hoping that for

now the topic would not be discussed. Millie was emotionally exhausted from the conversation with her parents. Hector's parents instinctively understood and moved ahead with lunch preparations.

"My wife made a very special dish for us, Miss Millie," Teófilo said, hoping to change the subject. "We are going to eat *guilotas con chile verde*, doves with green chile sauce," he said as he passed the colorfully painted ceramic plate filled with the tiny birds in the dark green sauce. He passed the chicken, rice, and the refried beans next. Millie could smell the pleasant aroma of the food. As she ate, she came across a chicken foot in the rice. Hector noticed her prized finding. "If you don't want it, I'll take it," he said, trying to help. She used her fork to pass the long, skinny foot to her sweetheart. Hector immediately began savoring the tiny bones on each of the toes. It reminded her of eating barbecued ribs in miniature.

"Tomorrow is your last full day here, Señorita Millie," Teófilo added as he tried the jicama and orange salad. "We are going to miss your presence," he continued. "We also expect you to return to your humble home soon." Teófilo smiled at her. She knew he was the happiest man on earth. She could only imagine his dismay at identifying the bodies of her parents and bothers, and finding a member of the family missing.

"Natalia, how about if we have a farewell party for Millie and Hector tomorrow?" Teófilo sounded as if he had rehearsed the question.

"If you're having a fiesta, make sure it's not early. I'm taking Millie on a short trip," Hector added his two cents' worth of advice. It was obvious to Hector that his father and mother had already spoken about this party before it was brought up at lunch.

Hector and Millie took a long walk through different parts of the town after lunch. In the evening, they visited the main plaza and ate enchiladas, tacos, and buñuelos from the street vendors. Upon their return to the quiet of home, they ended their day on the old wooden benches on the patio. "Make sure you get some rest for tomorrow's trip," Hector told her. The moon gave the couple its silver blessing as they retired to their rooms.

PIEDRAS EN EL VOLCAN
Rocks on the Volcano

Hector had planned a surprise trip for Millie for some time. During the revelations at Amapola, he had seriously contemplated postponing his plans. He knew that the melodrama of this trip would be as exciting as yesterday's. He finally decided to carry out his meticulous plans, but refused to tell Millie the details. He borrowed two canteens from his father and filled them with water.

The local taxi came to drive them through the Tarascan Indian land and up into the sierra. The taxi followed the curves of the main, paved road until it made its first turn. Millie wasn't paying much attention to the road but was looking at the plants and trees. She wanted to stop at the Indian towns but Hector suggested they visit them another time. When the car turned onto a small dirt road, Millie saw the sign for Angahuan.

"Where are we going?" she asked.

"We're visiting an enchanted location that is for the eyes of only a few," he responded mysteriously. They traveled the dirt road for another 40 minutes. As the red and white, dusty taxi approached the main plaza of the small town, they could see a dozen or so skinny horses waiting with guides.

The cab driver dropped the couple off in front of the town church. The town was inhabited mostly by indigenous people. "Hector, you have to tell me right now! What are we doing here?" Millie begged.

"All right. We're going to visit the volcano," he told her. "I really want you to see this phenomenon, Millie. Paricutín erupted in 1943. You and I weren't part of history when it spewed its massive lava." Millie knew that Paricutín had been one of Hector's dissertation topics. Moreover, Octavio and Teófilo had met at this very place.

Her heart began to pound in enthusiasm. This volcano was very important to Hector. She realized that it must have taken Hector lots of inner determination not to say much about the planned destination. He was an expert on this topic and she was looking forward to learning more.

"We need to rent two horses for the day," he said.

She looked at the horses and then back at Hector. "We can't ride these horses! They're malnourished!" she protested.

"Millie, horses are skinny because they work hard. The people here are poor and they will feed their families before they feed the horses." Hector didn't really know how to explain to her that this world was different from the one she was used to. "These horses will do fine," he added in a reassuring voice. He escorted her toward a better-looking bunch of horses.

Hector knew that riding a horse would not be a problem at all for Millie. As a matter of fact, he was embarrassed that she could ride much better than he could. He didn't need to help her up but he did anyway. "Can I get off my horse and help you?" she jokingly suggested. The guide led them toward the volcano. As they rode through the dark-gray dusty streets, the Indian women and children looked at the twosome as tourists. "What kind of Indians are these, Hector?"

"They call themselves Tarascan and Purepechas and they are a very proud people," he told her. The women wore colored aprons over black gathered skirts. They wore comfortable-looking blouses beautifully decorated with flowers and symbols.

They rode a long way through the dusty backwoods and young citrus and avocado orchards. Hector wanted her to see for herself the famous volcano that erupted from a cornfield. During his studies, he had learned so much about the area and the people that he felt more like a guide. As they rode along, Hector amazed her with the wonderful story of the unexpected natural occurrence.

The horses had a rough time climbing the surrounding hills of sandy gravel. The volcanic ash had left an eternal impression on the land. Paricutín became more real as they approached its majestic stature. After several hours on horseback, they arrived at the base of the volcano.

The surrounding area was nearly barren of vegetation. The cone-shaped mountain stood alone like a wounded military general inspecting the devastation of the nearby lava-buried village. Only the tall spires of the Roman Catholic church stood above the ashes.

At Hector's insistence, they began to climb the volcano. The guide waited with the horses at the bottom while the young couple began their ascent to the steep ledges of the volcano's crater.

The climb did not look that difficult at first. But as they proceeded up the mountain, the sand and sharp rocks slowed them down. After forty minutes of climbing they stopped for a bird's-eye view of the land below and a much-needed drink of water from the canteens.

"Hector, are we crazy or what? I'm supposed to be on a relaxing vacation, yet here I am struggling up this volcano," Millie joked.

"You'll love the view from the top," Hector assured her.

"The other night I saw a picture of your dad and my father in front of a smoking volcano," she said. "Is this the same one?"

"Yes, my father helped the village after the volcano erupted. The man in the picture, your father, became my dad's best friend," he added. "Come on, let's get going."

They continued climbing at a very slow rate of speed. In a

few areas the climb was so steep that Millie had to use her feet, knees, and hands to move upward. "Look at these stones, Millie." Hector gathered samples to show her. "This one is called pumice rock. It's released by the volcano and then slowly cools, which causes the holes to form."

In several areas, huge deposits of smoldering rock still maintained their dignified threat. Smoke penetrated the hot rocks and smelled like a sauna. Hector was good at explaining the details to Millie. "You'll be an excellent professor," she told him. It was amazing to her that after so many years, the volcano was still smoking.

The couple, tired and battered, finally reached the top of the volcano. "Welcome to Paricutín," Hector said as he offered her his hand on the last few steps to the flat ring around the crater. Millie was out of breath. To the north she could see the steeples of the church of San Juan Parangaricutiro peeking through the lava that had buried the church.

Around the ring, several smoking areas remained. The volcano had created a vacuum or an inverted small cone of sand and rock. Only the wind could be heard piercing through the rocks at the top. A few crows rode the air in search of their next meal.

Hector held Millie tight and close. Because no one else was present he felt comfortable showing his affection. Only a high-powered set of binoculars could make out the embracing and kissing at the top of the volcano. Millie wanted his kisses so much, especially after the previous day's shocking events. She had missed his expressions of love over the last few days. The climax of reaching the top and being held by the man she loved was a very powerful experience.

"Let's find a comfortable place to sit for a little while," Hector suggested. They found just the perfect rock next to some smaller rocks that were still smoking away. Millie straddled the rock and Hector climbed behind as they faced the north side of the sandy mountain. He moved in close to Millie, putting his arms around her and resting his chin on her right shoulder. From a distance, they looked like they were riding a tired horse.

"Doesn't it seem to you that we are very close to the clouds up here?" she asked.

"Millie, I've been in the clouds ever since I met you," he quickly responded with a short laugh. "Since you are addressing the beauty of this view and since there are no interruptions, how about if I give you a quiz about Paricutín?" he suggested in a professorial tone.

"What?" she exclaimed. "After what I went through yester-day, I don't think I'll be able to test at your required stan-dards. Besides, I don't know enough about the subject." She tried to sway him from the idea of a test.

"Don't worry, I'll give you enough hints," he assured her. Hector cleared his voice several times before he began. He held her tightly with his hands wrapped around her waist.

"Ready?"

"All right, let me have the first question."

"The first question is, when did Paricutín erupt?"

Millie knew the answer to that question since the year had been repeated over and over again during the last few days. She acted like it was a difficult question and played the dunce. "You have ten seconds, Ms. Wolf." He strained his voice as he spoke.

"The year was 1943!" She yelled as if trying to beat the ticking clock.

"Correct you are." He kissed her on the nape of the neck before continuing.

"If you get this next question right, you win a special surprise." Millie was not up for more surprises. She had had enough of a surprise with her new grandmother and family. "All right, Ms. Wolf," he said, "next will be identification questions." He reached one hand into his pocket.

"Close your eyes while I place the rocks on the palm of your hand," Hector instructed. He had been collecting tiny rocks all the way up. He gently laid a piece of pumice in the palm of her hand. "You may look now," he said.

Millie was beginning to think that maybe he had planned this quiz. "Tell me the name of this volcanic rock." He was hoping to stump her with the unusual piece. She studied it closely.

"I don't give up but I need a hint," she said as she rolled the rock between her index finger and thumb.

"The name of this rock starts with a 'P' and has a plural mouse," he said, providing a clear but silly hint.

"Pumice rock," she blurted out, hoping to keep the test short. "That was a real good hint." She thanked Hector by turning her face toward his to kiss him lightly on the lips.

"Now, close your eyes again," he ordered. "What kind of rock is this and what did the Indians use it for?" Hector put a shiny black rock in her hand. "You may look now," he said. Millie looked at the rock and thought about the question. Hector began counting very slowly. "Give up?" he asked, hoping she would.

"No, I'm not giving up. Give me a hint?"

"Time's up," he said with a Cheshire-cat smile. "This is obsidian rock. Now answer the second part of the question."

"I need a hint."

"The rock can break your heart or provide food for you."

"Arrowheads!" she yelled out so that the crows could hear.

"You're right, Millie! Now close your eyes for the final question," he said as he jumped from the rock. He swung her legs around on the rock so that she was facing him. "I'm going to get down on this earth, Millie. I'm going to get a stone you will need to identify for me. If you get this final question right, I'll love you forever." She giggled at his words. Hector knelt in front of her. From where she sat on the rock, her knees came just below his tall shoulders. He reached down as if to pick up a rock from the volcanic floor. "Are your eyes closed, Millie?"

"This rock is very light-weight," she noted as he placed the object on her palm.

"Keep your eyes closed for the question," he directed. She pouted in a teasing way while Hector prepared himself. He took a deep breath. "Will you, Ms. Millie, Milagro Luna Wolf, be my wife from here to eternity?"

"What!" She opened her eyes to find a beautiful diamond ring in her palm. "Oh, Hector." She did not know what to say and so just smiled at him.

"Do you need a hint?" Hector asked. "If you answer 'yes,' you'll live happily ever after." Millie stood up on the stone and faced north.

"Hector, I will." She moved quickly, saying, "I will, I will, I will," toward each of the cardinal points. Hector gladly placed the diamond on her finger. He was relieved that she had accepted.

She jumped off the rock and embraced Hector in the most passionate way she had ever allowed herself. Hector began to taste her tears as they kissed passionately. "I love you,

Millie," he told her in a sweet, tender voice.

"I love you, too."

"I want you to be my wife," he said more assertively. "I don't want to wait too long." Hector admitted that he had planned the volcano trip and spoken to his father and mother some time ago about his plans to ask her to marry him. They were pleased to know that he would marry a beautiful and hardworking woman. Now that they had met Millie and learned her real identity, they were even more delighted by this unity.

Hector lifted Millie off her feet and walked her toward the path of descent. "What are we doing?" she asked, laughing.

"I don't know that I'll be able to afford a hotel, so I might as well carry you over the threshold now," he responded. "Don't you think so?"

"Will we have to wait that long?" she teased back. Hector revealed that he wanted to marry tomorrow, but Millie was more of a strategic thinker. She knew she had found the right partner to achieve her dreams. The time would be right to marry in the near future, she thought. She was sure it was evident that they were the happiest couple south of the Tropic of Cancer.

Hector carried his future bride to the path descending to the floor of the sandy mountain. "Now be careful when you take your steps," Hector said as he held onto her. They slid down the sandy path, their shoes sinking so deep that their knees dragged through the volcanic dust. They seemed to be moving in slow motion. They paused and smiled at each other.

"This is good practice for us, Hector," Millie said. "This looks like the aisle to the altar."

He had not thought of it that way but after she said it, it made sense. "Well, Future Mrs. Gil, please allow me to escort you down this aisle," he said, and they began to descend Paricutín. The trip down was joyous and short; they reached the base of the volcano in just a few minutes. The horses carried the weary couple back to the church.

"You had this all planned, didn't you?" she asked knowingly.

"Millie, I hope you didn't mind my asking you to marry me on the crater."

"I think it was the most romantic place you could have chosen, Hector. It has so much meaning for both of us. Do you remember the first time I met you?"

"We met by the university post office."

"No, I mean the first time. When you gave the lecture," she said. "I thought you were so cute and intelligent."

"I didn't know you were Ms. Wolf when I read the your term paper until after we introduced ourselves in the library. "You know, I almost decided not to do this after our visit to Amapola," he admitted. "I didn't want anything to interfere with such a special event."

"Don't worry about it any more, Hector," she assured him. "We'll have some really good stories to tell our children."

They returned to Tangancicuaro in the early evening. Hector's family was waiting patiently to find out Millie's response. They had worked diligently to keep it a secret. After the visit to Amapola, they weren't sure Hector would propose at this time. A quiet family dinner awaited the couple. Teófilo was the most excited about the upcoming marriage. He felt a that ton of weight had been lifted from his shoulders. A special toast was offered for Hector and Millie and many kind words were exchanged on behalf of their future union.

After dinner the family sat together and listened to Teófilo's memories of Octavio. His children had heard these stories often before but this was the first time for Millie. All the old photos were brought to the kitchen table so that Teófilo could tell about each one. Many stories centered on the volcano and the work the two men had done in the 1940s.

Teófilo also told Millie about the talents that blessed her parents. He pointed to the many pieces of furniture Octavio had crafted for him. *"Señorita Millie, en su cuarto está un reclinatorio y ese mero su papi también lo hizo para mi mamá. Mi mamá después se lo regaló a mi hermana, la monja,"* Teófilo said with pride and respect. (The kneeler in your room was also made by your father for my mother. My mother later gave it to my sister, the nun.)

Teófilo and Natalia also spoke about the religious promise they had made in 1957. They planned to go to San Juan

Nuevo next week to honor their commitment to the "Lord of Miracles" for finding Milagro. Teófilo told the story of when the Bishop from Zamora visited the church that was in the volcano's path. The Bishop removed the "Lord of Miracles" venerated by all the people in the area. The Bishop and the townspeople walked the cross to San Juan Nuevo, the new San Juan since the old one was now under tons of lava. The stories helped Millie feel more at ease.

As the night approached, she and Hector moved to the benches under the stars. The rain had ceased for one day and the night skies were very clear. The full moon stared enviously at the shine from Millie's engagement ring. It sparkled with the light from the stars and the twinkles from the fireflies.

"When can we get married?" Hector asked, hoping that tomorrow wouldn't be too soon. Millie thought for a moment and reminded him that they still needed to tell her parents. "I'm personally going to tell them very soon," he said. "I spoke to my father and told him that a week after you leave, I'm going to fly to Mexicali to ask your father for your hand in marriage. I want to do it soon so that you and I can begin planning our wedding and our life together," he added. "I also want to visit you, and I want you to visit me in San Diego. I need you very much, sweetheart." He held her close under the trees' evening shadows.

They agreed that Hector would keep the ring until Millie's parents were properly informed of the engagement. Hector felt good that she cared so much about her parents that she would include them in every aspect of her life.

"I'm going to miss you," she whispered in Hector's ear. Hector lifted her onto his lap. He could not get enough, kissing her all over while he held her right next to his heart.

By ten o'clock, the lights in the house were out and Hector escorted Millie to her room. He started to kiss her goodnight but instead she pulled him inside the room by his belt. She held her index finger over her lips to remind him of the need for silence. Hector followed the soft orders like a baby lamb. Quietly, he locked the door.

He pulled out several of the heavy saddle blankets hanging on the ladder leading to the attic. Millie was lighting another candle next to the bed; she wanted to see Hector. In the darkness she could not touch, see, and feel him the way she wanted. Hector did not mind the light. He was content that she needed him, too. He smoothed three blankets on the floor and took the pillow from the bed. He also took the neatly folded coverlet at the foot of the bed and spread it over the saddle blankets.

The thick blankets made the best bed possible. Slowly, Hector began to remove Millie's clothes. She rested on the soft bed cover while Hector removed his shirt and pants to warm her with his flesh. Hector was a grown man wanting everything that a grown man is supposed to have. He tenderly caressed her breasts and hips. Her eyes cried to him for more. She had been through a lot of emotion and this was just the sweet icing they both needed.

The fresh perfume of the flowers at the altar added to their arousal. Hector gently placed his entire body over hers.

Slowly his manhood grew deep between her legs. "Let's be careful, sweetheart," she told him ever so dearly.

Hector wanted so much to do what he needed to do, but he also wanted to take care of his woman. He wanted to wait until the right time. As he placed his hand on the bare skin between her thighs he could feel the flow of another kind of eruption. He used his fingers to investigate the source of Millie's soft, warm lava. He was so aroused he did not know what to do with himself.

Hector slowly reached where he had never reached before, cradling her with his lips. Millie squirmed tenderly at the delightful banquet of joy Hector was giving her. She was beyond herself. "I want more," she said without thinking of the meaning of her words. Hector was well aware of her request and wanted to take charge of his girl like no other time. But he continued to pursue with his hands what he knew was not yet his.

As Millie relaxed once more, they held each other close and fell asleep in a great field of belonging.

Very early, even before the roosters began their call for the sun, Hector kissed parts of Millie's body signaling the four cardinal points, then rushed to beat the family to the shower. He was satisfied with the attention he had given his future wife. He respected her and wanted to make sure he honored her request of waiting until they were married to feel fully free.

Teófilo had arranged for a group of Tarascan Indian musicians to play from noon to eight o'clock for the newly engaged couple. Teófilo had also ordered more than twenty chickens killed for the family to enjoy in *mole* (chile sauce). Hector's relatives were bringing large clay pots of rice, beans, and chiles. A bathtub-sized tin container was filled with ice and beer. They had several reasons for celebration.

The arrival of the musicians signaled the start of the party. Many friends, neighbors, and relatives enjoyed the festive ambiance. The party focused on the joy of the new couple and the welcoming of a new family member.

At dawn the following day, Hector and Millie took a taxi back to the Guadalajara airport. She had said farewell to the Gil family in the evening so that they would not have to get up early to say goodbye. Teófilo had handed her an envelope to pack. He told her it was a birth certificate in case she ever needed one. Millie carried the envelope in her purse.

She solemnly boarded the Mexicana Airlines flight. As the plane taxied onto the runway, she thought about her family landing here in caskets many years ago. She cried, too, at leaving Hector.

Shaking and nervous, she pulled out her own, original birth certificate. Carefully, she examined every detail on the yellowing piece of paper. It was obvious that Teófilo had carried the folded document in his wallet all these years. With her index finger she outlined the little baby footprint that once belong to Milagro. She tenderly kissed the paper certificate, folded and returned it to a secret compartment inside her purse.

During the flight she composed herself in order to greet her parents and explain the entire week of unexpected events. The week in Mexico was nothing like she had expected. She reviewed over and over the way in which her past had met her future. How could she ever have guessed that Hector would be her soul mate, so instrumental in helping her achieve a happiness she had never known before? As the plane flew along the western coastal beaches of Mexico, Millie realized that her life had been a gift to Jack and Katherine. They, in turn, had given her the best gift of all: love.

She wondered about the magic in her life. Her birth name was Luna, meaning moon, and her name now was Wolf. She wondered if there was some connection between her longing for answers and the legend of wolves and their cries to the moon.

• • •

JACK AND KATHERINE WOLF arrived at the Mexicali airport forty minutes early, anxious to hear about Millie's journey. The Mexican airport was crowded with passengers flying to Guadalajara and relatives expecting the arrival of family members from the interior of Mexico.

As the airplane began to cut eastward over the north coast of the Gulf of Mexico, Millie anticipated her parents' nervousness. Who could ever have imagined that she would meet members of her real family through Hector? She wondered what her parents would say first. She hoped they would fill in the gaps of her past. She figured that they knew they would have to tell her the whole story of their train trip that rainy day many years ago.

More then ever, Millie knew that she needed to tell them how much she cared for them and how much they meant to her. Hector's father helped her to understand the importance of caring for the folks who raised her. She felt the entire trip was intended as a lesson for her in compassion, understanding, and love.

Jack and Katherine's hearts sank to their heels as the airplane landed with a loud screech and hiss. The temperature in the Mexicali Valley was over 100 degrees, but the heat was no match for their excitement. As the plane taxied to a stop, Millie's hands began to perspire at the thought of seeing her parents again.

Millie could see people waiting inside the terminal building, and knew that her parents were among the crowd. They could see her as she stepped down on the airplane ladder and moved to meet her at the door to the terminal.

"Millie, sweetheart!" Katherine's voice ricocheted above the rest of the welcome yips and yells. Millie immediately acknowledged their presence with a wide smile filled with love and respect. The grin she sent from a short distance helped Jack release some of the pressure he had been building up inside himself.

"We missed you!" hollered Katherine.

"I missed you, too," she called to them. They were not

allowed in the arriving passenger area, so Millie retrieved her suitcases one at a time and slid them forward to Jack. When the last of the luggage arrived, she ran from the passenger area to hug her parents and share their tears.

She could feel the emotions of her parents as they embraced. "It's all right, honey." Jack tried to reassure her with his own tears streaming down his rosy cheeks. His eyes were glassy. "Let's get out of here before we melt." Jack carried the two largest bags to the waiting pickup.

"I love you so much," Millie said, hugging both of her parents again before they crowded into the front seat of the truck. Katherine and Jack were still a bit nervous, but the fact that Millie was so happy to see them made them understand that they had not lost her love.

Where should I begin? Millie thought to herself as they drove toward the border city of Calexico, California. She started with the story of Teófilo and his life. Her parents listened quietly as she related the knowledge of her early childhood years. She was unaware of Jack's strong feelings of guilt.

He had never developed the courage necessary to tell her all that had happened that night in Texas. Jack and Katherine both knew that Millie's real parents had been killed. They knew it but perhaps never wanted to tell her for fear of losing her.

They crossed the international gate into the United States and stopped at the historic De Anza Hotel to eat lunch. Millie was hungry. The overwhelming outcome of her trip to

Mexico had kept her mind preoccupied and away from the need for food.

While they ate, Millie continued to tell the story about her Mexican family. Jack and Katherine were astonished by what she had experienced in a matter of days. Katherine cried as Millie told them of her last visit to the graves of her real parents.

"At the cemetery, the family had saved a plot of land for me," Millie told her parents as they picked at their food and drank the tea glasses dry. "The village of Amapola is beautiful. I want us to go visit one of these days. More than anything, I want you both to know that what I learned in Mexico doesn't change any of my feelings for you. I'm just grateful that you took care of me at such a difficult time." She explained to them that her name was Milagro and that she was named in honor of the good crops in 1952.

She told them that her last name had been Luna and that both of her real parents had been very talented individuals. "Hector's family was very close friends with my birth parents," she added. "Neither Hector nor I had any idea of this connection until I began to flip through pictures they had stored in the room I stayed in." Nervous but strengthened by the very mention of her fiancé, she prepared to tell them the next big news.

"Mom and Dad, I really love Hector," she announced, changing the subject. Jack and Katherine had guessed that her friendship with Hector would lead to something else. They had been through the same thing. They recognized the little hints of love that she displayed in her speech and mannerisms when she mentioned Hector. They had seen in Hector all the signs of a young man in love and ready for marriage. They were ready for the next announcement.

"Hector was in shock to learn that I was part of the Luna family." She wanted to introduce the subject of Hector into the conversation carefully. "He helped me during these revelations, and was very kind during these days," she added.

Without much ado, Millie shifted the conversation from the past to the present. She could not think of any other way to break the news than just to break the news. Her candor had always surprised Jack and Katherine anyway. As a child she had brought home six new baby birds and placed them on the dinner table without warning. She wanted to feed the birds at the same time she ate her own dinner. She would have to be just as brave about the news of her engagement to Hector.

"Dad, Mom, I need to tell you that Hector asked me to marry him." Her parents froze for a split second. Their private discussions about Millie and her feelings for Hector had been accurate. "Hector will be visiting us next weekend to ask you for my hand in marriage, Dad," she said in a matter-of-fact manner.

"Millie, this is a major decision." Jack laid his fork on the edge of the plate.

"Dad, I really want to do this. I don't know when yet but we'll spend time planning the whole wedding." Millie tried to respond in a calm and collected manner to make her parents feel that everything was all right.

"Millie, your father and I will do anything to support your wishes," Katherine told her. "We're just nervous about not knowing Hector very well. We trust your judgment and we'll stand by you." Katherine looked to Jack for his approval. "Right, Jack?"

Jack was not going to admit that he was not feeling well. This whole idea of visiting Mexico and now the marriage seemed too fast for him. Then he remembered his own proposal to Katherine. They had met at the graduate students' orientation and began dating immediately. Jack had informally proposed to Katherine almost immediately after their first date. Within weeks, they had planned their wedding.

"Jack, are you all right?" Katherine asked.

"I was just remembering that we got engaged pretty quickly ourselves," he replied sheepishly. The family laughed together as they got up from the table.

"Let's go," Jack said, leaving a tip for the waitress. "We have lots of work waiting for us." It was rare that the family left the farm during daylight hours. With Millie's help, Jack would be able to catch up on fixing some of the tractors that were waiting for new parts.

At the farm, Katherine began to make the necessary preparations for Hector's visit. Millie would pick him up at the airport in Mexicali and bring him home for dinner. He would spend the night in her room and she would sleep with Grandma. Katherine's attention to the details was a wonderful example for Millie and a tremendous support for Jack during such an emotional time.

Jack's sense of guilt tormented him. For many years, he had questioned his decision to take the hurt child to heal in his own home. He worried that taking her amounted to abduction. On the one hand he was sure he had done the right thing. On the other, he felt culpability in denying Millie the attention of loved ones like the Gil family. He just assumed she was alone in the world. Now that he knew more of her background, he felt even guiltier for not having searched for her true identity. It hurt him that it had taken another family to fulfill his own responsibility.

For the first time that night, Jack confided in Katherine his anguish about the ordeal that their daughter went through. He felt irresponsible for not helping her learn more about her past. He cried like a baby for several hours as Katherine consoled him. She had not been aware of the deep scar his guilt caused. Millie had brought so much joy to their family that Jack never wanted to face the reality of losing her, so instead he hid his feelings.

"Jack, why don't you take Millie to the place you found her?" Katherine suggested. Jack's eyes were red as he looked at his wife in amazement. Katherine knew that he did not deal well with matters of the heart. He was a baby when it came to emotions. Katherine was always there for him when he needed her in tough situations. He smiled at her suggestion. Katherine carefully crawled over Jack like a mother hen hatching her precious eggs. On this night Katherine and Jack recommitted their love for each other. Somehow Katherine knew that Jack would soon be at peace with his past.

The following day, Millie brought her tired body to the dinner table. She had not worked so hard since she and Hector had climbed the volcano. Katherine had made the most delicious roast beef along with Millie's favorite carrot salad and Jack's favorite lemon cake. The family was very happy to be together again.

"Millie, here." Jack handed Millie two American Airlines ticket jackets.

"What's this?" she asked as she pulled the tickets out of the special folders. She was confused because she didn't expect to travel for a while. Hector would arrive in another six days. Jack had liked Katherine's idea so much that he had gone into town first thing in the morning to buy the tickets. He had also bought the maps necessary to get to the place where he had found his beautiful treasure.

Millie had never known that the Wolfs actually found her in Texas. Jack had never shared any information about Millie with anyone. For that matter, he rarely discussed the matter with his wife. He had tried to forget how Millie came to be part of their family. Now it seemed that going to Texas would be the right thing to do for himself and for Millie.

"Dad, what is this about?" Millie thought she could work on the farm and rest for the next six days. She thought that all of her surprises would be over by now. She didn't need any more news today. "What's in Texas?"

"Your mother is taking us to the airport tomorrow," he told her. "You and I are going to the location where we found you."

"We don't have to do this, Dad."

"No, I want to do it. This is important for me. Your mother and I just want the best for you. This trip will give you additional information, Millie." Jack excused himself from the table. He really did not want to debate the matter with Millie. As far as he was concerned, this decision was his and it was final. "We leave early so make sure you're ready," he added as he left the room.

"You'll be fine, Millie," Katherine reassured her, holding Millie's hands. Of course, Katherine did not mention this had been her idea. She wanted her husband to be responsible. "This will be a good trip for both of you."

"We don't have to do this, Mother," Millie insisted. "I'm all right. I don't need to do this."

"This trip is for your father, Millie. Why don't you let him do this for his good health," she whispered. "Has your father ever asked many things of you?" Katherine walked with Millie to her room to help her pack a small bag. She had already done the same for her husband.

In the quiet of her room that night, Millie finally understood that the pain Jack had harbored was the same as the pain that Teófilo had spoken so eloquently about. She could vividly hear Teófilo's voice telling the story of Milagro. Deep down she could feel the pain that Teófilo spoke of. *Why didn't my father speak of the same pain?* Millie wondered. *How could I not have noticed his pain over the years?* Millie had been so busy with her own activities that she could not notice the things her father would not verbalize. *How could I have been so blind to think that I was the only one who thought of my past?* Millie lay in bed appreciating her parents more and more and thanking the good Lord for the love they had given her. Silently she prayed the Our Father in gratitude.

What would have happened if the Wolf family had not been there? What would have become of me? she wondered. *Would I ever have come to the United States of America? How about Stanford? Would I have ever made it there without their financial support and perseverance? Would I ever have met Hector?* She fell asleep thinking about Hector and the next day's trip.

• • •

THE FLIGHT TO HOUSTON took a full three hours. Katherine stayed behind in San Diego to shop in preparation for the engagement dinner she was planning for Hector and Millie. Jack and Millie would spend the night in Houston and return to San Diego the following day.

Jack had a rental car waiting at the airport. They drove toward San Antonio and then got off the Interstate to travel west on rural roads. For many years Jack had relived the night of the train wreck in his mind. He had even searched in libraries in different towns, looking for information on the railways. It was as if he knew that some day he would be making this memorable trip. He stopped many times to read the map and recall the directions. Occasionally, he would hold Millie's hand to assure her of the direction they were traveling. She tried hard to remember, but nothing in this area looked familiar at all.

Jack followed the rail lines, deviating only to avoid dry river beds. From a distance, he spotted the large trees that signaled the site of the accident. The terrain had not changed at all. The semi-arid land with its cacti and manzanilla was still the same. Jack pulled the rental car to the side of the paved rural road and got out. He looked up to see dark crows against the hot Texas sun.

Millie got out to follow her father as he climbed the slanting bed to the tracks. They could hear the distant rumble of a coming train. Jack walked ahead to the crossroads leading north of the tracks. He recognized the wooden bridge that had marked the brutal deaths of Millie's parents.

"Over here," Jack called as he walked briskly toward the bridge. He pointed to the small road crossing the tracks. "The vehicle was coming from Mexico, headed in that direction," Jack said, pointing north. She turned to face north. "The rain was pouring, Millie," he added. "The train was coming from Houston. Katherine and I had been on our way to California after a couple of years in Ecuador. Your mother and I were getting ready to go to bed when we heard a loud screeching noise and felt a jolt." He cleared his throat. "The train hit the pickup here." He pointed to the spot where the pavement and the train tracks met, and then bent over to feel the smooth edge of one of the rails.

Jack knew every detail of the night his ethics, beliefs, and medical training had challenged him like no other time before. He told her of his decision that produced a family he treasured so much. He spoke with great difficulty. Jack was crying inside, the sighs of relief just beginning to escape his lungs and mouth.

He walked farther back to the small wooden bridge. As he approached the river bed, he signaled to Millie to join him. She was sad and resentful of the dry land and surroundings, and walked slowly.

"Millie, come! Hurry!" Jack called. In the dry bed, rusted pieces of metal from the old truck still poked through the dirt. Fearing rattlesnakes, Jack kicked at the dusty ground with his boots until a piece of the wreckage broke loose. Millie picked up the piece of metal and scraped off a layer of dried mud with her bare hand. The rain and sun had worn away much of the color on the twisted steel and replaced it with a yellowish rust.

Beneath the piece was an old scrap of rotted cloth. It reminded Millie of the *rebozo* in which Mexican women carried their babies. Only shreds caked with mud were left of the material but she knew it must have been part of her family's clothing. As Jack watched, she raised the shreds of cloth in front of her eyes. She wished she could hold the material close to her heart, to feel the warmth of the absent mother.

"Can I take this home?" Her father nodded his head in agreement. He had brought a plastic bag with him to carry anything that she might want from the site.

The scene was still too real for him. Had Katherine been there, he would have cried all over again. He remembered not being able to help a single family member when he arrived at the accident. He wished he could tell Millie every detail but did not want her to know the horrible way her family's lives had ended. Millie understood his anguish because Teófilo had cautiously described the conditions of their bodies to her. She hugged Jack so that he would know how much he meant to her.

"Let's move on." Jack pulled her from the site. As they walked toward the car, Jack told Millie how he had found her. They looked under the mature trees they passed to see if anything was left from the accident.

"Dad!" she cried out. Jack rushed to her side. Millie picked up a tiny, weathered shoe with a loose buckle. It looked like lions had mauled it. Jack remembered that Millie had been wearing only one shoe when he carried her aboard the train. This age-worn shoe was filled with mud and weeds. Millie shook the dried mud out of it. She knew it was her shoe. She had seen the other one in the box hidden in the closet. Jack tied a knot in the plastic bag to keep the scrap of cloth separate, and Millie carefully placed the shoe in and tied another knot.

Jack explained to her every detail of how he had found her and what her injuries had been. In a way, she wished he had told her long before today. On the other hand, she knew that she could deal with it better now. "You know, Millie," Jack admitted, "the hardest part of these past years was not being able to tell folks around us what happened. When your mother and I arrived with you in the Imperial Valley, we were very nervous about this little girl that was ours. But we thought we were doing the right thing."

"Of course you did the right thing, Dad." She put her arm around her father as they walked back to the car. Millie did not know that Jack had another place yet to visit. He was determined to free himself from the shackles of guilt which held him prisoner for so many years. He was so grateful to Katherine for encouraging him to take this trip.

They drove back to Houston to have dinner and check into a hotel. Millie was inspired by her father's courage to travel with her to the site where she was found. She would never have gone there on her own. "Dad, thank you for doing this for me," she said in gratitude for the difficulty of the journey. Jack just nodded. He knew what she was going through.

The following morning Jack drove Millie to the FBI head-quarters in Houston. He told her that if Hector's father had made every effort to find her in Texas, the authorities had probably filed a missing person report. After some time the report is considered an unsolved potential crime.

It all made sense to Millie now. Jack wanted to do everything possible to alleviate his guilt. She was determined to help. At the FBI building, Jack approached the information desk to seek the department of unsolved matters. The woman behind the half-moon-shaped counter referred them to the second floor.

Jack Wolf introduced himself and his daughter to the receptionist upstairs. They immediately got the feeling that their dilemma was not a priority for the department.

Jack politely insisted that the young assistant look at the files for the 1957 incident reports and unsolved accident reports. "Perhaps the information is in the 'missing persons' file," Jack suggested. The receptionist disappeared through a door and called for assistance.

"Hello, I'm Julio Castro, a special assistant with this department." A burly, bronze-skinned Hispanic man appeared from another office. "I understand that you want to report on an incident that happened September 12, 1957."

"Yes, sir. I'm Dr. Jack Wolf and this is Milagro Luna Wolf." Jack was polite but assertive. Millie was shocked to hear her father refer to her as Milagro Luna. "She was lost in an accident in 1957," he added. "I just want to assure the department that she is not lost."

Mr. Castro's eyebrows furrowed in confusion as Dr. Wolf spoke. He took a small note pad from the counter and pulled a silver pen from his left shirt pocket. He took notes as Jack spoke. "What time was this accident?"

"The accident took place in the very late hours. We believe that a missing person report was filed with the FBI afterwards."

"Just a minute." Agent Castro disappeared behind the door to a storage room. He was gone for several minutes before he emerged with two boxes wrapped in thick plastic. He pulled the aging plastic from the boxes. They seemed so familiar to Millie. The yellowing cardboard containers with faded pictures of pink marshmallow cookies on the sides awaited ownership. Her heart danced in excitement as she recognized the boxes belonging to her Mexican family. She remembered the candle she held while the boxes were packed, remembered now where her dim memories of candlelight came from.

The agent also brought a file with him. The legal-sized file was dusty. "A missing young child was reported by Teófilo Gil in October of 1957," he read from the report. "The sheriff and police reports indicate that all passengers in the vehicle were fatally injured. The child was nowhere to be found. We also have a written report from a priest, Angel," he added as he looked at Jack's and Millie's shocked faces. Jack had taken a risk coming to the FBI, and his decision had turned out to be the right choice.

"Now, you say this is the missing child?" agent Castro asked. "My, my, she certainly has grown quite a bit." He looked skeptical. Without the proper proof it would be impossible to close the case.

Millie could see where the conversation might lead. She immediately intervened. "I have proof that I am Milagro Luna Wolf."

She guardedly opened her small leather purse and pulled

out the battered birth certificate her godfather had saved since 1957. The neatly folded documents made enormous noise as she spread the pages before the agent. The FBI agent stared in surprise at the old document. It clearly matched the birth certificate in the file.

Agent Castro took the file and the document Millie had handed to him, and asked them to wait while he had the birth certificate verified. He disappeared into an office, where he quickly noted the similarities in the documents under a magnifying glass. He returned with a slight smile on his face. Millie was so glad that the document had been in her purse. Once again, Teófilo proved to be a wise man.

"Where did you disappear to?" the agent asked.

"My adoptive father, Dr. Wolf, has taken care of me since the accident." Millie sounded very convincing. The agent again looked at the birth certificate to compare it to the one that had been submitted to the agency in 1957. There was no question that the documents were the same.

"The documents match," he said with a broad smile. "You are one lucky lady today. But I need to see proof from you, too, Dr. Wolf."

Jack pulled out his wallet and provided a variety of impressive I.D.s. The card identifying him as a doctor was followed by his membership card for the cattlemen's association. Finally, Jack handed agent Castro a picture of Katherine, Millie, and himself in front of the farmhouse. Millie's face had not changed. Jack hoped that the agent wouldn't ask him for adoption papers, as he would not be able to comply.

"Dr. Wolf, I'm going to have you and your daughter sign the documents here, indicating the resolution to the initial report," the investigator said. Jack smiled broadly and signed eagerly before handing his pen to Millie. Agent Castro photographed father and daughter for the file.

"You're lucky that technology was not part of our department practices at that time," he told them. "We would have gone through much more than the identification requirement and signatures." He handed over the boxes to their rightful owner, and could see how happy Millie was to receive them. He knew he had done a tremendous favor by affirming this father and daughter team. Moreover, the department would have one old file finally resolved.

Jack was elated that the matter had been settled so quickly. He had not expected it to turn out so well. He figured they would give him bureaucratic answers, or maybe not even have the information he needed. He was just glad that his daughter was happy with the resolution of such a personal matter. Her life would have been so different had he reported her to the authorities that night.

Jack had tears in his eyes as they left the FBI headquarters. He was one hell of a relieved man and showed it. He never in his wildest dreams figured that this case could be closed. Millie walked quickly to the car, carrying the two small boxes protectively under her arms. She was anxious to open them and see the things her family had packed for their new life in the United States.

She opened the car door and jumped in the front seat, elated with her presents. She clearly remembered helping her mother pack things for the trip. The faded picture of the marshmallow cookies was barely visible. Millie placed her hands over the pictures of the cookies and laid her head on the boxes. She tried to feel the tender, warm love of a mother she never really knew.

"Thank you for bringing me here. I doubted coming to this place, but you were right," she told Jack as he got in the car.

"I'm glad things worked out this way. It's a tremendous relief for me, too."

Millie asked her father for his jackknife and carefully began to unseal one of the boxes. Over the years, the lid had adhered to the bottom part of the box. Jack watched with excitement as she opened the first box. Inside were adult clothes, two pairs of pants and a pretty flowered dress, neatly folded. Millie buried her head in them, and her tears flowed with joy, sadness, and relief.

Her cries were more than Jack could handle, and he wept along with her. He had never experienced such a bittersweet moment with Millie before. As she calmed down, she began to pry apart the corrugated cardboard with the tip of the knife. She remembered that she and her mother had hidden pictures somewhere in the edges, but she did recall which box. "I don't think I'm going to cut this open until we get home so that Mom can be part of this," Millie told her father. "Let's go catch our plane back home, Dad." She wanted to rush to the airport.

Katherine waited on pins and needles to hear about the visit to Houston. She did not know of Jack's plan to visit the FBI, but was not surprised when they told her. The Wolf family drove to the nearby harbor in San Diego for a fish dinner before heading east to the hot desert Valley.

Millie carried the boxes into the spacious restaurant. At the table she meticulously opened a box full of tiny clothes and dresses. Little crocheted baby shoes and socks were packed on the sides of the box. She used a steak knife to split the bottom of the box between the layers of cardboard. Katherine helped her slit the aging box open. To their amazement, pictures of the Luna family fell out from their hiding place. The baptismal records of the four children of Octavio and Dolores Luna were folded in halves. Millie had found herself a hidden trove and looked forward to sharing it with Hector. The Wolf family took long minutes to look at every detail of the photos and the clothing. Millie's baby picture was the greatest treasure for Jack and Katherine. They had never had one.

FIN